PRAISE FOR ZOJE STAGE

Mothered

"Compelling . . . This disturbing yet addictive read will keep you wondering what is real and what is madness."

—*Kirkus Reviews*

"Stage thrusts dread upon readers from her book's first sentences and continues to escalate the tension with every page. A great choice for fans of intense psychological horror where nothing can be trusted and no one can look away from the emerging nightmare."

—*Library Journal*

"Each of Stage's books explores the dark side of family bonds, all in their own extraordinary way. This one lays bare the true horror inherent in fables and folklore, and what Pandora lets out of her box seems negligible compared to what Grace unleashes."

—*Booklist* (starred review)

"Utterly harrowing . . . masterful."

—Criminal Element

"Ms. Stage's narration is a superbly navigated exercise in the lives of those we meet . . . [her] storytelling is powerful enough to force you to shift around in your seat because of how she is able to shed light on her characters' deepest horrors: the truth."

—*Pittsburgh Post-Gazette*

"Stage is a master at drafting suspenseful ~~~~~~~~

Chronicle

"*Mothered* is disturbing in the best possible way. A dark and unsettling thriller that had me glued to the pages. This is Stage's best work yet—horrifying and brilliant."

—Lucinda Berry, bestselling author of *The Perfect Child* and *Under Her Care*

"Zoje Stage expertly explores the blurred lines between memory and nightmare in this deliciously twisty and riveting page-turner. An eerily crafted chiller set against the claustrophobic isolation of the pandemic, *Mothered* is a must-read for psychological-thriller fans. No one chronicles the complicated, sometimes perilous intensity of mother-daughter relationships like Stage. Absorbing, unsettling, and magnetic—don't miss this dark gem of a novel."

—Heather Gudenkauf, *New York Times* bestselling author of *The Overnight Guest*

"Zoje Stage's *Mothered* sent me on an intense, visceral ride. Stage's straightforward writing easily paints the initial picture we all went through, life screeching to a halt during the quarantine. But while that initial familiarity and instant connection with the protagonist, Grace, hooked me, the story quickly veered in an unfamiliar direction. As Grace's anxiety and instability rose, my own claustrophobic sensation grew, and I found myself flipping the pages, needing to know what happens next. The underlying mystery of Grace and Jackie's history kept me captivated and unsettled until the book's end."

—Mike Omer, *New York Times* bestselling author of *A Killer's Mind*

Baby Teeth

"Unnerving and unputdownable, *Baby Teeth* will get under your skin and keep you trapped in its chilling grip until the shocking conclusion."

—Lisa Scottoline, *New York Times* bestselling author

"You won't blink until you read the last line."

—*Publishers Weekly*

"A chilling thriller that will definitely make you lose sleep at night."

—PopSugar

"I've been waiting for a thriller to capture the emotional depth of women for years . . . I can't recommend *Getaway* enough."
—Tarryn Fisher, *New York Times* bestselling author of *The Wives* and *The Wrong Family*

"Tense, unpredictable, and utterly compelling, Stage's complex story of friendship and survival is a must read."
—Karen Dionne, *New York Times* bestselling author of *The Marsh King's Daughter*

"A harrowing, heart-pounding thrill ride."
—Rachel Harrison, author of *The Return*

"Strap into your pack, and step into this inky darkness with Zoje Stage."
—Stephen Graham Jones, *New York Times* bestselling author

Wonderland

"Beautifully choreographed and astonishing . . . Eloquent and unflinching."

—*Booklist* (starred)

"Sublimely suspenseful . . . Stage is a literary horror writer on the rise."

—*BookPage*

"Stage's darkly lyrical writing style shines."

—*Publishers Weekly*

"Just as deliciously unsettling as her unforgettable debut, *Wonderland* is a must read for horror and thriller fans."

—Layne Fargo, author of *Temper*

Dear Hanna

ALSO BY ZOJE STAGE

NOVELS

Baby Teeth

Wonderland

Getaway

Mothered

NOVELLA

The Girl Who Outgrew the World

Dear Hanna

A Novel

ZOJE STAGE

THOMAS & MERCER

Published by Thomas & Mercer, Seattle

www.apub.com

Amazon, the Amazon logo, and Thomas & Mercer are trademarks of Amazon.com, Inc., or its affiliates.

ISBN-13: 9781662521003 (hardcover)
ISBN-13: 9781662520990 (paperback)
ISBN-13: 9781662521010 (digital)

Cover design by Olga Grlic
Cover image: © Ruben Calvo Calles / Shutterstock

Printed in the United States of America
First edition

For my readers,
who changed my life

PART ONE: THEN

1

Four Years Ago

Hanna had a feeling about them as soon as she saw them in the waiting room. The man, around forty, was well put together—fit, dressed in business casual, his hair starting to gray in that way that made men look dignified. It was the girl he was with who was here to have her blood drawn—Joelle Altman, age twelve. The normal panel, plus iron and B_{12} levels.

"Joelle?" Hanna called, summoning them.

The girl gripped the man's hand, and Hanna was certain now that he was her father. A quick glance at his left hand confirmed he wasn't wearing a wedding ring. And he looked like a man who wouldn't object to wearing a gold band if he had a reason to wear one.

"Hi there," Hanna said cheerfully to the slightly stricken-looking girl.

"Hi," she mumbled in reply.

Hanna led them into her cubicle. "You can sit here, in the big chair. And your dad can pull over the stool—you're her dad?"

"Yes," he confirmed. "Jo's a little nervous, she hasn't had her blood drawn before."

"Well my name's Hanna, and you're in luck, Jo." Being so chipper wasn't Hanna's normal demeanor—unless it had to be: she was trying to make the right impression, while learning what she could about Joelle

Altman and her father. "I happen to have a reputation as being very gentle. And I'll talk you through every step. First, I'm going to tie this purple rubbery thing around your upper arm—it'll feel tight."

Joelle squeezed her eyes shut as she clutched her father's hand. Hanna flashed a sympathetic smile at him as she tied the tourniquet around the girl's upper arm.

"Can you make this hand into a fist? Okay so far?" she asked, and Joelle nodded. "Good. Next you'll feel me tap your vein with my fingers . . . And this is an alcohol swab—feels cool but doesn't hurt."

Hanna's attention alternated between her work and the people in her cubicle, noticing as many details as her brief glimpses would allow. The girl's delicate gold earrings and necklace, her trendy tween outfit. The man's expensive leather shoes and well-tailored clothes. When Joelle's eyes were open, they were blue like her father's, but her hair was lighter than his. There were no signs of illness about her, and no hints that Hanna could draw on from the requisition form to determine why Jo was here. The man's watch looked expensive. He was thin but not scrawny, and she wondered if he worked out. His aftershave smelled nice. He was clearly a man who still made an effort with how he presented himself to the world. *Definitely single.*

"Do you like school?" Hanna asked, a distraction technique for what came next.

"More or less," said Joelle.

"Which is the more part?"

"I like my classes. But I don't really have that many friends."

"You don't need a lot of friends, just one or two good ones." Hanna and the dad exchanged looks of commiseration. She knew a thing or two about not having many friends, but fortunately, through thick and thin, she had her younger brother, Goose. "I'm going to count to three and you'll feel a little pinch. One, two, three . . ."

Hanna really concentrated now. There were reasons why she'd chosen to become a phlebotomist—reasons that sometimes had nothing to do with how gentle she could be. Yet, she was capable of doing her job extremely well, and used that competence to earn herself a good reputation. That way, no one suspected that sometimes she used her needle as a tiny weapon, hurting people—just a little—to vent her own frustrations. But she had a different agenda today.

"You can unclench your fist," she said, watching the vial fill with blood. "You did great, we're almost done."

Joelle's eyes popped open. "You did it already?"

"Filling the last vial now." Hanna grinned at the dad. "She did great."

"*You* did great." Was that a flirtatious gleam in his eye? "My name's Jacob, by the way. Guess I should've said that sooner, but . . ." He held up and massaged the hand that Joelle had been squeezing.

"Oops, sorry Daddy," Jo said to him. To Hanna she said, with glee: "It didn't hurt at all!"

"That's what I pride myself on." *Sometimes.*

She extracted the needle and pressed a wad of gauze on the puncture. "Just hold this here for a second."

Hanna spun on her stool to retrieve a roll of nonadhesive medical tape, aware of Jacob's eyes on her. She shot him a quick coquettish grin, confident that he liked what he was seeing. The long mahogany hair and dark eyes. She hated how plain her regulation black scrubs were, though it amused her that coworkers liked to joke about her being a sophisticated Wednesday Addams. It had bothered her when she was little that she looked so much like her mother, though a growth spurt at ten had given Hanna some of her father's height. Unlike her mother, who tried way too hard to have a perfect facade, Hanna never wore makeup—and knew she didn't need to. People trusted a naturally pretty face, an easy smile, and being perceived as approachable helped her move through life.

And people would *do* things for a pretty person who knew just how to ask.

"Do you live around here?" Hanna asked Jacob, making conversation as she wrapped the medical tape around Joelle's arm.

"Yes, right up on Beacon."

"Oh, that is close." And she knew there were some *big* houses on Beacon.

"What about you?" he asked.

"I live in Shadyside."

"Oh, nice."

Yes, it was nice. Because, at twenty, she still lived in her parents' spiffy, if spartan, house. Hanna could've gotten her own apartment, but she really didn't want to live in less comfort than she was used to. Her plan had long been to meet a man who could care for her to the standard her father had established.

Joelle hopped out of the chair, ready to go.

"Are you a runner?" Jacob asked, lingering, pointing to Hanna's running shoes.

"Yes, it's one of my main hobbies. I run almost every day."

"Me too. I run in Schenley Park a lot, usually in the mornings. Maybe I'll run into you, pun intended."

Joelle rolled her eyes, itching to leave. Jacob took the hint and started following her out—but not before the neon words came into focus above his head. Sometimes such words appeared to Hanna, helping her to understand other people's emotions and attitudes. As a child she'd been forced to study people, to learn to connect the dots between external signifiers and common human behavior. This was meant as an exercise in learning empathy, and Hanna had discovered she had a knack for reading people. It became a skill that helped her move through the world.

Now, she saw *horny* pulsing the brightest, accompanied by *intrigued* and *lonely*.

"Maybe so, I run there too sometimes." Which was true, though rarely, and she usually ran in the afternoons after work.

As they waved goodbye, Hanna was reminded of her teenage years, and how awkward all the rites of passage had been for her. Until she'd learned to play the game. Flirting had come easily once she'd put her mind to it; so had seduction.

She was cleaning up and double-checking the vial labels when Jacob ducked back in.

"Maybe it doesn't have to be random good luck," he said, holding out a business card.

"Maybe not," she agreed, plucking the card from his fingers.

Gotcha. Hanna grinned as he left.

She had a very good feeling Jacob was the man she'd been looking for.

2

Four Years Ago

On their first date, jogging through Schenley Park, they took a detour off the trail to find a private place to make out. They had sex on their second date, tiptoeing so they wouldn't wake Joelle as they made their way up to Jacob's attic studio in the dark. Hanna had been pleasantly surprised to discover he was a rather serious artistic photographer, working in black and white, and this was another thing they had in common: she was an artist, too, working primarily in graphite. He was a good enough lover (not that she had so many to compare him to), and his house—what she'd seen of it—was all she could've hoped for.

He was exactly what she needed. A kind, financially stable, somewhat interesting widower, with tangential points of mutual interest. He wasn't put off by her age (because she was already a "working professional"), and didn't seem to think it odd that she'd yet to move out of her parents' house (expressing his desire that Joelle stay at home "forever"). Hanna hadn't originally envisioned herself becoming someone's stepmother, but she was willing to give it a try. Her vision of mothering would always be to do the opposite of everything her own mother had done. But Joelle seemed to be such a sweet, easygoing Daddy's girl, and Hanna was much closer in age to her than to Jacob, so she figured they'd be more like sisters. Hanna could impart advice, and Jo would look up to her.

That could work.

For their fourth date, Jacob invited Hanna to join him and Jo at home for dinner—which would be the first time all three of them were together since Hanna had drawn Joelle's blood. Whenever possible, Hanna tried to avoid interacting with her parents, and the whole household kept to their own busy schedules. But her mother caught her in the kitchen making a cheesecake, at which point Hanna revealed that she was going to a man's house for dinner.

"What man?" her mother asked.

"His name is Jacob. I met him at work."

"He's a phlebotomist? You have to be careful about workplace romances."

Hanna kept her back turned so her mother wouldn't see the annoyance on her face. It was so typical that whatever Hanna told her, Snide Suzette only saw the negative side of everything she did.

"He's a real estate agent," she snarled in reply. And then, more tenderly: "And a wonderful person."

Sometimes Hanna didn't tell her mother the truth, but Jacob wasn't "practice," as most of her other dates had been. She anticipated that at some point, she might need to tell her parents that she was engaged, so better they knew the truth now that she was in a real relationship.

Slightly self-conscious of how youthful she could look, Hanna did her best to wear stylish but mature clothing in Jacob's presence (silently cursing when she caught herself resembling her mother in the mirror). For the dinner date she wore a pair of skinny jeans and a cowl-neck sweater that was slightly transparent (a camisole beneath it), and a pair of well-worn ankle boots. She parked in his driveway, as instructed, and carried the containers with her cheesecake and the strawberry compote to the front door.

Joelle must have been waiting for her. She whipped the door open a half second after Hanna had rung the bell.

"Hi!" Jo said, wearing an enormous smile.

"Hi yourself, how's it going?"

"Good." Joelle led her to the kitchen. "You look so pretty."

"Thank you, so do you."

Hanna could tell this was something of a special occasion for her. She saw the word *hopeful* bounding along above the girl's head. Jacob hadn't dated much since his wife, Rachel, had died three years earlier. Was Hanna the first person he'd brought home?

"Hanna's here!" Joelle called as they entered the kitchen.

It was a kitchen any chef would envy, much bigger than the one in her parents' house. At home, everything was stark and Nordic, but Jacob's house was styled a bit more traditionally, with a lot of warm browns and beiges. Joelle climbed onto one of the chic stools at the enormous marble-topped island, and Jacob came around to plant a kiss on Hanna's cheek.

"Hi, you look beautiful."

"That's what I said," Joelle agreed.

"Thank you—both."

"Here, let me take that from you." Jacob scooped away her containers and carried them over to the counter.

"What did you bring?" Jo asked.

"My homemade cheesecake and compote."

"Yummy!"

"Do you like to cook?" Jacob seemed endearingly flustered, as if he hoped to make an extra-good impression but wasn't sure how. Hanna liked seeing him this way. For one thing, it meant he was fallible—not just the suave middle-aged lover he'd so far presented himself as.

She also recognized the opportunity inherent in his question. "I love to cook."

It wasn't exactly true, though she *could* cook. And she saw how it would help slot her into the family—she could be as useful to them as Jacob would be to her.

"I wasn't sure if you might be a vegetarian, I never thought to ask." Which was Jacob's way of apologizing for the simple meal of cheese tortellini with salad and garlic bread.

"I'm an omnivore, I'll eat anything," said Hanna.

"Good to know." He seemed a bit calmer now that they were all seated around one end of the island.

"I tried to go vegan but my doctor was concerned I wasn't getting enough protein."

"That's why she was having her blood drawn," Jacob explained. To his daughter he added: "You can try being a vegetarian when you're a little older."

Hanna was used to eating her meals alone, which she thought she preferred, but found herself genuinely enjoying the easy camaraderie of this little family. She made a point of asking Joelle questions, so that most of the conversation was about or included her. Jacob expressed his approval in lingering gazes and admiring smiles.

Joelle and Jacob both lit up with delight as Hanna served them dessert plates of strawberry-topped cheesecake.

"Mmm—this is the best part of the meal!" Joelle declared, mouth full of gooey cheese and strawberries.

"Thank you."

"Hey," Jacob said in mock offense to his daughter.

"When do we ever have homemade cheesecake?" she replied in defense.

"Good point." He turned to Hanna. "It *is* delicious."

How wonderful it felt to be treated with such deference by these two near strangers.

"I'll be right back." Joelle abruptly got up and fled the room.

"What's that about?" Hanna whispered to Jacob.

"Dunno," he said with a shrug. Alone now, he reached over and took her hand, kissed it. "This is nice, I'm glad you could come."

"I'm glad you invited me. Supper was delicious, by the way."

He laughed. "Supper was basic. We're pretty down to earth—" He seemed to notice the size of the kitchen. "The house notwithstanding. This was more Rachel's style."

"You have a beautiful home."

A moment later, Joelle appeared in the kitchen entryway, where she sheepishly stood rather than returning to her stool.

"Joelle?" Jacob sounded as puzzled as he looked.

"Um, I think I just got my period?" Jo directed the hesitant words at Hanna.

Jacob uttered a startled "Oh," and then tried to hide his clumsy response by giving her a totally cringe thumbs-up.

Hanna got off the stool, grinning her best welcome-to-the-club smile as she went over to Joelle. "It's a pain in the ass in a lot of ways, but a sign of moon-goddess power." Hanna turned back to Jacob. "Have you stocked up for this? Have anything ready?"

"Yes, there are some pads in the upstairs closet." He looked relieved when Hanna put a hand on Joelle's shoulder and Jo led her away.

Hanna waited on the top step while Joelle changed into clean panties in the bathroom. The girl came out a minute later and sat beside her, breathing a sigh of relief or frustration—Hanna couldn't tell which.

"Okay? Do you feel any stomach pains or anything?"

"No."

"That's good. But it could happen, and then you ask your dad for some Advil and a heating pad—heating pads really work."

"Okay."

"And speaking of pads—I'll tell him to order some of those reusable period underwear, okay? I think they're much more comfortable and practical."

"Yeah, this feels weird." She squirmed a little, tugging at the crotch of her jeans, obviously unaccustomed to having a sanitary pad between her legs.

"Ready to go back down? Finish your cheesecake?"

Joelle emitted another sigh, and stood up. "Yes."

As they neared the kitchen, Hanna felt as Jo slipped a hand into hers and gripped it.

"I'm glad you were here," the girl whispered.

"I am too," Hanna whispered back.

The look on Jacob's face as he watched the two of them return to the table was almost rapturous. And Hanna knew then and there: she had won. This was going to be her new family.

3

Four Years Ago

Dear Hanna,
I'm very happy to hear you're getting married. I'm
sure you will look beautiful in a white dress. Mommy
thinks it's very fast, but Daddy says sometimes love
works that way. I hope you will send me lots of
pictures—I wish I could be there, but I know you
understand.
Love,
Goose

4

Dearest Goose,

I wish you could've been there! I think it's very mean of Mommy and Daddy to make you stay at school on my big day—but it's typical of them, right? You probably would've enjoyed the wedding much more than they did. Daddy seemed a bit like a smiley ghost, and Mommy kept looking toward the door like she wanted to run away. It was small—just both sets of parents, a few of Jacob's friends, and a couple of my coworkers. And Joelle, of course. She was the maid of honor, the best girl, and the ring bearer rolled into one. We rented out a restaurant and had it decorated with flowers, then had a nice big meal after the ceremony.

For a wedding gift, Jacob got me a professional drafting table, which he set up in the spare bedroom that I now use as a studio. I had hardly anything to bring over from Mommy and Daddy's house—just my clothes, some art supplies and years of sketchbooks, and a few personal things. For now my studio is pretty empty, but that's okay. I haven't shown much of my art to Jacob yet—I'm kind of afraid of what he'll think. His photographs are very . . . what's a good word . . . esoteric? (Do you know what that means? Kind of mysterious.) And my drawings, as you know, can be a little . . . I was about to say gruesome, but that's just what other people think. Seeing that being a wife means *sharing* and *compromising*, I might need to explore some less graphic ways of expressing myself— at least so I'll have some pictures to share with him. It will be good to expand on my creative ideas!

I think of you a lot, little brother. I cherish every one of your letters and store them in a keepsake box! I keep them in order, and sometimes I go back and reread them. Because, as you know, I love you very much.

Yours,
Hanna

5

Two Years Ago

Dear Goose,

Happy 13th Birthday, baby brother! I know you don't like it when I call you that, but that's exactly why I'm doing it because you're a TEENAGER now and I can't believe you're so OLD! ;-)

How are you? How is school going? What's the most fascinating thing that you can't stop thinking about?

I'm always afraid of boring you by writing too much about my domestic life, but what can I say? This is my life, and it's pretty darn good! My days have a very regular routine, which might sound dull, but I like knowing exactly what to expect.

During the week I get up super early and Jacob and I go for a quick run. It's nicer than I would've thought to be out so early in the day. It's so quiet then, the streets and park are empty of people, and the light (or lack thereof) is often quite captivating. I always enjoy this time with Jacob, it's kind of our special time, just being together, breathing in unison. Maybe that sounds cheesy, but for me, running in sync with him feels more productive than a conversation ever could.

After that, I take a quick shower and head to work. I know a lot of people (Mommy, Daddy, you?) thought it was a strange career choice, but I love it—and not just because I think blood is the most beautiful color. It also feels rewarding to do something you're good at (remember that when you start thinking about what sort of career you might like to have). Right after work I pick up Joelle and take her to one of her classes. She's becoming SO good! Her singing has gotten so strong and consistent, and though she's thinking about quitting ballet, she's doing great with contemporary and jazz. There's a viewing window at the dance school where the parents can watch, and for her voice lessons I sit on the other side of the room and look busy with my phone (which maybe I am, but I'm also listening). Maybe it's because I didn't take any sort of enriching classes when I was a kid (I know—that's on me), but I love seeing how much better she's gotten over the two years that I've known her. It's kind of inspiring.

When her lesson is done, we come home and I cook while Joelle sits in the kitchen, keeping me company as she does her homework. We try to eat dinner together as a family every night, though occasionally Jacob has to work (and once in a while Jo is at a sleepover with her dance friend, Maya). In the evenings we prefer to watch a movie rather than television, and I've proudly introduced both Jo and Jacob to a plethora (that means an excessive amount) of indie and foreign films that they never would've selected on their own. Now it's something we really enjoy doing together and it makes me feel like I'm contributing something genuinely interesting to their lives.

Our weekends are a bit more free form, and if Jo has to be somewhere, Jacob will take her (unless he has an open house). I do most of my drawing on the weekends, and I think we all need time, especially on Sundays, to decompress. The best thing to do on a Sunday is cuddle up on the couch with some snacks and watch a movie or two and order in pizza. Everyone needs a Lazy Day!

There, that's my whole life in a nutshell . . . Which I know is why you prefer to talk about ideas and crazy random thoughts and life philosophies and whatnot, but I find it comforting to know that you can envision how I spend my days. I really wouldn't mind at all having such details about your life, if you ever want to share them? That would be a comfort, too, being able to imagine you in your classes and doing after-school stuff. No pressure—but I would NOT find that boring!

All right . . . I hope you have a wonderful birthday! I had to fold it to get it in the envelope, but I included a little drawing, a self-portrait—and not a weird one, but one where I think I look calm and at peace. I miss you!

Yours,

Hanna

6

Dear Hanna,

I love you, but for the love of Einstein, I'm just as capable of using a dictionary as you are—and I already knew what *plethora* meant! I think sometimes you forget how smart I am—dare I say brilliant? I'm not trying to brag, I just want you to know that I'm not a little kid anymore and you can use Big Words and say Serious Things and my brain won't explode.

I like hearing about your life—in fact, I sorta love it. I didn't think I'd miss having a normal family life when I went away to school, but maybe that's because I really don't miss our parents (I miss you, though). But what you describe . . . Well, that sounds genuinely nice and I am very happy for you. You deserve a nice, normal, happy family. And yet . . . You are right, I don't wanna talk about the blah-blah-blahbity-blah of my own routine. The best I can say is, it's about what you'd imagine. ;-)

Did you know that dogs can hear your heart beat? People say that dogs can sense when you're scared of them, but that's not technically true—they can hear when your heart speeds up, and I guess when you're scared your heart beats faster.

I've been thinking a lot about animals lately. Specifically, I've been thinking about all the species that have gone extinct. And how 99% of the time it's because of human activity. I gotta say, it's making me think less and less of the human species. The animals are innocent, and they have just as much right to live on earth as we do—if not more! I mean, they don't HUNT us, they don't DESTROY our territory, they don't EAT us, they don't POISON the land and water and everything they touch, and they certainly aren't the cause of catastrophic climate change. Really, it's so unfair how much all the animals suffer because of humans. It makes me very sad sometimes. And very mad that people are so cruel and indifferent.

Thank you for the self-portrait! My sketching skills are a little sketchy (ha ha) in comparison to yours, but I've enclosed a doodle of a red wolf dancing with a Japanese wolf. Yeah, it looks like a pic of two skinny dogs fighting, but that's the best I could do in five minutes (I wanted to send this off to you sooner rather than later). Both of these animals are extinct, so I'm just trying to do what I can to keep their memories alive.

Yours,

Goose

PART TWO: NOW

7

For lack of being able to slip a little dog shit into the woman's kombucha, Hanna dug the needle all the way through her vein. The woman in the chair winced, and Hanna clicked her tongue in sympathy.

"Sorry. You have really small veins."

"I know," the woman agreed. She death gripped the bottle of kombucha in her free hand and averted her eyes from the needle as Hanna tried again.

The words *vain* and *insecure* flashed in their holographic way above the woman's head. Her yoga pants and trendy tea functioned as a visual hashtag for an aspirational lifestyle, and the *vain* arrow hovered over her fake eyelashes. The *insecure* arrow pointed to her bedhead hairdo, artificially red and tousled, and the muted tie-dyed sweatshirt—a fashion necessity of the teen set, not the thirtysomethings. She was trying hard not to seem like she was trying *too* hard, and Hanna pegged her as a disappointed millennial who wanted to hang on to her youth.

"There we go," Hanna said, nimbly inserting the needle on the second try.

It wasn't the woman's fault that Hanna was having a bad day. She almost snickered thinking about the people who self-harmed to relieve a little stress; *inflicting* a little harm was so much better. This person and this day weren't the *worst*, but her overall frustration level was on the rise.

That morning Jacob had gone on a run through Schenley Park without her. Again. It had become the norm. Since autumn he'd been picking times when he knew she was unavailable—like, before she woke up, or five minutes before she had to leave for work. He said it was because his sleep schedule was off, but since Hanna's own actions were very intentional, she assumed her husband's were too. Whenever she would ask him why they didn't run together anymore, he would shrug and say they'd get back on track soon.

As the tubes filled with blood, the woman periodically leaned away to cough into her shoulder. On the third tube, Hanna glanced up long enough to notice the fine cracks in the skin around the woman's lips—a telltale sign of a cigarette smoker. And her clothing emitted the faint scent of skunk. Hanna imagined her sitting in her car, smoking weed, before heading in for her blood draw. The poor creature was less pretty and less healthy than she desired to be. But *vain* and *insecure* presented an opportunity when Hanna was in the mood to hurt someone.

Such women liked hearing about their small veins: their small veins made them feel special, and in some cases they took it as a compliment—those *thin* veins. As if thinness—somewhere, anywhere—was desirable above all else. Hanna was grateful to be free of such self-doubt. She'd witnessed firsthand how her mother had mentally tortured herself; all that worrying and fussing only tarnished a person's natural beauty.

"All finished." Hanna removed the tourniquet as she pressed the gauze against the slightly bleeding puncture.

The woman smiled and thanked her. They always thanked her. Hanna's parents had thought she was crazy when she'd announced at eighteen that she wanted to become a phlebotomist. But they'd paid for her program at the community college, and supported her while she built her résumé volunteering at the blood bank and the Red Cross. And she'd proved them wrong: she'd stuck with it, and still loved drawing blood, perhaps more than was normal.

8

Dear Hanna,

No, I don't think you're horrible for being . . . hmm, what's the right word? Disillusioned? Irked? It was too good to be true, and I haven't wanted to say this before, but married life sounds like a giant pain in the ass. No offense—I know you had good reasons for choosing Jacob—but even a decent man, a reliable and financially stable man, is still a *man*. And I say this as a *boy*! But you know that men of a certain age are set in their ways—accustomed to being king of the hill and all that. And I don't blame them—someday I want to be king of *my* hill—but you're not exactly one to bow down. Honestly, it's gotten harder for me to even picture the domestic life you describe.

Sister dear, I love you—and this isn't an "I love you *but*" but an "I love you *and*"—I love you and . . . I've been having some concerns about your long-term happiness. You're only twenty-four! Four years of marriage already, stepmother to a sixteen-year-old—yeah, you liked Joelle when she was an awkward twelve-year-old who needed your advice, but come on . . . I'm fifteen, I know exactly what teenagers are like and I suspect it's gonna keep getting worse—unless you can hang in there until she pirouettes off to college. (Though, from everything you've said about Jacob, I'm guessing he'll want his baby girl to go somewhere local.)

That all sounded extremely cynical and a bit angry. I care about you—that's what I'm trying to say. And if you're unhappy, I'm unhappy.

No real news at this end. Mom and Dad are unrelentingly predictable. They ask about you when they see one of your letters, but I try to keep everything tucked away when they come to visit so I don't have to answer too many questions. Like seriously, how many more times can they comment on how "eccentric" we are for exchanging snail mail in the twenty-first century when we could email or text like regular people? Mom, of course, thinks it's just an "artsy affectation." Sometimes I think she's happy that we communicate this way—a safe outlet for our weirdness. But other times I know it bothers her that we can't be more like Usual Children, normal and well adjusted. And Hanna really: Must you refuse every invitation? Every family event, every holiday? I mean, they get it: you have your Own Family now. But it hurts their feelings. And then I have to hear about it.

Maybe hurting their feelings is the point?

Anyhoo . . . You know I love the physical act of writing a letter, and receiving a physical one in reply. It makes me feel like we're ageless, living in another dimension, so sophisticated and urbane . . . Yeah, so I'll just fart on this before I stick it in the envelope . . .

Yours,
Goose

9

Dear Goose,

What would I do without you? (Look, I'm "unrelentingly predictable" too!) But . . . sometimes I wonder if I'm putting too much pressure on you. I don't mean to sound weird, or condescending . . . I just mean you're young and you have your own life.

You should be sharing yourself with your friends just as I should be sharing myself with my husband. I guess I'm supposed to be the more mature one here and set better boundaries. But since half the time I can't, you should tell me if it's ever too much—all this crap I tell you. As you know, I don't trust very many people, and that is a bad trait. But you didn't ask to be my confidant, so you have to promise to let me know if/when you need me to find another pen pal or otherwise fuck off. (I would understand, and I'd never hold it against you!) Until that day, please know how much I cherish your gentle heart and reliable ear. And I always appreciate how outraged you feel on my behalf.

That's my preamble for what I'm about to admit. Maybe I've gone too far this time to deserve your support. It wasn't just a hypothetical rant. I really did it:

I told Jacob I'm pregnant.

It was a little unnerving watching the emotions shuffle across his face. I saw him wanting to ask *How?* ('cause, you know, birth control). But he's old and wise enough to know that's a bad first response. Then I saw him trying to read me, trying to gauge if I was excited or . . . ? I endeavored to seem as neutral and matter of fact as possible so his reaction wouldn't be about *me*.

Naturally, we've talked about if we'd ever want to have a child of our own. And I truthfully told him I wasn't sure—leaning toward probably not. I've never gotten the sense that he was eager to have another child, so our conversations about it were brief and noncommittal. But with the reality in front of him . . . I have to say, he handled it admirably. He gently gripped my shoulders and gazed into my eyes, still trying to decipher my feelings. (Give him credit for that.)

"We weren't expecting this. But you've been a great stepmom to Jo."

I literally saw him then picturing a little brother or sister for Joelle. His face grew brighter, happier . . . it was shockingly easy for him to visualize a future with a baby. It almost made me feel guilty. He was so tender with me in that moment, so loving. It was the first time in months that he'd really been present, focused solely on me.

"You're not mad?" I asked. (Yes, I admit that was passive aggressive: he clearly wasn't angry and I was just hitting him up for more lovey-dovey reassurances.)

He wrapped his arms around me, pulling me closer, and smiled down at me. "I would only be mad if you were mad. And if you were upset this happened . . . you know I'd honor your choice."

I married him in anticipation of behavior exactly like this. Admittedly, I felt a tiny sting of regret while basking in his devotion. I'd hoped my plan would produce this reaction, and maybe this will get me a few weeks (or months?) of more considerate and attentive behavior. But now that he's imagined holding a new little daughter or son, it's going to hurt him when I proceed with the second part of my plan and "lose" the baby. Though, if I'm appropriately crushed by the loss, perhaps he'll fuss over me endearingly for a few more weeks (or months) . . . ?

Brother dear, please: do as I say and not as I do. Someday I want you to fall in love for *real*. Don't be as impatient as I was. I don't regret the path I've chosen, but you know I want only the best for you. No one's life is perfect, and there may be unavoidable spasms of suffering along the way. But I want you to experience all those giddy and sickening things that I've heard described about falling in love—apparently it's great? In spite of the nausea?

Speaking of nausea . . . perhaps I'll "suffer" from morning sickness. Obviously I don't want to miss work, but it would be lovely to see Jacob take a little more effort with food preparation. Would my queasy stomach inspire him to think about gentle, easy-to-digest foods? Could it propel him, perhaps, to set some toast or a bagel beside my morning coffee?

I admit I made a big mistake back in the day when I told him I loved to cook. I laid it on way too thick (not unlike a job candidate at an interview), repeatedly telling him and Joelle how I liked to express my love with well-prepared meals. I was concerned then, having never been in a real relationship, about my ability to sustain a nurturing front. And I didn't anticipate that it would lead to years of being responsible for every meal, day in and day out. I guess the upside is I'm a really good cook now? A good baker too. Sometimes I even bake the famous Jensen cinnamon rolls—though I guess that wouldn't impress you, seeing how you're the one person on earth who hates cinnamon.

Send me some more of your drawings when you get a chance? I love seeing the dark, wordless recesses of your mind. I try to pretend that our artistic talent wasn't hereditary . . . Oh well, I guess it doesn't matter where we got it. I love that Jacob gets jealous of me sometimes—he can spend weeks redeveloping a single negative (or weeks without shooting a single photograph), while I fill sketchbooks with the worlds inside my head. I wish we could visit them, you and me . . . disappear into another realm.

Yours,

Hanna

10

Hanna pulled up in front of the Bloomfield coffee shop, a place with a retro-diner vibe on a block of cool storefronts. Her 8:00 a.m. to 3:00 p.m. schedule had always worked well for driving Joelle places after school—maybe a little too well. Jacob had handled such duties before Hanna came into the picture, and his career in real estate afforded him a lot of flexibility. But, as with many domestic duties, once he saw how competent Hanna was at managing their daily routine, he left more and more things to her.

Gradually it had become a burden, and she was tiring of it. They weren't even enjoyable errands anymore, like taking Joelle to and from her voice and dance classes, which had been fun to watch. Now Hanna wasn't allowed to observe Joelle's classes and was forever ferrying her to rendezvous with her friends. Something happened to Jo the summer between ninth and tenth grades. Jacob described it as a butterfly emerging from a cocoon. Hanna didn't think the girl's metamorphosis was that beautiful, or that profound.

She'd liked her stepdaughter better when the girl had been more hesitant about the world, more skeptical, and generally more confused. *That* Joelle had claimed she didn't care about following the trends, being pretty, or having a ton of friends—after all, Hanna was there when she needed someone to talk to. *That* Joelle had loved going to the Mattress Factory with Hanna, wading together into the cosmos of surreal art installations. *That* Joelle had been in awe of Hanna's eclectic movie-night selections—documentary-like family dramas from Belgium and Denmark, art films from Korea and Mongolia, heartbreaking films from Romania and Afghanistan. They'd traveled the cinematic world together, and then had all sorts of interesting things to talk about as a family.

Joelle was bored of that now. Her interests had narrowed and shrunk, so she could quibble with her friends about the Marvel and DC universes. Like a moth drawn to the brightest light, Jo now sought the loud and colorful spectacle of computer-generated entertainment. Even Jacob was being lured away from cinema verité in favor of action and superpowers. Without Joelle's interest in her—and their once-mutual fascinations—Hanna was feeling more and more like the odd one out. And it didn't help that she'd become an unpaid chauffeur—especially when, at sixteen and nearly halfway through high school, Jo was more than capable of taking the bus.

Hanna had talked to Jacob about it multiple times, but he'd shrugged it off. "She'll be driving on her own soon enough."

As if a future driver's license negated the ability to ride public transportation. Both Jacob and Jo seemed to prefer to let Hanna do all the schlepping.

She texted to let Joelle know she was outside waiting. Jo had gotten a ride to the coffee shop with a friend, and Jacob had asked Hanna to pick her up when he found himself running late after showing a house in Fox Chapel. Contrary to what she'd told her brother, Hanna was starting to regret her life choices as she sat there in the car with the hazards on. This was supposed to have been a day off from errands; she had better things to do than lose the rest of the first sunny day in March—the first sunny day in eons—to the tedium of domestic life.

Told you, Goose whispered in her ear.

The yard and the back deck were calling to her, promising her good light and fresh air. She'd promised her TikTok followers she'd go live and show them in real time how she brought her detailed graphite images to life.

Finally Jo pushed open the coffee shop's glass door, waving good-bye to friends inside as her coin purse—cluttered with goofy key chain doodads—dangled from her wrist. There were only eight years separating them, but sometimes Joelle's exuberant demeanor made Hanna feel old. The fact that Hanna still had her black work scrubs on didn't help. Here was Joelle, shiny and awash in pastels. Here was Hanna, miserly and monotone.

Just as Hanna was getting ready to put on a smile of greeting, Jo's boyfriend hurried through the doorway, clearly intent on following her to the car. Jacob hadn't mentioned that Hanna would be picking up Boyd too. Not that it was an unusual occurrence, but she didn't like Boyd. His beefy boy body and gummy mouth. The way the strings of spittle always connected his top lip to the bottom one. It made Hanna grimace and shudder to think of her sweet stepdaughter kissing that gross mouth.

Joelle clambered into the back seat, and Boyd crawled in after her. (As if Hanna, alone in the front seat, needed more reminding that she was the chauffeur.) He reddened a little as he caught Hanna's eye and said hello. It always amused her that Boyd was so abashed by her presence. Jacob attributed it to her beauty—"perfect features on a flawless canvas." (Sometimes Jacob's words of endearment were a little cheesy, but Hanna never demurred.)

"Staying for supper?" She glanced at Boyd in the rearview mirror as she merged back into traffic on Liberty Avenue.

"Yes," he mumbled with his gummy lips.

"How was school?" she asked Joelle.

"Good," she replied, chipper but absorbed in her phone. Jo turned to Boyd, her tone turning conspiratorial. "Did Grayson send you that text?"

The two of them beheld their phones, looking separately at presumably the same thing.

"The monster in the woods?" he asked.

"Yes!"

"That's not real—he totally edited that."

Hanna listened to the coded nothingness of their conversation for the rest of the drive home. As Joelle slipped deeper into the tribe of adolescence, with its secretive tongue and rituals, Hanna was increasingly reminded of her own childhood. She remembered feeling distrustful of the words people spoke. She remembered seeing her parents' eyes ablaze with furtive life, yet their mouths uttered pabulum in a syrupy attempt at deflection. Young Hanna never quite understood what anyone meant.

It wasn't until they sent her away to Marshes, a place she described—to herself, to Goose, to Jacob—as a school for peculiar children, that she started to learn the language of partial truths that other people accepted as normal. Even the exchange she'd just had with Joelle would have confused her back in the day—Jo confirming a "good" day at school. Her body language, mood, facial expressions made "good" a shorthand for *I can't tell you everything that happened.* "Good" meant there were good things, frustrating things, normal things, things she was stuck with whether she liked it or not.

Hanna had kind of hated Marshes, but in many ways the school had taught her how to be a functioning person. For the three years that she was there, all she'd wanted was to go home. That hadn't prevented her from being an excellent student—though she probably hadn't learned the exact lessons her teachers had intended.

11

When he was finished eating, Jacob excused himself and retreated to his home office to do some work. Without being asked, Joelle and Boyd slipped down from their stools and started clearing away the supper dishes. It was one of the nicer perks of being "pregnant" that Hanna didn't have to beg anyone to do their chores now.

Joelle had been surprised but happy about the news—relayed to her by her father, though Hanna had asked him not to tell anyone until after she saw a doctor. When Hanna had come up with her little attention-seeking plan, she hadn't thought about how it might impact her stepdaughter—because Jo wasn't supposed to know about it. Oh well. Really, if Jo got upset later, it would be Jacob's fault for announcing the pregnancy too soon.

With everyone otherwise occupied, Hanna wandered off to the living room to check on her newest TikTok. The room's soft browns always felt cozy in the lamplight; she snuggled into her corner of the sectional couch, spacious enough to seat a sports team. Around her, the walls were adorned with their framed art—Hanna's drawings, and Jacob's enlarged photos. Blurry and slightly abstract, his pictures made her think of cinematic watercolors. That they both worked in gray tones gave a uniformity to the artwork that was displayed throughout the house.

Hanna had been forced to abandon her plan to work on the deck and live stream the creation of a new drawing. Supper preparations had required too much of her attention, and it had gotten colder out as evening set in. Instead, she'd created a sort of time-lapse video with short snippets edited together—condensed footage of herself sketching in the kitchen, shot during breaks in the cooking process. People liked seeing Hanna on screen as much as they liked seeing her artwork, and only occasionally did it annoy her when they complimented her appearance rather than her work. Her style was different—more earnest—than what most TikTokers bothered to do, but her followers appreciated the creative touches she added to her videos. In the new one, the drawing segments were intercut with quick flashes of sunlight—glistening on an empty flowerpot, streaking through the bare branches of a tree, fracturing into rainbows as she pointed the phone lens toward the sun.

After only two hours the video already had more than eight thousand views and six hundred likes. Even though she had almost eighty thousand followers, she made sure to use trending music and the right hashtags in an attempt to appeal to the algorithm. Her TikToks regularly got twenty-five thousand views or more, usually in the first day, though sometimes an older video suddenly sprang back to life—and sometimes a video went viral, with views in the hundreds of thousands. She genuinely enjoyed sharing her work this way and seeing people's reactions. Her pencil and charcoal drawings got an infinitely broader audience online than she could ever get by displaying her work in local art spaces. She'd tried to win Jacob over to the possibilities of modern technology—TikTok had niche communities for almost everything, including real estate. But after making an initial flurry of videos, he'd lost interest three weeks later.

———

Jo slunk into the room, clutching Boyd's chubby fingers. Hanna imagined they felt rubbery and slightly greasy, like sausage links, but she'd never verified it by actually touching them.

"Is it okay if we hang out in my room?" Jo sounded so meek and innocent. So hopeful, and yet so doubtful even as her tone promised nothing but wholesome activities. But Jacob had established a firm No-Bedrooms rule after coming home from work early one day and catching the two of them on her bed, fully clothed but entangled in lust.

"What would've happened if I hadn't come home?" he'd asked Hanna that night as they discussed the matter privately, naked on their king-size bed.

"I'm guessing you know the answer to that."

Jacob had shut his eyes. "Yeah."

"I've talked to her. Many times," said Hanna. "Maybe you should talk to her too, give her some life lessons from the male perspective."

"She doesn't want to talk to me about that stuff. And she just turned *sixteen*," he'd whined.

Hanna allowed him the hypocrisy of thinking his daughter was too young to be sexually active, never mind that he'd been sixteen his first time. *Being* sixteen felt much older than *watching* sixteen. Joelle often seemed immature for her age, and Hanna alternated between disapproving of how Jacob sheltered her, and admiring how he'd helped to preserve her innocence when the world around her was a catastrophic shit show.

Somehow Joelle didn't live in fear—of droughts or fires or tornadoes or pandemics, of low wages or diminishing returns, of school shootings or extinction. From Hanna's diverse selection of films, Joelle had learned a lot about the human condition, yet she managed to stay sanguine in spite of everything. But there was one area where Jo wasn't as blithe as she'd once been: her burgeoning interest in sex. Their girl talk was getting more awkward as it shifted away from the theoretical to the practical; gone were the days when Joelle had a million questions about *everything*. Yet, even recently, she'd insisted to Hanna that she wasn't ready to "go all the way"—to which they'd both cringed that every euphemism for sex was so *ugh*.

Now Hanna gave her a half-squished smile that she hoped said, "*I trust you, but my hands are tied.*" Aloud she added, "Your dad makes the rules."

"I know," Joelle sighed. She wasn't upset, merely disappointed.

Jo and Boyd plopped onto the couch and turned on the TV. Within seconds their limbs were fully intertwined, a two-headed human pretzel. Hanna wrote a final quick reply to one of her video's comments, and then extricated herself from the sofa. She headed down the hall toward Jacob's office, resigned to what she was about to do.

———

When she'd first moved in to Jacob's place—a few months after they'd met, and a few weeks after they'd gotten engaged—she'd thought of his house as a mansion. She'd always admired that winding stretch of Beacon Street, where many of the houses, including Jacob's, looked like they deserved to sit atop a hill on a private parcel of land. But it was in a city neighborhood within walking distance to restaurants, coffee shops, synagogues, specialty stores—and much more modest homes. Hanna and Jacob were in agreement that they loved Pittsburgh's varied architecture—it was part of why Jacob had gone into real estate—and Squirrel Hill showed it off so well.

By comparison, the house she'd grown up in in Shadyside, no matter its clean and modern sensibilities, seemed narrow and confined. In Jacob's home there was ample room for everyone and every activity: four sizable bedrooms on the second floor (one of which Hanna used as her art studio), and a little-used game room and guest suite in the finished basement. Jacob had long ago claimed the cavernous attic as his creative space, with its open lounge and work area, and the once-tiny bathroom was now the spacious darkroom where he developed his moody, black-and-white photos.

With her process of analyzing people and sorting out their prevailing characteristics came the awareness of the similarities between

Hanna's parents and Jacob. Well-educated, upper-middle-class East End residents with a certain aesthetic: in more ways than one, when Hanna left home she hadn't gone far. Her mother was an artist, as was Jacob. Her architect father had claimed the attic, the best room in the house, as his workspace, as had Jacob—though he also had a more perfunctory office on the first floor, for his day job tasks.

Jacob's taste in furnishings wasn't as austere as Hanna's parents', though his late wife, Rachel, likely deserved most of the decorating credit. When Goose was little, Hanna's mother had relented a little in her design choices, allowing for bright toys and plush throw rugs. But she'd reverted back to her old ways—white and wood—when Goose started first grade. (How happy Mommy had been when Gustav—well behaved and amiable—had started school! A normal school for a normal boy. Unlike troublesome Hanna, who got kicked out of every school she was enrolled in until they sent her away to Marshes.)

Sometimes it was a source of embarrassment for Hanna that she'd gone from her parents' house to her husband's. While she thought the move was clever and practical, other people—coworkers, Jacob's friends—judged her for having married at twenty to a widower two decades her elder. They judged him, too, dubious about his reasons for choosing such a youthful (*hot*) stepmother for his daughter. So what if he was in it for the sex and she for the money, if that's what they all thought. That was part of it, for both of them; there was no denying it. But they were also companionable and got along with relative ease—which was more than could be said for most of Jacob's quarreling and divorced friends.

Hanna had a general fuck-you attitude in regard to people's hypocritical expectations when it came to families. She knew better than most that it didn't matter how much money you had or how perfect you looked from the outside. Family units were complicated and notoriously dysfunctional, and she still considered herself lucky, more often than not, that she'd found such a workable alternative to living in her parents' house. Perhaps some young women desired independence;

Hanna had no interest in living alone. Sometimes she thought of herself as a constellation—an arrangement of stars that didn't actually look like anything until someone looked skyward and connected the dots. In spite of her ambivalence about the human race, she needed to be around people.

As she approached the open door to Jacob's office, she placed a hand on her abdomen. She'd been doing that a lot in recent weeks—in her husband's presence—to remind him of the baby that was supposedly growing inside her. Now she did it in part to quell the mini firecrackers of nerves that were mostly excitement, but partly apprehension, about the events that were about to unfold.

12

"Hey babe?" As Hanna stood in the doorway to her husband's office, she couldn't help but notice how cluttered it was, folders and stacks of papers everywhere. But he had a system, and except for the floors, she never cleaned in here, lest he accuse her later of messing up his system if he couldn't find something.

Jacob looked up from his computer, but the smile that started growing on his face faltered. Hanna often thought of herself as an actor in a scene, and for this one she needed to seem tired, and maybe a little worried. It wasn't just how she arranged her face that mattered; her body equally needed to manifest the right presentation of feelings. It would be a poor show, indeed, if her face appeared grim while her limbs jittered with excitement.

"What's wrong?" he asked, with the requisite concern of a good scene partner.

"I'm not feeling well." She pressed her hand against her belly, rubbing it as if something hurt. (That part, at least, wasn't a complete lie: she always got a little crampy with the onset of her period.)

Her husband pushed his ergonomic chair away from his desk, making room for her on his lap. Hanna never thought of sitting on his lap as a childish thing—she'd stopped sitting on her father's lap when she was seven. She sat sideways across Jacob's thighs and wrapped her arms loosely around his neck. Their heads touched as she leaned in.

"What's wrong?" he asked again, softer. He'd grown tender with her over the past few weeks, like he'd been during the first year of their relationship. Now that she'd resurrected the trait in him, would his tenderness last even if she wasn't "with child"? She didn't want it to go away, but she didn't think it was smart to stretch the ruse much longer; he was excited to go with her to the doctor's and see the ultrasound.

"I don't know. I feel a little . . . squiggly inside. Can't really explain it."

"Something you ate?"

She shrugged. "I want to go upstairs and lie down—"

"Yes, you should take it easy." He shifted, ready to launch her from his lap. Was he too eager to get rid of her, or trying to be helpful?

"But Joelle and Boyd are watching TV . . ." She left him to picture the two of them in the living room, unattended.

Jacob patted her hip, a go-now, don't-worry gesture. "I just need to send off an email."

She wasn't sure if that meant he'd head to the living room in a minute or an hour, but at least he couldn't blame her if he later found his daughter canoodling on the couch. The God of Hormones was either very clever about the progression of adolescence—where horny teenagers lacked access to private, comfortable quarters—or very cruel. Hanna was glad not to waste another evening in front of the TV pretending she didn't see Boyd's hand sliding over Joelle's ribs, slithering under her shirt. It seemed inane to her to babysit two teenagers and she wished Joelle and Boyd would spend less time at home. But Jacob liked having them where he could "keep an eye on them."

What Hanna really wished was that Joelle would dump Boyd. Why did she like him so much? A dull lump of boy flesh.

"Call me if you need anything." He gave her a kiss on the cheek as she readied to depart his lap.

He meant that quite literally: the house was big enough that it was easier to text or call each other if they were on different floors. She beamed an appreciative smile at him as she left the room. But Jacob's attention was already back on his computer screen.

———

Their en suite bathroom was another aspect of her married life that often reminded Hanna of her parents, because of its similarities to one in her childhood home. Her mother treated her own all-white, pristine bathroom as a sanctuary. (Mommy used to lock herself in there to get away from Hanna whenever she was getting on Mommy's nerves.) For years Hanna and Jacob had been batting around renovation ideas to make the room less stark and more user friendly. Neither of them used the separate bathtub, and they both liked the idea of an extra-large shower with multiple showerheads. And Hanna wanted more color. Soft greens or blues—something that was more alive, gentle hues that whispered of a needed oasis.

Jacob was firm on waiting until they knew where Joelle would be going to college, in case she picked an extravagantly expensive one. The real estate market had been up and down in recent years and Hanna agreed, at least for show, that they should avoid any reckless spending. Their bathroom, like the rest of the house, was beautiful—its real crime was triggering memories of Hanna's childhood. (She remembered knock-knock-knocking until Mommy whipped open the door and screamed in her face.) For now, Hanna had added some teakwood accents and foxtail ferns. And she'd replaced Jacob's (or were they Rachel's?) light-gray towels with a set the color of robins' eggs.

For the sake of what she needed to do, she slipped into a pair of older panties—and didn't replace her panty liner. The start of her period made it the perfect time to "miscarry" her pregnancy with some amount of gory authenticity. She hoped Jacob wouldn't wait more than an hour or so before coming upstairs to check on her. In case her period came on too strong before he got there, she grabbed a towel from the linen closet—and left her soft jogging pants on the bathroom floor—so she wouldn't stain anything important. She flipped off the bathroom light and headed for her side of the king-size bed, where she spread the towel atop their downy comforter.

It wasn't that she didn't like to sleep next to her husband, but she was glad they had such a large bed and could sleep without touching. Physical intimacy didn't come naturally to her, unlike sex; sex was easy because she got something out of it. But she'd had to train herself to rub Jacob's knee when they sat side by side, to caress his cheek when they were face to face. In truth, skin—other people's skin—bothered her.

As a child she'd come to think of skin as a living suit of clothes, which then made her see clothing differently too. She had imagined the dresses in her darkened closet growing imperceptibly every night. When her socks got too stretched out, Hanna had believed they'd grown. She'd worried on such thoughts, and wondered what unexpected things human skin, a costume of cells, did when the body was asleep and no one was looking. Did it wiggle and wrinkle and contort itself in strange ways? Or maybe it molded its pliable folds into an alternate face.

It had been all too easy then for her imagination to breathe life into unlikely things—inanimate objects that became her friends, or people from history who became companionable ghosts. Adults had described her as creative and naive. Now, when people saw her artwork, they often labeled it as fantasy or horror and complimented her ingenuity. Hanna didn't correct them, but she thought of many of her drawings as *memories*. Once a vivid image settled in her mind—whether as a child or an adult—it lived there forever. Skin, and to a lesser degree clothing, still seemed alive and strange to her at times. Sometimes when she traced her fingertips back and forth along Jacob's bare shoulder blades, something he enjoyed, she pictured her nails as scalpels, delicately dissecting the layers of skin and peeling away the mask of his outer self.

She lay on her side, facing the door. As she scrolled through her TikTok feed, she kept the volume on her phone low: she needed to be ready to run to the bathroom when Jacob headed down the hall toward their room. A half hour had passed when she heard the front door open.

And then voices, half-inside and half-outside. Boyd's father must have come to pick him up after finishing his shift as a security guard. Both of Boyd's parents worked erratic hours—his mother was an ICU nurse—which made Jacob disinclined to let Joelle go over to their house.

As a teenager, Hanna wouldn't have wanted her parents to schlep her all over the place. The tiny private high school she'd attended had been within walking distance of her house. She'd had no real friends at school (but no enemies either). Back then she'd had no need to pal around with people; if she behaved, her parents gave her whatever she wanted. (Joelle had been like that once, and Hanna had assumed her stepdaughter would *always* be a person that she intrinsically understood.) While Hanna had kept to herself and done her work, she'd plotted her future. It wasn't until she went to the Community College of Allegheny County—the first step in becoming a phlebotomist—that she started socializing, and even then it was only practice. Rehearsal for the adult self she envisioned presenting to the world.

Moisture bubbled between her legs and she clamped them together in an effort to keep the blood from spreading. Bored, she tossed her phone aside, ready for the next act in the living theater of her married life. She really didn't consider, or care about, the dishonesty of the script she'd written. Didn't everyone play a role when it suited them?

Finally she heard Jacob call down to Joelle from the top of the stairs and knew he was on his way. Hanna sprang from the bed and tossed the towel into the laundry basket as she headed for the bathroom. For a moment she kept her ear pressed to the closed bathroom door, waiting for her husband's arrival.

13

When she yanked down her underwear and sat on the toilet, she smiled, ever so briefly, at the sticky smear of plummy blood. Then she rested her elbows on her thighs and hung her head, ready for an audience. Between her parted legs she saw red droplets splashing into the water below, filmy designs that spread in concentric shapes along the surface. Needing to summon tears, she concentrated on how appreciative she felt—and made the tears in honor of her body and the beautiful, ephemeral collaboration it was creating with the toilet bowl. In that moment she felt powerful. Indestructible. Everything was falling into place. *Will it stay there?*

"Hanna? Honey?" Jacob's voice grew louder as he neared the bathroom door. He tapped it with his knuckles.

As she inhaled, readying herself for a gasp of sobs, she caught a whiff of the eucalyptus bouquet on the vanity. "Babe?" she squeaked, her voice broken and pathetic.

Jacob eased his way through the door with the caution of a man who feared a honey badger might pounce on his throat. By mutual agreement, they weren't a couple who liked to use the toilet in front of each other. "Everything okay?"

Hanna burst into tears. Ready for the reveal, she sat up straight, spreading her legs a little wider to give Jacob the best view of the ruin inside her panties. His eyes and mouth popped open in surprise.

"I lost . . ." The sobs overwhelmed her, and Jacob rushed to her side.

"Oh honey!" He knelt on one knee beside the toilet, his arms akimbo as he embraced her. The position was made even more awkward by his attempts to avert his eyes from her stained underwear.

Sometimes Hanna forgot that other people weren't comfortable around blood. Though, in this instance, perhaps his fear was of seeing a tiny mass, a clot that had once promised a different future. Hanna pushed the panties down to her ankles so he wouldn't have to see the blood anymore.

She reached behind her and flushed the toilet. Jacob gasped, an inhale that might have been the prelude to tears or the sound of shock. Had she just flushed their fetus down the toilet with less regard than one might give a goldfish?

He turned his face away from her. Hanna was out of her depths with the dos and don'ts of postmiscarriage protocol. She swiped at her tears with the back of her hand. It was time to move the show along—they needed to get away from the toilet. As she stood, Jacob stood with her.

"Can I get you anything? Do you need to see a doctor?"

She shook her head. "I wasn't very far along." She wished she could ask him to make her a whiskey sour. Perhaps, given the circumstances, he'd understand her desire for a stiff drink, but it set a better tone to maintain a somber mood. "Maybe just some chamomile tea? Feeling a little crampy—I guess that's what I was feeling."

"Of course." He fled the room. Hanna resented his quick departure—was he too eager to get away from her? Or just trying to be helpful?

She balled up the panties and threw them in the garbage. Quickly cleaned herself up. As she got fresh underwear from her dresser, she wondered if she'd miscalculated. Would Jacob have been more responsive—more present—if she'd made the show less visceral? She'd thought the blood would be more convincing, more dramatic. But maybe she'd grossed him out.

———

She was sitting in bed, tucked in like a good little unwell wife, when he returned.

"Thank you," she said as he set the mug on her bedside table.

He walked around to his side and sat on the bed, one leg tucked under him. Neon labels flashed around his head—*uncomfortable! Itchy!* The *itchy* label meant he wanted to run away but a sense of duty told him to stay. Hanna saw this in him whenever an intense moment required him to do or say more than he felt able to follow through with. She'd witnessed it for the first time at her very first dinner at the house, when Jo had gotten her period. More than once since then she'd wondered if she'd made it too easy for Jacob, handling the stuff he simply didn't want to do.

Had that been his game all along?

Maybe it wasn't fair to think that way, but if she could be calculating, so could he. He'd relinquished a lot of responsibilities to her, and maybe it wasn't simply a matter of her being competent and efficient. Maybe he just didn't like getting his hands dirty and had found a young woman willing to do anything to get out of her parents' house. And perhaps, as she was, he was growing bored of his game, and was ready for something else. As Joelle got more independent—even in slowly permitted increments—both she and Jacob seemed to be drifting away from Hanna. Even right here and now. Hanna saw how he was perched on the bed, the physical subtext indicating his desire to leave the room.

"Do you have more work to do tonight?" she asked, giving him an out.

"No . . ." He hesitated, perhaps realizing he'd missed his chance to escape the awkward denouement. Then he surprised her and inched closer, taking her hand. "We can try again. If you want. Try to have a baby?"

Oh. *Oh!* It was a confounding turn of events. He sounded hopeful, and his eyes searched hers. What was she supposed to say? Weren't they supposed to mourn their lost embryo before they started planning for another?

"Do you really want . . ." She tried to sound inquiring and not pissed off. He'd never expressed a strong desire to have a child with her. "I didn't think . . ."

"I know. I know, but . . . it wasn't real before, and this . . . almost was. And Joelle will be on her own in a few years. You're young. And I'm not that old."

As he added up his reasons, Hanna wanted to smack the beseeching look off his face. This was *not* what they'd talked about. His eagerness for her to get pregnant—for real—felt like a betrayal. Being supportive of an "accident" was one thing, but suddenly Jacob was acting needy, fearful of a future when he couldn't be a father on a daily basis.

An image came to her, sharp and unwanted. Her precious daddy. Driving away. Leaving her behind in a puddle of tears at the school for peculiar children. Before that, he'd been a Good Daddy. It was never the same after that.

She knew from experience that a man's joy in being a father could change. Jacob was ignorant of that reality. With a daughter as good natured and reliable as Joelle (despite the heavy petting), his fathering had only ever boosted his ego, made him feel like he was doing every-thing right. Hanna had seen her parents struggle; she hadn't been an easy child to raise. And once Goose came along, his presence affirmed for them that the problem, all along, had been Hanna. (Stupid Mommy deserved a *lot* more of the blame.)

Some women bore a child to please a husband, to keep him from tugging too hard on the leash. Even if it was something that Jacob now really wanted, Hanna wasn't sure if having a baby was worth the risk. What if she gave birth to a child who was as sensitive and creative and misunderstood as she was? She would hate to be as impatient a mommy as her own mother had been. And she would hate to be the reason why a sentient creature had to endure a miserable life. And . . . she shut out the other reasons.

"We can think about it," she said meekly. "I'm sorry, it's just . . . I didn't expect to feel this way, but . . ." A tear slid down her cheek and she pressed her lips together as if to keep dammed a deluge of emotions.

"Yes, I'm sorry, I don't mean to rush you. I just wanted you to know—if you wanted to try again . . ."

He left the sentence as open ended as the possibility. It was a worrying development. Hanna realized then that even if she played her part well in the coming days, Jacob wasn't going to be responsive or invested in "mourning" this loss. He was ready to move on, eager to do it right this time—even if that meant taking their marriage in a direction it was never meant to go.

14

Dear Goose,

Scene from a marriage:

The young wife, still in her black scrubs, leans on the kitchen counter making a shopping list. She has just finished Swiffering the floor, as someone left crumbs everywhere. In her left hand is a fresh, cold drink—a whiskey sour (extra lemony and sugary). She sips the drink as she double-checks the contents of the refrigerator.

The middle-aged husband enters through the door from the garage, wearing a sweaty long-sleeve T-shirt and joggers. He's a little out of breath. His running shoes are muddy and he leaves them by the door.

They make eye contact as he crosses to the refrigerator. The young wife is irritated that once again he went for a run without her, at a totally random time. The middle-aged husband looks irked, too, but the cause is less clear.

He fetches himself a glass of cold water and gulps it down.

"I guess you've decided to wait to try getting pregnant again."

So there is the source of his displeasure—but what the hell? When the young wife glares at him, clueless, he gestures toward the whiskey sour.

"You've been drinking more recently."

"Have I?" she asks, unaware that her intake of alcohol was being monitored. "So?"

"Alcohol and babies don't mix."

This, dear brother, is the shit I'm dealing with.

I know you're going to suggest this is all my fault—but how could I have known that losing an accidental pregnancy would make him really, really want the real thing? I was expecting some sympathy, maybe a little coddling, but it's become dangerous for me to act broken up about the miscarriage because Jacob's only form of reassurance is to tell me we can try again. If that had been a real loss, about which I'd been genuinely shattered, I'd be going nuclear on him for his shockingly insensitive behavior. But, for obvious reasons, I'm not really in a position to point that out.

I know the conclusion you're drawing as you read my pathetic words: lies are more trouble than they're worth. Yes, yes they are. But you know that's why I save lies as a tool of last resort. Ah, famous last words . . . *It seemed like a good idea at the time.* But seriously, I didn't know what else to do. I feel Jacob and Joelle both pulling away, growing less interested in me. I thought this would be a tidy little drama, with a beginning and an end. Now I have to wonder . . .

Should I seriously try to get pregnant????????

Yours,

Hanna

15

Dear Hanna,

What if you spawn a mutant? Or a serial killer? Or a compassionless conformist? What if you get pregnant with quadruplets? Or twins conjoined at the face—or the butthole? What if you have some sort of horrible complication during delivery and bleed out and die? Alternately, can you imagine having a greedy little mouth stuck to your tit, sucking on it till it bleeds? Do you really want to spend your days mucking around with a tiny screaming monster's shit and piss?

And these are only the most obvious pitfalls, the things everyone who watches horror movies (or reality television) knows about. I'm sure there are other potential disasters that happy-go-lucky would-be parents shut out of their minds as they roll the dice. But if you're going to contemplate this, you need to consider every horrible possibility—'cause you'll be stuck with it after the fact.

You're welcome.

Seriously, Sis. Don't have a kid for a shitty reason. Don't have a kid for any reason less than it's the only thing that will make you happy—and even then, think twice. Have you seen the state of the world?

Dad thinks we're about five years away from having to buy an insurance plan that will guarantee an individual's access to fresh drinking water. And you and I will probably have to pay for the honor of breathing by the time we're senior citizens—when the rich people buy up the oxygen and leave the poor people to suffocate. (And yes, Dad's doom and gloom about the climate crisis and corporate greed is getting to me. Betcha a million dollars he eventually convinces Mom to move to Sweden. "They recycle everything!")

If none of this deters you from stretching out your vagina for the benefit of overpopulation—you know "conservatives" are opposed to abortion because every new human brings corporations more profit, right?— then I will support your decision. And by *support* I mean I will cheer you on, and listen to you complain. But you know you can NOT count on me to babysit—babysitting is something I'll never do, so let's make sure we're clear about that.

I really don't want to hurt your feelings . . . but I would be remiss in my brotherly duties if I didn't drag you back to reality. And that reality is: Hanna, do you really think you've got what it takes to care for a baby, *24/7*??? I love you, but I say this as a once-little kid: you might not have the proper attention span to be responsible for someone who's young and fragile. What are you going to do when you get bored of looking after him/her/it? Storm off to your bedroom for some alone time? I'm not trying to shame you for being a terrible babysitter, but having a baby requires a lot more than a three-hour commitment. ;-) (See, the winky face softens the blow.)

I think my work here is finished, but if you need more pep talks, you know where to find me.

Yours,

Goose

PS Here's a quick sketch of a goose drowning in an oil spill.

16

Goose's letter took up residence in her thoughts. Made her question who the hell she was to even consider having a baby.

Hanna remembered being called into an unscheduled family-therapy session during her second year at Marshes; she had recently turned nine. She'd entered the room tentatively, clutching her little friend Skog to her chest, unsure if she was about to hear good news or bad news. One time she'd been called in to be told she was going home—only for a long week-end—but it was a pleasant surprise. The next time she was summoned it was to tell her that *Farfar*, Daddy's father, had died. This time Daddy and Mommy were all smiles as she sat across from them. Just as Hanna noticed that Mommy was plumper than she'd ever been, the therapist proceeded to explain that she was pregnant.

"You're going to have a little brother!" Mommy said, cautiously watching to see how Hanna would react.

"Don't worry, we have plenty of love for both of you," said Daddy.

Everyone was afraid Hanna would be jealous, angry. But just like Daddy and Mommy, Hanna wanted someone new to love too. She fell in love with baby Gustav. Each of them thought of Goose as *theirs*—Mommy's normal child, Daddy's baby boy, the sibling Hanna never had. That didn't mean things weren't weird when Hanna finally got to go back home to live. Goose was almost a year old by then, and Hanna was ten and a half. All she ever wanted was to hold him, to pet his downy blond hair. But Mommy never let her. Mommy was always tense, watchful, ready to spring up and snatch Goose away whenever Hanna came near him. Only under careful supervision had she been allowed to hold her brother's pudgy hands as he learned to walk.

In the intervening years, Hanna almost forgot that her unease around babies had been planted then. By her mother. Her mother's distrust of her. Mommy had planted that seed, that Hanna posed a danger. And Hanna had internalized it, and a part of her feared, then and now, that she would accidentally do the wrong thing. Was it true that she wasn't capable of caring for a baby, or had she been infected by her mother's anxiety? Parents were allowed to be imperfect, to make mistakes—more than one therapist had explained that to Hanna. So wasn't she allowed to make mistakes too?

Maybe not.

When Hanna made mistakes, no one could ever forgive her. That was another thing she'd learned as a child. Now she wasn't sure if she could ever risk having a baby. Joelle had come into her life half-grown. Would Hanna have ruined her somehow if Joelle had been younger? Hanna needed to make Jacob see that their family was fine as it was—he didn't need a midlife crisis baby. And the last thing she wanted was for Jacob to start seeing her as an untrustworthy demon, like her parents had.

So that's that.

It felt good to have clarity.

———

She changed out of her work scrubs into comfy joggers and a loose top. As usual, the laundry basket was full, so she carried it from her bedroom to the small room next door and put the load in the washer. Such were their lives—with work clothes, running clothes, lounging clothes—that there was always laundry that needed to be done. The load of Joelle's that Hanna had put in the dryer that morning was still there. She quickly folded everything, gazing out the window as she returned each piece to Jo's basket.

It was a decent enough day that Hanna had walked to and from work and thought she might go for a run after getting home. But as she contemplated the backyard, she wasn't sure. It had been a soggy April, gray and wet for weeks. Today the precipitation was more like a fine mist, like the spray at the base of a powerful waterfall. But it was finally warm. The grass popped out of the earth in brilliant green spikes. The trees were still the ragged bones of winter, darkened by moisture, but the branches were dotted with little green knots, waiting to unfurl. She opened the window and took a deep breath.

Wet earth emitted a certain perfume, an almost tangible blossoming of life. She imagined the worms churning through the soil. Then a squirrel chittered and chased another one up a tree.

Squirrelly girl.

That had been one of her nicknames once. But after her dad became afraid of her, he stopped calling her precious things. She liked squirrels, though. They were fuzzy and cute (even if they did eat most of the seeds in the bird feeder).

It wasn't warm enough to leave the windows open for long, but she decided that instead of a run, she'd air out the house. Now on a mission, she strode down the hall and deposited the basket of folded clothes outside Joelle's closed door and then headed for her studio. Hanna opened the window farthest from her drawing table—so no rogue droplets could splatter her mishmash of sketchbooks. Next, she jogged down the stairs and threw open the window on the landing.

In the living room, she slid open the door to the patio, which ran the length of the house from the living room to the kitchen. Again she faced the backyard and considered it—the wild green of an evolving, living canvas. Early spring was a liminal time, no longer winter but not yet the heart of a new season. The thought of things pushing up through the mud enchanted her: dormant plant life, the skeletal reaching hands of—

"Hanna?"

She spun around. With her back to the room, she hadn't seen Joelle come in.

"Hey." Hanna grinned. "Getting a little fresh air. It smells like spring today."

Jo knit her fingers together. One socked foot fidgeted against the wood floor (like a worm, finding resistance in the soil). Big glowing words hovered above her. *Worried. Scared.*

"Is everything okay?" Hanna asked, suspecting it wasn't. She and Joelle moved toward the couch at the same time.

"Is Daddy working?" Jo sounded hopeful. And Hanna understood she needed him to be gone to say whatever it was that was on her mind.

"Yup, it's just us for supper tonight. No Boyd?"

Joelle shook her head, tucking her feet under her as she sat on the couch. Hanna sat a cushion away from her—close enough, but with a little space between them. Though Hanna hadn't experienced the full catalog of normal teenage obsessions—such as the all-consuming desire to have a tight ring of friends, or the contradictory need to establish a unique identity while conforming to the likeness of the peer group—she'd learned a lot from movies. And she was an expert in how unfair and disappointing adults could be—teachers, therapists, parents.

She tried to imagine now what was causing Jo such angst. Had Boyd done something? Had a friend or classmate started an ugly rumor about her? Or might she be unhappy with her father? Eventually every girl felt oppressed in her father's house.

"What's up?" Hanna asked, hoping to give her stepdaughter a gentle opening.

They hadn't talked like this recently, just the two of them, private and intimate. Hanna thought back to past troubles: Joelle, a perfectionist, worried about a class; Joelle, then timid, wondering what to say in various social situations. Everything to a young girl was *so important*, so consequential—yet so insignificant in light of greater injustices. Perhaps Hanna had done her job of confidence boosting a bit too well; Joelle was part of an in crowd now, and rarely sought Hanna's reassurance. But here they were, like old times. Back then, after one of their girl chats, they'd watch a film together. Hanna quickly thought of some options for what they might watch, should it go that way now. She needed to stay in the moment, yet she looked forward to sitting side by side, silently bonding as they viewed the foreign landscape of other people's lives.

Joelle hesitated. She used a finger to press her bottom lip against her teeth so she could gnaw at it.

"Seriously Jo, what's going on?" Hanna was getting a twinge of concern. Joelle's coloring was off, and her expression had a glazed quality, the frozen features of a porcelain mask. Whatever was bothering her, it seemed to be more serious than usual. "You can tell me, I won't judge you."

"It's not that."

"And I won't tell your dad, if it's something you need to work out without your father's overbearing concern." Hanna grinned, hoping it made the comment as lighthearted as she'd intended.

Jo gave her a weak smile. "It's not that either. I wanted to talk to you . . . but I didn't want . . . I don't want to say something that would hurt you."

Oh. That possibility hadn't occurred to Hanna. Was Joelle upset with *her*? Was she the one being an annoying parent? Hanna tried to think of what she might have done—or not have done, since a person could feel slighted by a thing left unsaid or a promise unfulfilled. She didn't like being criticized. The dread that she was about to be ambushed made her feel less charitable than she had when they first sat down to talk.

"It's okay," Hanna said. "I'm not made of glass."

Maybe Jacob said something. The thought popped into her head. Would Jacob do that? Talk about her behind her back with his daughter? Hanna had sensed for a while that Jacob was keeping things, thoughts and feelings, to himself. Had he opened up to Joelle instead of her? She braced herself for whatever her stepdaughter was about to say.

Joelle chewed on her lip for another moment. "I'm pregnant."

17

Another thing Hanna didn't like: surprises. Surprises made her feel out of control. She remembered surprising Jacob with this same unexpected announcement, and he'd handled it so well. But she was unsure what to do, what to say, or even how to rearrange her face. Conflicting possibilities warred inside her.

Embrace your scared stepdaughter.

Scream at her for fucking up her life.

But a larger part of her was confused. Now Hanna understood the instinct to blurt out *How?* The how of it, in this instance, being *where?* Had Joelle and Boyd rendezvoused in the school locker room for a quick shag? Or slipped into the bathroom together at the coffeehouse? She imagined sticky-floored movie theaters and the spider-infested basements of pimply friends. The possibilities were a little gross, and sad.

This wasn't what Hanna wanted for Joelle. Especially not with that lump of a nothing boy. Boyd Bland—not his actual surname, but it might as well have been. Inoffensive in demeanor, but borderline lifeless. He wasn't an academic, or an athlete, or an artist. He wasn't the goofball, or the daredevil, or the pothead. Hanna had considered him an okay-ish choice for a first and temporary boyfriend—harmless—but this changed everything.

Joelle gazed at her, waiting for a response. Hanna wasn't prepared for this. Her brain whirred, trying to land on any suitable reaction. As a child, at Marshes, she'd been taught certain techniques for dealing with situations when she couldn't understand why something was happening or what was being asked of her. She'd practiced asking for time to sit and think. They'd role-played ways that Hanna might express her confusion and request more information to help with her understanding. But none of those things could be applied here, and Hanna was expected, as an adult, to respond appropriately. And she knew she was failing.

The one thing she did understand was that Jo had hesitated to tell her because she feared Hanna would be hurt. And Hanna was hurt—disappointed that Joelle had not, in fact, ever really listened to her stepmom's good advice. About becoming sexually active. Or using birth control. Yet, Hanna saw in Joelle's sweet, wounded face the girl's concern over Hanna's recent miscarriage. That's what Jo thought would hurt her: the possibility of a baby in the house that wasn't hers. And, for any number of reasons, that was a problem, though Joelle's sensitivity was misdirected.

"What about all those times you told me you weren't ready, that you and Boyd didn't want to rush into anything?" It came out angrier than she'd intended. Hanna clamped her jaw tight to keep from saying more.

Jo gaped at her like a cornered deer. Hanna took a deep breath.

"I'm sorry, I'm just . . . I wasn't expecting this."

"I know." Joelle tugged at one of the frayed strings at the knee hole of her distressed jeans. In barely a whisper she added, "I feel really stupid."

Stepmother Hanna was supposed to immediately counter with "You're not stupid," but her tornado of thoughts was busy stirring up other angles to consider. Like, what if this was a ruse—a bullshit tale, not unlike her own? A ploy for attention. A test of Hanna's devotion. A device to elicit some sort of emotional (or material) payoff. Maybe it was trending on TikTok, *Ways to Torture Your Stepparent*. The whole conversation was playing out like a scene in a TV show or a young adult novel, right down to Joelle's perfect, nervous fidgeting.

"Are you sure?" Hanna asked, testing her, doubting her.

"We took three tests."

We. So Boyd already knew. So Joelle wasn't performing. Not that Hanna could imagine how such a deception would benefit a strait-laced teenage girl like Joelle, but did anyone really understand all the rites and rituals of adolescence? Hanna would have preferred for this to be an insane prank, a dare thought up by one of Jo's popular pals. Unfortunately, she needed to accept reality—and stop withholding the support Joelle was waiting for.

"See, this is why I didn't want to tell you." A plump movie-star tear dripped down Jo's cheek. "I knew you'd be upset—you just lost your baby. And here I am . . . stupid and pregnant."

"No, that's not . . ." To the best of her ability, Hanna stilled the cyclone of out-of-control thoughts. "I'm sorry for being—I know you were nervous about telling me, and I don't mean to be so . . . I don't want to ask, 'How did this happen?' But I have to assume now that you've been lying—to me, to your dad."

Joelle hung her head.

"Girls have sex," Hanna continued. "It's a natural part of life—which I'd wanted, I'd hoped, to better prepare you for. The lying is the part I'm hurt by."

That sounded like an appropriate thing to say. An hour ago, she hadn't considered the possibility that good-girl Joelle possessed the instinct to lie. Now Hanna wondered: How long had Joelle been lying? How often did she lie? In a way, it made her stepdaughter more relat-able. But Hanna didn't let on that that part was a relatively easy thing for her to understand. It seemed likely that everyone lied. Everyone contained multitudes, and it wasn't that long ago that Hanna had been a young person tormented by people's inability to truly understand her. Perhaps Joelle wasn't so much a liar but a hider, afraid of what people—her father, especially—would think of her multidimensional self.

Yet, if Hanna was being honest with herself, it did kind of hurt to be at the receiving end of Joelle's deception. With their closeness in age—with Hanna being more like a cool older sister—she'd assumed that Jo would keep her in the loop. It was probably selfish that in this moment Hanna should feel injured: that Joelle hadn't come to her to get birth control, that Hanna hadn't anticipated the need for it.

"I'm sorry." Jo sniffled, bringing Hanna back to the problem at hand.

"Jo . . ." She opened her arms, and Joelle flung herself into Hanna's embrace.

"You're not mad?"

Hanna sighed. "I'm not mad. This isn't what I wanted for you, but I'm not mad. And I'll help you, of course. Abortion is still legal in Pennsylvania. And it's up to you if you tell your father."

Joelle quickly pulled away, her face once again a frozen mask. "I didn't say I wanted to get rid of—"

"I thought . . . I mean, you're not even halfway through high school." A flame ignited at the base of Hanna's spine—the warning sign that she'd made a mistake, and someone had caught her. But she didn't understand why Jo was looking at her so warily. "Don't you want an . . . ?"

Hanna hesitated to say the word again. The word was divisive. The procedure had been demonized by a scientifically clueless portion of society—people who maddeningly confused the projected sound waves of a machine for a heartbeat. Maybe Joelle didn't understand that. Hanna reached out and took her hand.

"Don't let the controversy scare you. A bunch of dividing cells is *not* a *person*, a child. When it lives outside of the womb, that's a baby. Don't let anyone tell you your life isn't as important. *You're* the one who's alive *now*—and you're the one who's most impacted."

"I know." Turbulence splintered Joelle's features, one part of her face disagreeing with another as different emotions emerged.

"What about your dancing?" An image came to her of Joelle performing onstage with a big pregnant belly and top hat and jazz hands. "You can't . . . Weren't you thinking about musical theater? Broadway?"

"I dunno. I haven't decided, it was just an idea. I can still sing even if . . ."

"I know it's not an easy choice," said Hanna, "but the alternative is harder. You don't have to give up all of your dreams. You can take a pill—it doesn't have to be anything scary."

Joelle withdrew her hand. Hanna watched her retreat within herself, like an animal descending into its underground burrow. A new word hovered over Jo's head. *Disappointed.* In some manner Hanna had let her down.

"That's not why you came to me?" she asked, as stricken and defeated as Joelle.

"No," she said softly. "I came to you first so you could tell Daddy."

18

Hanna didn't tell Jacob. Instead, for the time being, she'd convinced Joelle to really think about it—to really ponder a future where she was forever responsible for someone else's life. It would've been easier if Hanna could've made a copy of Goose's letter—see if it had the same effect on Jo as it had on her. But Joelle didn't know Goose; she might not feel the warmth of his heart behind his sardonic words. The best Hanna had been able to do was paraphrase the essence of his warnings about unpredictable offspring. And she'd gravely counseled her about the physical realities of carrying and delivering a baby. And how the trajectory of her life would be utterly changed. Hanna hadn't been trying to scare her, or exert her own opinion *too* much. But she'd wanted to be clear: terminating the pregnancy was a good option.

A week later, she was still watching Joelle out of the corner of her eye. Hanna kept expecting to get a furtive nod, a signal that she was ready to put this mistake behind her. But every day Joelle performed with flawless normality. She kissed her daddy's cheek each morning before heading to school. She did her homework and loaded the dishwasher and asked for permission to go somewhere with someone to do all the normal somethings. Boyd hadn't been around quite as much, and Hanna hoped that was a positive sign. Whatever Jo thought about her lump of a boyfriend, Hanna knew she'd be better off without him.

On Sunday morning, Jo came into the kitchen looking pasty, her hair disheveled. *From vomiting over the toilet bowl?* Though Hanna's first thought was morning sickness, she stayed quiet, sipping her coffee, watching the interplay between father and daughter.

"Feeling okay?" Jacob asked as Jo gulped a glass of water.

"Yeah. Didn't sleep that great."

"You look a little pale. You getting enough protein?"

Joelle looked at Hanna, and they both rolled their eyes. Protein was Jacob's perennial concern regarding his daughter's health and her meat-free diet. He'd relented to her desire to go vegetarian the previous year, and Hanna prepared many nutritious vegetarian meals with beans and nuts and leafy greens (and cheese, cheese, cheese, because everything tasted better with cheese). It wasn't her fault if Joelle's food preferences leaned more toward french fries than tofu—though her diet was the least of her current problems.

"I'm fine, Daddy. I'm on my period, if you must know." She cut a quick glance at Hanna, acknowledging her intention to keep the truth a secret.

"I'm just concerned for your well-being. It's better than being unconcerned."

She kissed his cheek. "I know. I had a healthy supper and I'll get fresh spinach and feta on my pizza, how's that? Gotta jump in the shower." Her sigh turned into a weary groan as she deposited her empty glass in the sink. "I wish we'd picked a later time."

"Have fun," said Hanna.

"See you later," Jacob said as Jo trudged off to get ready to go out.

She'd told them she was meeting friends for lunch, but now Hanna wondered if that was true. Who knew what Joelle was doing when she left the house?

"I gotta go too," Jacob said, getting off his stool. "Wish me luck." He gave Hanna a quick peck on the cheek—the Altman family's preferred gesture of affection.

Hanna tweaked his jacket collar and smoothed down his tie. "You don't need luck."

"Just need a buyer," they said in unison. He was holding an open house for a new listing, a fully remodeled four-bedroom on Northumberland Street.

"I'll be back by five—unless we get an offer," he said, already halfway out the door to the garage.

"Love you."

"Love you too."

Finally alone, Hanna could release the smirk she'd been holding in. What a show they'd all performed. Jacob, the Busy, Clueless Dad. Joelle, the Sweet, Duplicitous Daughter. She most certainly was not on her period, and Hanna had watched her eat a supper of Cheetos and Skittles while watching a movie with Boyd the evening before. Her lies flowed so smoothly. She must've had a lot of practice. Hanna remained torn between feeling betrayed and impressed.

———

When Hanna got home from work on Thursday, she found Jacob in the kitchen, putting on his running shoes.

"Give me a sec to change?" she said. "I'll come with you."

"Great!" He seemed genuinely pleased—almost surprised—that she wanted to join him for a run. It was a welcome reaction, if a slightly baffling one.

Hadn't she lamented aloud, multiple times, that for months he'd been going on runs without her? It made her question if somewhere along the line—once, on a day when she'd been too tired or too busy—she'd expressed a lack of interest? Or maybe she'd needed a little more sleep? For weeks she'd puzzled over whether he'd come to prefer running alone, or if he'd somehow come to believe she didn't enjoy it anymore. It worried her a little that sometimes she wasn't certain if she'd actually vocalized all the thoughts she'd meant to say; it was useless to debate with *herself* the things she meant to discuss with her husband. But her memory of actual conversations could be a little slippery.

Oh well. Less than five minutes later, they were side by side, crossing Shady Avenue as they headed down Beacon Street toward Schenley Park. They ran in comfortable silence for a block.

"A little birdy told me we might need to prepare for something," Jacob said.

"What kind of something?" It wasn't yet four o'clock, but it felt twenty degrees cooler than it had earlier in the day. She picked up the pace a little, eager to feel the warmth of exertion.

"About a certain daughter. And a special event."

Hanna glanced at him. He was in way too good of a mood for this to be about the thing *she* knew about a certain daughter. "What are you talking about?"

"I saw pics of fancy dresses. On her phone. I think Joelle's heading to her first prom." He beamed, full of pride over the milestone. (Hanna had never been to a prom, but from pop culture she'd gathered the impression that proms were an expensive, overly dressed form of foreplay.)

They jogged in place as they waited for the light to change, then crossed the street and headed into the park proper. Hanna rarely remembered that Boyd was older—seventeen, a junior. He seemed ageless and unfocused. But yeah, it made sense. Joelle was the kind of girl now who'd want to go to prom.

"Maybe I can take her shopping," she said. "Help her pick out a dress."

"Yeah, I'm sure she'd like that."

Once on the park trail, they picked up additional speed, their strides perfectly in sync. Hanna didn't know anything about prom dresses—weren't they frilly and garish? Or maybe the modern style was more about promising a reward of flesh: the well-cupped breast, the too-high leg slit that made it easy to reach for the prize. While Hanna would gladly take her shopping, the dark part of her—whom she thought of as her Other self—opined that what Joelle really needed, more than a dress, was an abortion.

———

Jacob kept smiling over the eggplant parmigiana, as if expecting a terrific secret to soon be revealed. Hanna, on the other hand, had a better read of the room. It was apparent to her that this Friday-evening family dinner—the three of them plus Boyd—was not going to result in a prom announcement, as Jacob had previously suggested. Joelle and Boyd seemed to be having problems swallowing their food, in spite of Hanna's eggplant parm being one of everyone's favorites, and kept glancing at each other while avoiding eye contact with Jacob.

Fuck fuck fuck. These two were preparing for a big reveal, and it had nothing to do with hitting up Daddy for limo money or a slinky dress.

When Joelle met her eye, Hanna gave a little shake of her head, wanting to warn her off. Jo squinted a question at her—*What?* Hanna clenched her teeth together and tried not to audibly growl. The last thing Jacob needed to hear over dinner was that his baby girl had been screwing around and was now with child. In Hanna's opinion, that was a conversation better suited to the living room, with its plush cushions and soft lighting, not the kitchen with its shiny pots and sharp knives.

Hanna hated the tension in the room. She pushed her plate away and reached for her wineglass. It pained her to think that Joelle had spent the last week and a half contemplating her options and once again had taken none of the advice she'd been given. Unless there was a chance she simply meant to come clean to her father? And then proceed to sort out the problem with his support?

Boyd cleared his throat and turned to Joelle. She held out her hand, and he clutched it. It struck Hanna as an interesting twist if in fact Jo was forcing Boyd to do the heavy lifting of communicating the situation to his girlfriend's father.

Jacob, sensing the moment, wiped his mouth and set his napkin aside, ready with a smile.

Hanna glanced at the counter to make sure no knives were within arm's reach.

"So, um . . ." Boyd looked to Jo, who gave him an encouraging little nod.

Hanna watched Jacob, concerned about his reaction, as surely it wouldn't be as sanguine as when *she'd* announced a pregnancy. She almost felt sorry for him; fatherhood had gone fairly smoothly for him so far (the loss of Jo's mother notwithstanding), but that was about to change.

"I, we, wanted to let you know . . . ," Boyd stammered. "I asked Joelle to marry me and she said yes."

Joelle grinned. Hanna did a spit take with her wine.

19

"What? You can't be serious!" She never yelled at Joelle. And she hadn't intended to react first, let alone lash out. Flustered, Hanna dabbed the wine droplets off the island's marble top and turned to Jacob. But if he'd even heard her, it wasn't obvious.

Dumbfounded, his shocked gaze flitted back and forth between Joelle and Boyd. Then his face cracked open into a lopsided grin.

"Very funny," he said, once again failing to read the room. "I'm going to assume that's code for 'we're going to the prom.'" Oblivious or in denial, he resumed eating. He shook his fork at them. "You got me, but that's not a cool thing to joke about with your dad."

Boyd and Jo looked to each other in startled fear. *Now what?*

"I think they're serious," Hanna said, mortified.

"I wasn't spying on you," Jacob said to his daughter, "but I saw over your shoulder, when you were looking at dresses on your phone. I think Hanna would like to take you shopping—"

"Jacob." Good God, how could he be so clueless.

"Daddy . . . those were wedding dresses."

To her credit, Joelle looked sufficiently stricken, and Hanna was almost glad she'd dug herself a deeper hole. One stupid mistake after another. These were not the actions of someone who should be entrusted with bringing a baby into the world—and surely Jacob would see that, once he knew the rest.

"You're way too young to get married." Jacob sounded dismissive and annoyed. "I know, first love and all that, but come on, this really isn't funny."

"It's not funny," Hanna agreed, glaring at her stepdaughter.

"Mr. Altman." Boyd cleared his throat again. "I know I should have asked you first, but I was really trying to step up." He turned a loving gaze on Joelle. "So you know that everything's going to be okay."

Hanna rolled her eyes. "Jo—what are you doing?"

This wasn't what they'd talked about. Ever.

"Daddy, we're gonna wait until I'm eighteen, after I finish high school. But Boyd and I . . ."

Here it comes.

"Boyd and I are having a baby."

Time stopped as they all watched Jacob. An earthquake rattled the landscape of his thoughts and his eyes blinked and bounced, trying to get the new world in focus.

"Are you messing with me?" he asked his daughter.

She shook her head.

"Your plan is to get married—because you're *pregnant?*"

She nodded meekly. In a whisper she said, "It was an accident."

"You're having a baby—you're definitely pregnant?"

She nodded again and melted against Boyd. He cast his eyes downward, and his cheeks were pink and inflamed, as if they'd been slapped.

"Did you have sex in this house?" Jacob barked at them.

"No, of course not!" Joelle insisted.

"That's not really the important thing here," Hanna said through gritted teeth. She'd wondered the same thing, but was disappointed that Jacob should fixate on such petty incidentals.

"Weren't you using birth control?" he demanded.

There you go, that's better.

"Boyd said . . ." She turned sheepish eyes to her boyfriend, and Hanna knew what Jo was about to say. ". . . condoms were uncomfort—"

"Oh for fuck's sake." Hanna hadn't meant to blurt it out, but still she was surprised when everyone looked at her. She didn't usually swear aloud or let out her caustic thoughts, but didn't she have good reason to be pissed off?

Jacob spun his ire toward her. "Didn't you take her to get birth control? The pill? Or a thing in the arm like you have?"

Hanna wanted to scream, squirm out of her skin. "Why are you yelling at *me*?"

"You should have taken her—"

"She said she wasn't having sex!"

"It was only a matter of time, Hanna! Even *I* could see that!"

They kept looking at her. Like this was her fault. Like the teen wedding could've been avoided if only Hanna had done her job.

"This is not my fault! I trusted Joelle to be honest with me!" She bulleted a glare at her stepdaughter, and then at Jacob. "Do you grasp what's happening here? She's pregnant. And thinks she wants to get married."

"Well obviously that's not happening."

Finally, the voice of reason.

"See," she told Joelle. "Your dad *also* thinks an abortion is a reasonable idea—no need for an engagement." Believing they were a unified team now, she turned to Jacob. "Maybe she'll listen if it comes from you."

Again the table went quiet. Hanna didn't understand why everyone was staring at her, radiating an atomic, combustible heat. With drama all around her, she'd lost sight of the flashing signs hovering over her husband's head. Now she couldn't decipher the jumbled letters. Had she misread something? Needing to get away from the chaos, from the confusion of the moment, she stood up and started grabbing plates.

"You knew about this?"

She ignored Jacob's roar and stomped over to the sink. The dishes clattered as she dropped them. She turned the water on full blast, wanting to drown out her husband's anger. As he marched toward her, she clocked the location of the nearest knife—a tiny paring knife, on the cutting board—just in case. Steam rose from the water pooling in the dirty plates, but Jacob's breath on her ear felt hotter.

"What's wrong with you?" Something like disgust slithered in his tone.

"Daddy?"

In unison they turned toward Joelle. She and Boyd tiptoed to the doorway.

"Jo, please go to your room," Jacob told her. "Boyd, we'll talk about this again, but not now."

Boyd nodded, understanding it was his cue to leave. He gave Joelle a hasty peck on the cheek and fled.

"Daddy?" Joelle said again after Boyd was gone.

"Later. I need to talk to Hanna."

The weepy look Jo cast her was apologetic. But it was little help. Joelle disappeared, leaving Hanna alone in the bewildering fallout of Jacob's rage.

20

Joelle's absence gave them a reprieve from speaking. They didn't have to be diplomatic, or maintain their composure, or have an answer. Hanna and Jacob cleaned up the supper dishes in bitter silence. As he scrubbed the marble countertop with excessive zeal, Hanna had a flashback of her mother. Scrubbing was how Mommy had tried to put order back into her world—usually after Hanna had done something to make her feel unhinged.

But what was happening now wasn't Hanna's fault.

Jacob had a lot to process. His little girl had pecked her way out of her shell, revealing that she wasn't a fluffy yellow chick but a bantam velociraptor. Hanna tried to have sympathy for the revamping of his reality.

"We should talk," she said softly.

"We should." He didn't look at her.

The kitchen still felt too severe, like too dangerous of an environment. She grabbed his hand and led him toward the softer surroundings of the living room. He wouldn't allow his hand to be held, but he followed her.

———

I've turned into my parents. The thought made her feel old. Here they were, medicating their parental turmoil with wine, sitting on the sofa like bookends too flimsy to keep the heaviness between them fully upright.

"I know you're disappointed with Joelle's decisions," Hanna said, using every bit of the finesse she'd learned from years of therapy. She hoped the wine would help Jacob mellow a little.

He shook his head, still not looking at her. "Jo is a teenager. I expect her to make questionable decisions—it's her job as a teenager to make questionable decisions. It's *your* decisions I'm disappointed with."

"I don't know what it is you think I've done so horribly wrong." Alarmed by the implied magnitude of her mistakes, Hanna felt that flame ignite at the base of her spine.

"I know you don't, that's part of the problem." He reached for the wine bottle and topped off his glass.

Hanna envisioned grabbing the bottle from him and smashing it against his skull. No, that was too violent a thought. *Excessive.* She rewound the footage in her mind and imagined dumping the cabernet over his head instead.

"When did Joelle tell you she was pregnant?" he asked.

"Last week. I talked to her about her options. And advised her to really think about it."

Finally he looked at her. "You advised her to end the pregnancy."

She shook her head, not in denial but in uncertainty; she'd never seen Jacob like this before. That he contained unseen personalities wasn't a complete surprise—he was human, after all. But she still didn't understand what she'd done to summon this cold, judgmental version of him.

"I advised her to think about what her life would be like, how it would change. I don't think taking a week to think about it is a crime—"

"You had an obligation to tell me." His eyes locked on hers.

She accepted the stare-off challenge. "I had an obligation to give her real-world information."

"She's a sixteen-year-old child. *My* child."

"And do you seriously think she's ready to have a baby?"

"I think if you'd told me about it a week ago, she and Boyd wouldn't have had time to cook up wedding plans."

Hanna looked down at her hands, forfeiting the stare off. Joelle had wanted Hanna to be the one to tell him. In hindsight, maybe that would've been better—maybe Jacob would've directed his anger more appropriately.

He sighed and threw his head back. "Seriously Hanna, this is so fucked up."

"I know."

"Jo is too smart for this. She doesn't make careless mistakes. Do you think . . . Do you think this was some sort of reaction to *your* pregnancy?"

"How . . . ? That doesn't even make sense." How did he keep finding ways to make this *her* fault?

"Maybe she felt weird about having a younger sibling, not being the only child anymore—we never really talked to her about that. What if it made her feel . . . pushed aside. Like she wasn't part of what was going on."

"I really don't think she's that insecure, and I wasn't pregnant for that long." And it was *his* fault that Joelle knew about it at all.

"Still. The timing. Maybe she thought if it was okay for you to get pregnant, then it was okay for—"

"Are you being real right now? This wasn't a conspiracy. She has a boyfriend. They apparently screw around. Why aren't you mad at him? Or her?" *Because Joelle is Daddy's girl.*

Hanna wasn't anyone's girl anymore.

"Because their screwing around was predictable! Why wasn't she on birth control?"

"I don't know, Jacob—did *you* discuss it with her? Did *you* take her to her pediatrician? Is this my domain because I have a uterus and it was singularly my job to handle everything that involves girl parts?"

That shut him up for a minute.

The house was eerily quiet. Hanna felt the darkness in the unoccupied rooms, a presence like a mob of eavesdroppers. Were they there to protect her, take her side? Or were they part of her husband's army, there to smother her if she made too many mistakes?

"I'm gonna go develop some film." He sounded depressed now, and pushed himself off the sofa like a man with arthritic bones. "Go develop film" was one of those expressions that meant more than its surface words. Sometimes, like now, Jacob used it as a warning: *I'm going somewhere where you can't follow me; don't open the door; I need to be alone now.*

"Okay." She didn't mind that he was abandoning the conversation. Maybe doing something meditative, like working in his darkroom, would help him come to terms with the situation.

He stopped in a shadow where the living room met the hallway. "Maybe you're right. Taking some time to think might be good advice."

It was a lame apology for blaming everything on her, but it was the best she could get for now. Hanna arranged her face in the expression she thought he wanted to see: the sympathetic yet weary smile of the understanding wife.

She dropped the smile the instant her husband turned his back and left.

While it was true that Hanna didn't feel fully qualified to be a parent in this moment, she also knew she was absolutely right: if Joelle had this baby, nothing in the Altman household would ever be the same. The cozy little world Hanna had built for herself would be destroyed. And she would never be the center of any of their attention again.

There was no way she could handle being a "grandmother" at twenty-four.

21

"She's never had her blood taken before," the mother explained.

Seventeen-year-old Kami was barely in the chair and already hysterical.

"I promise it isn't as bad as you fear." Hanna spoke in her most dulcet tones, to hide what she was really thinking. *Obnoxious twat.*

Sometimes she was able to summon sympathy for patients who were afraid to have their blood drawn: young children, people with genuine phobias. But Kami was merely an attention whore. The type was easy to spot. She had an entourage with her—her mother and her best friend—who were tasked with holding her hands and cooing over her incessantly. And the row of piercings along the cartilage of her right ear made Kami's claim of being afraid of needles a complete hoax. The signs above her head flashed, *Look at me! Coddle me! Spend all your energy on me me me!*

Hanna pegged her as shallow (in addition to being an attention whore), as clearly the girl would sit still for a needle if it contributed to her "look," but for her health . . . ? Not so much. Kami whimpered like a cornered animal as Hanna tied the tourniquet around her arm.

"You'll just feel a little pinch. One, two . . . three."

The girl all-out screamed as Hanna drove the needle hard through her vein. While the friend and mother provided comfort, their eyes on Kami, Hanna dug around with the needle for a another second or two—well aware it was the *wrong* way to draw blood, and that it hurt.

The neon *me me me* winked out over Kami's head, and Hanna was glad to see her shed real tears. Hopefully the brat had learned a lesson about creating unnecessary drama.

Hanna deftly inserted the needle correctly and drew the first tube. "Almost finished," she said, cooing in an imitation of the entourage. "See, not so bad."

She pressed gauze to the puncture, and then wrapped it tightly in a strip of self-adhesive bandage. When Kami left the cubicle, clutching her mom and friend, she was subdued. Quite different from the girl who'd overplayed her hand just a few minutes ago.

I won.

Before going to the waiting room to summon her next patient, Hanna hurried to the tiny break room for a quick bite of her apple. Raven was there, leaning against the counter and texting on her phone.

"Real or a faker?" Raven asked without looking up. The cubicles were divided by curtains; everyone could hear the criers. All the phlebotomists knew about people like Kami, who made everyone's jobs harder with their overwrought behavior.

"Faker." At least that's how she'd started out. Kami might be genuinely afraid the next time she needed to get her blood drawn.

"Don't you hate people like that?"

"Yup." But Hanna silently thanked the Goddess of Human Attributes for people like that, as they gave her an outlet for her own frustrations. She sighed, refreshed, and put the rest of her apple in the minifridge. "See ya later."

"Later."

"Tell Drew he's a lazy douchebag," Hanna said on her way out, assuming that, like usual, Raven was texting her boyfriend about getting off his ass to do something other than play video games.

Raven smirked, still focused on her phone, and gave her the finger.

Hanna stood at the threshold to the waiting room. To her dismay, it was polluted with flashing words, labeling the unpleasantness of all the nervous people in the chairs. It had been like that all day. She consulted the paperwork in her hand.

"Larry?" she said to the room.

When the next patient stood, Hanna's brain issued a torrent of profanity. She couldn't afford to be reckless with any regularity—couldn't let the stresses on the home front interfere with her job. But as Larry approached, Hanna questioned if she'd skewered the wrong patient.

Fiftysomething with a beer belly and an unkempt mane of gray hair. Underdressed in a filthy T-shirt with tufts of smelly armpit hair poking out. But personal hygiene aside, Larry's actual crime was the faded but still legible motto on his shirt.

MILLIONS OF BATTERED WOMEN AND I'M STILL EATING MINE PLAIN

What sort of disgusting asshat would own such a shirt—and wear it in public? His clothing was spattered with paint, and it was probably an indicator that he'd come to the lab in the middle of a workday. She could hear Jacob in her head referring to his outfit, perhaps with sympathy, as *schmattes*—one of the Yiddish words he'd learned from his grandmother. Jacob would consider it normal and fine to put on *schmattes* to do messy work, but this shirt—and perhaps the schmuck who wore it—should be tossed in a bonfire.

As she led Larry to her cubicle, she prayed she couldn't find a vein. She prayed she'd have no choice but to stick him three or four times with as much force as she could get away with.

22

Dear Hanna,

You better wrangle in those pesky demons. You're gonna be super sad if you fuck up your job.

And speaking of demons, someday we should have a little show-and-tell—I'll draw my demons for you if you draw yours for me. I'm immensely curious about what yours look like. Craggy, dark skeletal monsters with taloned hands? Or cherubic baby doll faces whose Cupid's bow lips hide extra-sharp teeth? Or maybe you have a romantic streak and they look like hot gentleman (or gentlelady) vampires who are gentle only until they sink their fangs into someone's neck. Or possibly you mentally skin the faces off your enemies to make punching bags for your pent-up rage.

Perhaps not surprisingly, many of my demons are oddly reminiscent of UnderSlumberBumbleBeasts— and specifically of your old friend, Skog. I was afraid of your cherished beanbag buddy when I was little. I know you swore he was cute, but to me he looked like the remnants of a dwarf who'd survived several unhealthy minutes dancing with the blades of a garbage disposal. I still appreciate, however, that you took the time when I was six to help me make a

BumbleBeast of my own. I know it didn't turn out so great, but I understood you were trying to share a mutual interest, and give me a loyal companion to keep by my side.

And speaking of loyal . . . I can't believe you still have Skog! How old is that little bastard now, seventeen? He's gonna pack up and move away from home soon, ha ha. (Just kidding! I know you couldn't get along without him, even if you do keep him in a padded coffin like the aforementioned vampires.)

Anyway . . . go on an extra run or two (with or without the husband). Go to one of those places where they give you protective goggles and a sledgehammer and let you crush the dishes and coffee tables that people used to donate to Goodwill. You can't control everything, Hanna. Shit happens and all that, blah blah blah.

Don't forget that Love is Hate's dearest bedfellow—or is it the other way around? *Bedfellow* is my new favorite word.

Yours,
Goose

23

Dear Goose,

First of all, Skog doesn't live in a *coffin*—it's a fancy velvet-lined box, meant for treasures. A bed with a lid, really. And when he's in there with the lid closed, he's in stasis, so he doesn't get claustrophobic or feel like he's missing out on anything. You may mock my devotion to him, but keeping him safe was one of the things that gave me purpose while I was at the school for peculiar children. Sometimes loving someone is what gets you through the hard times. (And unlike you, I wasn't worthy of a fancy boarding school.)

I appreciate your advice—running, and smashing things, are both mature outlets for when a person is overstuffed with thoughts and anxiety. I am not, however, as mature as you are, little brother. I know your intention is to encourage me in the right direction—but your faith in my ability to take the high road may leave *you* feeling in need of a sledgehammer. (Please do not use it on my head!)

I think Joelle and I were both afraid of how Jacob would take the news of becoming a grandfather a decade+ ahead of schedule. But while she's relieved by his acceptance of the situation, I am not. He's made exactly zero effort to convince her to terminate the pregnancy, and he's indifferent about her engagement. In private he calls it "the so-called engagement" because he doesn't believe "for a second" that they'll still be together in two years. And he says that if they are, "it will prove something significant about Boyd."

But that will still leave him with a mutant grandchild spawned by Boyd Bland. Boyd the Boring. Boyd the Blob. I do not understand Jacob's passivity in all this. I guarantee you if I had gotten pregnant at sixteen, Mommy wouldn't have even asked before shoving the abortion pill down my throat. She would've checked under my tongue to make sure I'd swallowed it, and then made me an appointment to get my tubes tied. Even Daddy, with his great efforts at being Mr. Super Chill, wouldn't have just waved it all away with a *Things happen,* lilla gumman. *I'm sure it will all be fine.* I do not understand Jacob's capitulation!

Joelle's "plan" (I use the term loosely, as it's really more of a fantasy) is to finish up her school year, and do virtual school next year. And then maybe return to Allderdice for her senior year if she has "good day care options." Is she—or Jacob—thinking of *ME* as the good day care option??? For reasons you fully understand, that CANNOT happen. Meanwhile, Boyd is insisting that he'll be there every step of the way, supporting her and pitching in to take care of the baby. He's announced his plans to get a summer job, and see about getting his GED so he can start working full time. It all sounds wonderful, doesn't it? So perfect and easy?

For fuck's sake, has no one in this household watched any of those pregnant-teen reality shows?!

I watched them as a teenager and they were a good deterrent—against baby making *and* boyfriends. Or maybe Jo and her friends do watch them—and now they believe all pregnant teens are rewarded with a starring role in their own well-paid drama.

I'm hearing you telling me to take a deep breath . . .

In through the nose, out through the mouth . . .

I just don't think Jacob is thinking about the implications of all this. Does he really think this won't impact Jo's musical-theater dreams? And never mind that her commitment to dancing has lessened over the last year, does he think it's okay that she starts compromising her goals—college, career—so young? (I'm pretty sure, even if she stays on track in school, that she's not going to live in the freshman dorms with a toddler.) Is Jacob really ready to convert the basement guest suite into a love nest and nursery for his sixteen-year-old daughter (as he mentioned to me in private)? Has he thought at all about what it would be like having Boyd at the house twenty-four hours a day? And has anyone, other than me, thought about who will be taking care of this baby while the teenagers are busy being teenagers and the grandpa is busy with his career and his hobbies?

It's making me crazy that I can't fix this. Everything feels so topsy-turvy now and I can't handle it.

You've been so patient with me, dear Goose—the least I can do is honor your request. I've enclosed a sketch of an endearing little demon named Phloppy Philip. Don't be fooled that he resembles a frog; he can flatten himself and squeeze between the crack where the wall meets the floor. He lives in the water pipes and likes to pop his head through the drain hole in the bathtub. His tongue emits a caustic poison and he's especially fond of ankle bones.

    Yours,
    Hanna

24

The Wednesday-afternoon excursion wasn't exactly meant to be a bribe, but Hanna felt the need to repair things between her and Joelle. Things at home had been a little awkward and tense since Friday's cluster bomb of announcements. Their first stop at the Waterfront was DSW, where they each picked up a pair of shoes: white Doc Martens boots for Joelle, new running shoes for Hanna. They were almost to the register when Hanna decided to dash to the men's section to get a matching pair of running shoes for Jacob. She wanted the gift to symbolize that they were a team and she was fully invested—in their shared hobby, and their family responsibilities.

"I'm a little hungry—up for a snack?" Hanna asked as they put the shoes in the back of her car.

"Sure."

"What sounds good?"

Joelle chose Eat'n Park. Hanna's mission to the Waterfront had really been about this next stage: talking with Jo in a harmless, neutral setting—without her dad or her boyfriend. They sat across from each other at one of the family-size booths, and ordered a big plate of fried zucchini to share and two Diet Pepsis. For a few minutes they chatted about the normal things—classes, schedules—until Hanna was ready to tiptoe into the murkier business.

"Been feeling okay?" she asked casually, not completely sure how to navigate the conversation.

Joelle nodded, gulping down her soda. "Mostly good. Had a few days of feeling like crap in the morning."

There were no indications, by her posture or attitude (or hovering words), that Jo was anything but relaxed and at peace. Good. She wasn't a defensive girl by nature, but Hanna wouldn't blame her if Jo harbored some resentment about how her dad—and stepmom—were handling the news of her pregnancy.

Jacob put on a fake smile when he was around, but he'd developed a pretty obvious habit of avoiding everyone. He was always scurrying off to his office or darkroom. Or running out for mysteriously urgent errands or an oddly timed jog. He didn't want to look either of them in the eye. Jacob had the privilege of being aloof because Hanna was there to keep the household running smoothly. But she knew she should be behaving with more warmth toward Joelle, make more of an effort to seem supportive. If she and Jacob withdrew too much, even if only because of their own wayward feelings, a sensitive girl like Joelle would think they were rejecting her—which would only push her deeper into Boyd Bland's open arms.

"Have you guys talked to his parents?" Was there any chance Hanna would find an ally there? Someone to talk these kids out of their crazy plans?

Before Jo could answer, the waitress set the plate of fried zucchini on the table between them. Their eyes lit up.

"Haven't had this in eons," Jo said as she speared a long slice onto her plate.

They devoured their first few bites in silence. Joelle liked her zucchini dipped in marinara sauce; Hanna preferred squeezing a lemon wedge over hers. She wasn't sure if Joelle was going to answer her question at all, but then:

"We talked to Boyd's mom and dad a few days ago."

"How did it go? How'd they take it?" Hanna hoped they'd taken it badly, and behaved worse than she and Jacob had.

"Okay. They weren't thrilled of course. But Boyd's older sister became a mom at seventeen, so they've done this before. It wasn't like a shocking catastrophe."

Was that how Hanna and Jacob were reacting? Like it was a shocking catastrophe?

"So you've definitely decided? No chance you're going . . . to not have it? I needed you to know you had options, that's all. And there's still time."

"I know. But yeah, Boyd and I don't believe in . . ."

In what? Hanna didn't understand how a medical procedure had become a belief. Joelle apparently wasn't sure either. She shrugged.

"From what I've read," said Hanna, "Judaism doesn't have a problem with freedom of choice. Your faith supports doing what's best for the mother."

"I know, it isn't that."

"And medical procedures exist to help people."

"It doesn't sound very helpful." Joelle sounded bored.

"That depends on what your goals are—and I don't just mean your ambitions in life. And sometimes of course it literally saves a woman's life, or spares her from suffering unnecessarily."

"Yeah, I get that." She lost a piece of zucchini in the marinara sauce. Fished it out and scooped it into her mouth. "If it was an emergency. But it's not an emergency for me."

Not an emergency for her. Because she had a daddy with a big house and a cushion of cash. Like so many other things, this wasn't something Joelle viewed as a crisis, as something she should be overly bothered about. The only part of it that had really troubled her was telling them the truth, and feeling a little stupid.

"Boyd's parents said we can live there if we need a place."

Would having Joelle out of the house be a solution of some sort? It might only benefit Hanna, make her workload a little less. But she really did care about what happened to her stepdaughter. And wanted to save her from making any more terrible mistakes.

"I don't think your dad would be too keen on that."

"I know, but, just in case. It felt good to know that was an option. I'm still not really sure about what you, and Daddy . . ." She quirked her eyebrows at Hanna in an unspoken question of annoyance.

"Your father would never, ever kick you out." Hanna didn't think it was her place to suggest they could live in the basement; she'd let Jacob offer that when he was ready.

"No. But if it's just going to be stressful, and everyone's miserable. That's not the sort of environment I'd want for my baby."

Her baby. Was Joelle really this maternal? Or were these merely the words a would-be mother should say?

"You know we're going to do the best we can," said Hanna. "It might take a little time to get used to. We all need to adjust. But we're going to be there for you, no matter what."

Hanna sounded a bit more sincere than she felt, but her efforts seemed to have the desired effect. Joelle nodded, grinning as she took out her phone.

"We decided—we're going to prom. I wasn't sure I wanted to, but no one knows I'm pregnant yet—other than Malika and Gwen—and it might be my last chance to look nice before I get fat."

Like a dutiful stepmom, Hanna oohed and aahed at the pictures Jo showed her of sparkly dresses.

"This is my favorite." She enlarged the pic of a short hot-pink dress. "It'll go great with my new white boots, don't you think?"

Yes. Hanna could see it: Joelle in her bright, super-cute prom outfit. Like a doll, all dressed up.

In that moment, Hanna fully grasped that Joelle might not be a girl capable of understanding the peril she was putting herself in. She wasn't mature enough, and she hadn't experienced the right kind of hardships to make her wary of giving her life away, or her heart. If Hanna really couldn't influence her toward not having the baby, then the second-best option was to make sure her stepdaughter didn't get stuck with Boyd. Only once in Hanna's life had she been truly infatuated, truly devoted to a man—and even though he'd been her father, he still hadn't been capable of loving her unconditionally.

———

Before they headed home, Hanna ran into the Giant Eagle to pick up a few groceries; Jo stayed in the car, texting with Boyd. As Hanna pushed the cart down the medication aisle, on the hunt for Jacob's allergy pills and a new bottle of ibuprofen, her daring Other self whispered an idea:

What if you acquired the abortion pill on your own? Could you dissolve it secretly into Joelle's food?

Hanna proceeded through the store like a zombie, barely aware as she dropped necessities into the cart. Could that work? Was it safe?

As a child she'd tampered with one of her mother's medications—dumped out the contents of the capsules and filled them up with flour. At the time Hanna had believed her mother would die if deprived of her daily medicine. But Mommy had only gotten a little sick because, as Hanna later learned, the capsules were never meant to keep her from dying; they simply managed the symptoms of her Crohn's disease. Jo would feel unwell after ingesting the pill—that was inevitable: if taken correctly the result would look like a miscarriage. But Hanna didn't want to *hurt* Joelle.

She needed to know how far along her stepdaughter was, and she needed more info about how a medical abortion worked. She told herself that no harm would come from doing a little research. Due diligence. Just to know if it was a viable option.

25

Never mind that she would wake up at five thirty so she could get a run in before going to work, Hanna was determined to stay up until Jacob came to bed. It was already midnight. She'd barely seen him for a couple of days—an unconscious lump beneath the blanket, or crossing paths as they came and went—and it was time to undo the knot of acrimony that was keeping them from communicating. Perhaps Jacob had hoped that she would be asleep when he finally came down from the attic at 12:24. But Hanna was sitting up in bed, sketching in a small pad.

Of late he'd been withdrawn—not overtly angry, but something more like depressed. Defeated. He grinned a hello at her that looked more like a grimace and headed for the bathroom, pulling off his shirt. Hanna was ready—sitting on his side of the bed with both shoeboxes on her lap—when he finished brushing his teeth. In nothing but his boxers, he walked over and sat beside her. She admired his physique. He was naturally lean—he'd probably been a scrawny kid—and he exercised just enough to retain some muscle definition. His furry chest hair had gone salt and pepper, like the hair on his head. He looked good. Good enough to fuck. Maybe one thing would lead to another. But first:

"I got this for you, while Jo and I were shopping." She handed him a shoebox.

As he opened his, she opened hers—so he could see the contents were the same. A tired grin bloomed on his face as he held one of the running shoes.

"Matching?" he asked.

"That wasn't the most important part. But I wanted you to know we were in this together. And I figured you were about ready for a new pair."

"I am." He leaned over and gave her a peck on the cheek. "Thanks, babe. I know I've been . . . distant."

"You've had a lot to think about."

He nodded, and gathered the shoeboxes and set them on the uphol-stered bench at the foot of the bed. Hanna scooted over, plumping up the pillows as she reclined on her side; she sensed him wanting to talk. And he did, though he stayed at the edge of the mattress with his back to her.

"I have been thinking," he said, "about a lot of things. I know this isn't what we wanted for Joelle. I'm sorry if it seemed like I was blaming you. Mostly I've been . . . I'm mad at myself. Maybe I wasn't paying enough attention to her, or the things happening in her life."

"This isn't your fault." Just like it wasn't *her* fault. She leaned toward him, wanting him to face her so she could keep track of his expressions.

He shook his head. "I just can't stop thinking about how disap-pointed Rachel would be."

Hanna retreated into her pillows, unnerved that he'd brought Rachel into it. There were a few photos of Jacob's first wife in Jo's room, but they didn't talk about her much—at least not in Hanna's presence. Rachel had died in a car accident when Joelle was almost nine. She was alone in the car and had been drinking, and she'd injured a bicyclist before swerving into an oncoming bus. The story had made the local news at the time, but Hanna, then seventeen, had no recollection of it.

The sketchy details of Rachel's life and death painted a less than impressive picture, and Hanna had a generally low opinion of Jacob's first wife. But whenever he did bring her up, he made Rachel sound angelic, nearly perfect—an accomplished attorney, a doting mother—except for that one unfortunate night after her friend's bachelorette party. Her distraught friends told him afterward that Rachel hadn't seemed drunk, that she'd only had a couple of glasses of wine. But they'd probably been too drunk themselves to assess Rachel's ability to drive herself home.

"I can't stop thinking that Rachel would've been able to stop this from happening," said Jacob. "She would've understood what was going on with Jo, even if she wasn't telling us everything. She would've gotten her on birth control." He turned to Hanna, not accusingly but sheepishly. "The pediatrician referred us to an ob-gyn—Jo's appointment is Monday. I can take her."

"I don't mind taking—"

"You were right though. I did just let you handle the girl stuff."

"I think we should let Jo pick who takes her to the doctor. Just in case she's feeling any awkwardness about it." It was more important than ever that Hanna seem supportive—especially if she decided to go through with her plan. Her husband and stepdaughter needed to see only the *good* parts of her, so they'd have no reason to doubt or suspect her.

Jacob nodded. "Jo might want that. Rachel, too—I'm sure she would've been with her every step of the way."

It was taking all Hanna's self-discipline to remain calm and rational. Inside she felt like a dragon ready to obliterate a village with a tantrum of flames. She didn't believe for a minute that Rachel had possessed the prescience or empathy that Jacob was crediting her with. Rachel had only ever mothered a *child*. Jacob had no clue how she would've handled a tween, a teen, a sophomore with a steady boyfriend.

"We can't really know what Rachel would've done," she said, as diplomatically as possible. "Joelle is a good girl."

"She is. I know. But . . . the one thing I'm sure Rachel would want—would want *us* to do. This is another thing I've been thinking about." He shifted position, finally moving toward Hanna so they were face to face, ready for a deeper level of intimacy. "We should offer to raise the baby. If not outright adopt it."

Adopt Jo's baby?

Hanna forced the muscles in her face to freeze in a position of neutrality. Now that Jacob was looking at her, she had to be extra careful about how she proceeded. It was a terrible, appalling suggestion on so many levels, but she couldn't let him see how horrified she was. Had he considered Joelle's wishes at all? She didn't seem the least bit inclined to give up her baby. And for Hanna's part, she'd only recently come to the conclusion that she should never be a mother, that she fundamentally wasn't equipped to care for a helpless creature who would rely on her for everything.

She heard Goose gently reminding her, *I'm not trying to shame you for being a terrible babysitter.* And she responded in her head, *I know.* Goose was the only young child she'd ever been around, and even though she'd loved him, she *had* been a terrible babysitter. She wasn't a moody teenager anymore, but she didn't want to add to the family lineage of unfit moms.

How could Jacob think this was the answer to their problems? What she really heard him saying was, *We'll make it your problem.*

And in the layer beneath that she heard, *The domestic duties are your job—isn't that what you're here for?*

And beneath that, *You aren't the priority here, so it doesn't matter what you want.*

26

Jacob was staring at her, waiting for her to say something. He'd probably expected an enthusiastic *What a fantastic idea, honey!* But the moment stretched, sticky and unforgiving.

His brow furrowed. "What's wrong? I thought you'd be happy."

"Why would I be happy?"

"You just lost your . . . We wanted a baby, we'd talked about—"

"We never said we wanted a baby." Reproach spiked her words.

"We were thinking about trying again."

"Yes. *Thinking* about. You can't just replace . . ." *My fake baby with Joelle's real one.* Oh how the dragon wanted to roar. "I'm not . . . I can't—I can't, Jacob."

"Why? Jo isn't prepared to raise a child—regardless of what she thinks. But we're mature, stable adults. This would let Jo be part of her child's life, without all the responsibility. This is the perfect solution." He sounded heartfelt and reasonable. And ridiculous. And then he made it even worse by adding: "Rachel wouldn't hesitate—"

"Rachel isn't here."

Now he was the one who looked ready to blast her with a gusty breath of fire. With a tense jaw he asked, "Why were you okay with the idea of raising *our* baby, but seem nothing but angry about this one? Don't think I haven't noticed how pissed off you get every time it comes up."

Hanna felt herself melting inside. Her foundation was crumbling, and she didn't know how to make him understand. All the truthful explanations were secrets. But to avoid the quagmire that came with lies, she had to tell him something that was at least adjacent to the truth.

"I've come to realize . . . I'm not mom material."

He quirked a look of doubt at her. "Hanna, you keep our whole house running. You're a great mom."

She shook her head. Focused on mobilizing a few tears. "I'm *organized*, that's not the same thing . . ."

It was mind boggling to her that they were at this crossroads. Could Joelle's unplanned pregnancy be the undoing of Hanna's marriage? She couldn't see herself sticking around to play permanent Mommy to her teen stepdaughter's baby. And even if she stayed and tried to fake it, there was the very real risk that Hanna's mommying skills would reveal hereditary defects. What would happen when Jacob witnessed that? If he thought she'd dropped the ball with Joelle's birth control, what would he say if she dropped a squirming baby on its head? Or stormed off to her room for some alone time? *Goose wasn't wrong.*

"Jacob . . . I know I haven't talked about my upbringing very much. There were things that were really hard for me." Her voice got soft and foggy.

She didn't dish out sob stories with any regularity, but she'd learned a long time ago that personal admissions could elicit sympathy—which in turn could mollify a person's anger. She'd used the tactic when necessary at Marshes: if she got caught stealing something—from the art room or the kitchen or her therapist's office—she'd burst into tears and gush about why she'd needed that thing so very, very badly, because she was "hurting inside."

Everything she'd said then—and would say now—bore elements of truth. She'd needed those crayons and yogurt cups and manila folders to make her art; her art became a vital way of expressing herself, and without it she might have exploded. People liked to hear other people's hardships and say, "There, there." They liked to grant forgiveness and understanding because it made *them* feel like the better person.

"That's why you cut ties with your parents," Jacob replied, engaging with Hanna's chosen script. "I know, I understand."

He was fully invested now, hopeful of hearing Hanna's confession. Confessions were a currency better than gossip, and almost better than sex.

———

"My mother . . . I don't even know where to start. She hated me." She thought Jacob might refute her, or at least look doubtful. But his gaze remained steady, and he waited for her to say more.

The only real time he'd spent with her parents was at their elegant but tiny wedding. He thought they'd seemed like "nice, sophisticated people." Those nice, sophisticated people hadn't understood Hanna's urgency to get married five months into her first relationship; they'd asked if she was pregnant. Jacob had agreed not to bring up Goose's name—the missing member of the Jensen family (though going forward Hanna took her husband's last name). She informed him that her mother, especially, was sensitive about perceived criticism for sending her children away to school so young. As the parents of the bride, Suzette and Alex had gone through the motions, and more or less accepted Hanna's new life.

"I gave up trying to figure you out a long time ago," her mother had said.

Since then Jacob had respected Hanna's boundaries and the distance she wanted to keep. Every once in a while, they crossed paths with her mom and/or dad at Trader Joe's, though Hanna avoided most of the places that she knew her parents liked to frequent. Early in her marriage she'd anticipated seeing her mother pop up at the wrong Giant Eagle or the wrong library; she'd thought Mommy would want to spy on her. It was stupid, but sometimes her mother's complete lack of interest in her felt like rejection, even though Hanna was the one who'd walked away.

She couldn't, given the seriousness of the matter at hand, come across like nothing more than a petulant young adult complaining about her shitty parents. It was important that Jacob see how her experiences had *hurt* her, and that she wasn't merely pissed off or hateful. As far as Hanna was concerned, Mommy and Daddy had committed a terrible crime against her when they'd exiled her for three years. But she'd never fully explained that to Jacob, and probably never would. To do so would mean revealing to him the events that turned Daddy against her, which in turn led to her being sent away to Marshes. She didn't think Jacob would be very understanding of why, at seven, she'd wanted to kill her mother. Although Hanna believed her reasons were sound.

Now she understood all the mistakes she'd made, but at seven she'd been naive and impatient. Now she knew that if you were going to kill someone, you needed to be both more competent and more subtle about it. As a child she'd been a tangle of explosive impulses and hard-to-quell desires. But it was still hard for her to put into words just how wrong everything with Mommy had felt.

Maybe Goose would like me to draw him a picture of my Mommy demon.

"I don't even remember when the war between me and my mom started. We were just always at war. And not to sound like a brat but I have to assume she started it—and maybe when I was still a baby. She always wanted me to be . . . different. Someone other than who I was." Hanna imagined how an actor in a movie would interpret this moment, and attempted an appearance of similar angst. *See, I was a helpless child.*

"What about your dad?" Jacob asked. "I know I don't really know him but he seems warmer, friendlier."

"He was, for sure. I worshipped him when I was little. Like, over-the-top worshipped him. But I was wrong to do that. I saw him as *perfect* because my mother was so imperfect. And when I needed him most, he abandoned me."

"When they sent you to school."

She nodded. That's what he believed, that in their frustration to parent her, they'd sent her off to a better school. He didn't know it had been a residential treatment center for severely mentally ill children.

"My mother planted a lot of ideas in my head. About how bad I was. And then after my brother was born . . . It's amazing Gustav and I even have a relationship. If it had been up to my mother, we'd never have even been in the same room together. She treated him like he was sculpted out of tissue paper and I was a hot ember. I *loved* Goose, but Mommy did everything she could to keep me away from him. And it left me feeling, even now . . . like I'm a danger." In a tiny voice she added, "A danger to small children."

"That's why you're not sure about having a baby—or raising a baby? You're afraid?"

She nodded. "I don't want to hurt—even accidentally—a fragile little child."

Jacob took her hand and squeezed it. "Oh Hanna . . ."

It had worked. Jacob looked at her with pity.

For the first time in what felt like weeks, he wasn't disappointed in her—because now he could blame her mother. And now he could feel like a good person for being so understanding.

"I think everyone's afraid at first," he said. "Afraid of not being a good enough parent. Afraid of messing up their kid, in whatever way. That's normal—a normal thing to question. But you get the hang of being a parent, like everything else. Some things are second nature, and some of it you have to keep working on. It's not a bad thing that you have doubts—it means you care, you want to be a better parent than your parents." He smiled at her, with real warmth. "And Gustav is fine. Your mom was paranoid, and you and Goose, by all accounts, have a good relationship—you're a good big sister. It's wonderful that you write to each other the way you do. And I really hope, in spite of everything else with your family, that sometime when he's home from school I can finally meet him."

Jacob believed that sending the kids off to boarding school was the Jensen family tradition. That little lie was like the oil that lubricated a complicated machine.

"It's because I love Goose that it concerns me so much. What if my mom's right?"

More honesty had bubbled to the surface than she'd anticipated: she *was* afraid that her mother was right. Hanna believed that as an adult she was in full control of the parts of herself that were dangerous—but what if she was wrong?

Jacob wrapped his arm around her, and she snuggled against his bare torso. He kissed her forehead. "She's messed with your head enough, Hanna. You can't let her stop you from doing what you want to do."

"It's hard," she said, "to go from having her voice in my head my whole life to . . . I'm just not sure. That I'm ready for a baby."

For a moment they didn't speak. Hanna raked his chest hair with her fingers while Jacob caressed her shoulder.

"Maybe . . . ," he said, ending the lull in their conversation. "I know you haven't wanted to see your parents, or have them involved in your life. And I understand that. But maybe if your mother saw how good of a stepmom you are—how well you're doing. She shouldn't have this power over you. Maybe showing her would dispel this curse you think you're under."

"I don't need to prove myself to her."

"No, of course not. But her doubts have made you insecure. If she saw what a great life you have—maybe even just a few positive words from her . . ." He shrugged. "It might change something about how you feel. It might be worth a try."

"I'll think about it," she said, to satisfy him.

Once upon a time getting the upper hand over her mother had been Hanna's singular goal. But she couldn't be bothered with that now, and Jacob was wrong: Mommy was mostly out of sight and out of mind—and she wouldn't boost Hanna's ego with compliments. No, the person Hanna needed to get the upper hand over was next to her on the bed.

The current confessional tactic had been a good one. Jacob was being affectionate, concerned. He pulled her closer, nibbling her cheek with kisses until he reached her lips. She still didn't have a solution to the monkey wrench Jo had tossed into their lives. But Hanna could keep milking her own troubled story, to create the excuses she needed. For now the conversation had put them both in a better mood.

She reached between her husband's legs, ready for a quick fuck before going to sleep.

27

Joelle sat on the exam table, absorbed in her phone as she waited for the doctor to come in. A nurse had already taken her vitals and had her pee in a cup. Hanna sat in a chair against the wall, her legs tightly crossed, trying to maintain a neutral expression. She was supposed to be there as a supportive adult, but doctors' offices made her nervous. She'd kind of hoped Jo would want to go in alone and she could stay in the waiting room, with the nauseating daytime talk show on the TV and the advertising-filled magazines. *Rachel would never have sent her in alone.*

Jacob and Hanna had agreed that Boyd wasn't allowed to go to Jo's doctor's appointment, that the nature of the appointment was too intimate for an underage bystander. They'd appeared a united front, though Hanna had other reasons for keeping Blobby Boyd away. She didn't need to witness him playacting the expectant daddy, pretending as if the sperm he'd implanted was a virtuous accomplishment. Hanna longed to remind everyone that an acorn-size cluster of cells was *not* a baby, but first things first: maybe Joelle had a hormonal condition and wasn't actually pregnant. Or maybe the fetus had already aborted itself, as many early-stage embryos did. Such a tidy solution would require a pound or two of luck; Hanna hoped her crossed legs would suffice for crossed fingers.

After being denied her first choice of bringing Boyd, Jo had settled on Hanna—and she'd agreed to come, of course. But it was bringing up a lot of memories. Mommy had dragged her to all sorts of specialists when she was little—for CT scans and tests and exams—trying to understand why she couldn't (wouldn't) speak. When Hanna thought about scary places, she didn't picture graveyards at midnight or derelict murder houses. And she wasn't afraid of vampires or werewolves or even ghosts (some of whom might have legitimate grievances). She was afraid of medically trained men and women in white coats. Skilled practitioners of torture with lying smiles and sterilized tools.

When the doctors finally ruled out physical abnormalities, Hanna had been diagnosed with selective mutism. By the time she was a tween, she'd graduated to being reticent (though, when no one was eavesdropping, she spoke openly with Goose). Speaking in a broadly normal fashion came a couple of years later, a strategy she adopted when the time was right to move through society more effectively—though to this day she felt words were often gauzy and inadequate. It frustrated her that the intricate drawings she created were interpreted in simple, shallow ways. The commenters on her TikTok posts liked to sum up her drawings in a few words or a sentence—"creepy and hilarious," or "diabolically whimsical," or "a hand grenade of powerful yet sad observations." In Hanna's mind each image told an entire story that a handful of adjectives was inadequate to tell.

Then again, perhaps she'd only know what people really thought of her work if they drew a picture in response. Sometimes Hanna thought she'd be a very different person if she lived in a dimension where people communicated in imagery.

There was a tap on the door and the doctor came in—a middle-aged woman with a severely straight bobbed haircut and neon-tortoiseshell eyeglasses. From the neck up she could've been the owner of an art gallery, but the collection of enamel Mickey Mouse pins on her lab coat ruined her otherwise sophisticated look.

"Hi Joelle, I'm Dr. Levine. Nice to meet you." She carried a folder with her, open to the background info Joelle had provided.

"Nice to meet you," Jo mumbled, tucking her phone next to her thigh.

"Is this your big sister?" the doctor asked, smiling at Hanna.

"I'm her stepmother, Hanna." She didn't think she and Joelle looked anything alike—a young princess and a beautiful witch—but this wasn't the first time they'd been mistaken for sisters.

"Okay. So I think you already guessed this, but the urine test confirmed you are, indeed, pregnant."

Shit.

"How does it do that?" Jo asked, displaying a level of curiosity that surprised Hanna—forgetting, for a moment, how good of a student she was (given the girl's predicament).

"It measures the levels of a hormone called human chorionic gonadotropin—we usually just call it HCG—which is primarily produced by the placenta. Hence our ability to confirm a pregnancy. Are you interested in science?"

Hanna tuned them out for a minute. The confirmation wasn't a surprise, but it still revolted her to imagine clammy Boyd between Joelle's thighs, hammering away. It was too easy to hear in her head the slap-slap-slap of their flesh connecting. While the doctor got a little personal info about Jo's life, Hanna unlocked her phone and checked her email. Two nights ago she'd ordered the abortion pills online—just in case, and aware that the clock was ticking. She checked the shipment tracking; it would arrive in discreet packaging, but everything would be easier if she got to it before anyone could ask about it.

She'd learned some important things about how the medication worked when she'd placed the order. The process involved two pills, one each of two different medications, mifepristone and misoprostol. They needed to be taken within forty-eight hours of each other, though taking them together was also an option. Hanna now understood the two crucial factors that would impact the effectiveness of the pills: the age of the embryo, and the complete ingestion of both pills. The medication was safe during the first ten weeks, and the earlier in the pregnancy, the higher the success rate. But if someone swallowed the mifepristone and then chickened out—or neglected to take the misoprostol—it could result in a dead fetus that the body didn't expel. Without medical intervention, it could lead to sepsis and death.

"Based on the date of your last period . . ." The doctor consulted her paperwork. "That puts you at about nine weeks."

"Is that accurate?" Hanna asked. That made for a small window of opportunity.

"Fairly. We can schedule a dating ultrasound—that's usually done during the first trimester. And at that point we can give you a more accurate due date."

Dr. Levine asked gentle, diplomatic questions about Joelle's plans, and Jo told her about Boyd and doing virtual school next year and getting engaged.

"It sounds like you've got it all figured out." The doctor smiled at Joelle and then turned to Hanna, silently questioning her young patient's version of things. Hanna flashed her a tight-lipped grimace and half rolled her eyes.

"For now I'd recommend you start taking prenatal vitamins, and avoid caffeine," Dr. Levine said, her focus once again on Jo. "I'll have the nurse give you a sheet with the dos and don'ts. And I'd like to order some labs—just the regular blood work to make sure everything's okay, and we'll set up your next appointment. Sound good?"

"Can Hanna take my blood?" Jo asked with some urgency.

The doctor tilted her head, as if she didn't understand.

"I'm a phlebotomist," Hanna explained. "And Jo's a little uncomfortable with needles."

"Ah! Well, we've got a lab on site," said Dr. Levine. "But if you'd rather go elsewhere, that's totally fine. I'll send the nurse in with all your paperwork. And I'll plan on seeing you monthly. Okay?"

Joelle nodded; Hanna didn't. But they both thanked the doctor as she left the room.

"You don't want to just get the blood work done now?" Hanna asked. "I'll hold your hand?"

"No, I want you to do it."

"Okay, you can come by the lab after school tomorrow."

It made Hanna feel fuzzy and pleased that Joelle held her in high esteem. She'd picked Hanna to be with her at the doctor's, and didn't want anyone else sticking her with needles. Hanna truly did have Jo's best interests at heart. And hopefully, once she wasn't pregnant anymore, her stepdaughter would confess her relief, and resume the life she was meant to have.

28

Dear Hanna,

Here's something I've been thinking about a lot recently: there is a certain kind of man who was once fawned over and is now irrelevant. These are mostly older men, mostly white, and were highly accomplished in their fields—like, lots of artists, actors, film directors. Now their legacies are ruined and they're in the Bad-Man file alongside the nonfamous lecherous old men. Once upon a time the Bad Boys could do whatever they wanted. They power tripped on their badness—and everyone's blind acceptance—in an endless cycle of feeding their ego. Now we look at them and scoff, "Whatta piece of shit!"

I've been thinking about this for two reasons. First, there's something both fascinating and tragic about someone who was once revered, successful, living the high life . . . who is now a pariah. Aren't some of those old fuckers in prison now? They're probably all shaking their heads and screaming into their pillows, "What HAPPENED?!" Because they got away with their shit for decades—centuries? millennia?—and nobody cared. Long live the penis! And then all of a sudden, people took their blinders off and started to care. I can't figure out which is weirder, that the dick behavior was accepted for so long, or that one morning it suddenly wasn't okay anymore.

There's like this reverse fairy-tale quality for these men. They weren't frogs who turned into princes but kings who turned into Demogorgons.

The other reason I've been thinking about this? Well, I'm a guy with some artsy-fartsy dreams and I'm not gonna get to be the dickhead I might like to be. Gone are the days when I could expect anyone to peel my grapes or massage my toes or otherwise tolerate my bombastic horseshit. No more casting couch or wearing a hot dame on my arm like a diamond-studded accessory. What—women aren't *objects*, there for the taking?!

I know I'm not supposed to say this out loud, but being a total asshat sounds like it was a lot of fun. All the more so for being surrounded by a gaggle of people who placidly (or eagerly) put up with the handsy, moody, didactic Artiste because they believed he was a *Geeenius*. Isn't that weird that "genius" and "bad behavior" went together like peanut butter and jelly?

I know, I know—you're appalled by my cavalier attitude. And now you want to lecture me (or scream at me) about privilege, entitlement, patriarchy, etc. etc. But Hanna, can you imagine the FUN it would be to be taken So Seriously—and respected so highly—while being absolutely the *worst* person?

Sigh . . . Rest assured, it's not that I desire to be the worst person, but it sounds so freeing, so tantalizing, to do whatever you want. No rules. No repercussions. I think I would've very much enjoyed being an emperor. Though my current views may be clouded from watching too many shows about Henry VIII. (Hey, at least Harvey Weinstein and Bill Cosby never had anyone beheaded, am I right?)

Yours,

His Royal ~~Highness~~ Hubris,

Goose

29

Dear Goose,

Wow. I don't know what to say. I know you don't want a lecture, but I would like to discourage you from aspiring to dickheadedness. You can be a genius without molesting anyone. You're better than that. You don't need to saddle your talent and ambition to wickedness. Please lil bro, I know you're joking . . . but I also know that behind such jokes is a tiny bit of envy.

You've demonstrated the ability to discern right from wrong, and that means you can *choose* who you are and what you do—and I like to think that makes you inherently better than these dickheads from the near and distant past. They had small ideas about other people's intrinsic worth. But really, to be so dismissive of others is to make *yourself* smaller, don't you think? What sort of person needs to act that way—someone who's cowardly and insecure, right? You've never struck me as someone who's cowardly or insecure.

End of lecture.

You have this way of making me feel like I owe you something. And now I owe you something questionable from my own cobwebbed corner of reality—something I've only mentioned to you in cryptic passing. I'll draw a quick sketch below, but here it is transcribed into words (as this image comes with a bit of history):

Sometimes I feel the presence of someone else inside me.

When I was little, I tried to turn the Other self into something like an imaginary friend. I gave it the name Marie-Anne Dufosset—which was pretty stupid on my part, because Marie-Anne was a real person who lived a long time ago (and was one of the last people burned as a witch). I found her on the internet while googling all sorts of stuff about witches. I couldn't put it into words then, but I connected to Marie-Anne because she was obviously terribly misunderstood. So misunderstood they burned her to death!

Anyway, the Other presence inside me . . . it both *isn't* me and *is* me. She is someone I don't understand at all, and someone I have everything in common with. I love her more than anything and I despise her for being such a wicked little monster. She keeps me company and she makes me feel alone. She isn't an "alternate" personality but her own separate being . . . who happens to live inside me. I am her house. She is the inhabitant of my body, the house.

Weird, right? She's what makes me feel different, freakish . . . but also unique. When I was little I'd named it, but she doesn't have a name. Or if she does, she doesn't trust me with it, even after I've spent my whole life with her. Sometimes I feel her presence so strongly, a physical thing inside me—not unlike what a heavily pregnant woman must feel. But the being I house isn't a child, and was never a baby. She is older than I am, though I am unsure of her exact age.

There are times when she feels like a stomach-ache, like something I ate that doesn't agree with me. Other times it feels like a tumor, hard and bony, and every now and then she stretches up toward my throat. It's hard to swallow then. I've rushed to the bathroom on more than one occasion, on the verge of vomiting or choking. And I've stood in front of the mirror and opened my mouth so my jaws felt ready to unhinge . . . and this is what I've drawn. Me with my mouth open. And fingertips emerging from the dark cave of my throat, followed by an eye. Sometimes I wish she would crawl out so we could speak face to face. I want to know her better, and I want to know her less. I want her at my side, and I want her to disappear. The best I can do is imagine on paper what she looks like—though I'm certain she's a shape-shifter. And maybe I see her every day and don't recognize her.

Yours,
Hanna

30

Rain beat against the windows. It was so ferocious that Hanna wondered what the ground had done to deserve its watery punishment. Could spring flowers survive such a thrashing? Cloud cover had swallowed all traces of the sun, and it was dreary in her studio even at four in the afternoon with all the lights on.

She worked at her drawing table on a large sheet of heavy paper. The textured paper felt good beneath her fingertips, and she liked the way the indentations absorbed the dusky silver of her graphite stick. For Hanna, this was as close as she got to meditating. Her artwork had served so many purposes when she was a child at Marshes. The therapists had used it as a tool to help her communicate, to help her calm herself, to help her understand the world. In this moment she was drawing to center herself—to prepare for what she was about to do. She'd silenced her phone; no one on TikTok would ever see this piece. It was for her—and, in a way, it was for Joelle.

It had been a risk to wait three days; Joelle was already so close to the limit of being a candidate for a medical abortion. But Hanna wanted to time it in a way to cause as little disruption to her stepdaughter's life as possible. Fridays were a light day at school for her, so if Jo needed to take tomorrow off to recuperate, she wouldn't miss anything important.

Hanna let her hand wander while she tried to clear her mind, which was cluttered with the variables she'd carefully weighed. It hadn't been possible to find answers to some of her questions—like, did the tablets have a strong flavor, and would the medication lose its efficacy if it was exposed to heat? In the end, Hanna ruled out putting the pills in anything that needed to be cooked. Instead, she'd made a batch of garlicky hummus for a little dinner appetizer. She planned to make bite-size crostini, topped with a smear of hummus and a teaspoon of chopped olives and tomatoes. At the risk of appearing stingy, she'd initially serve them each only two crostini—and Joelle's would contain the pulverized pills, mixed together. Hopefully the concoction would sufficiently mask any medicinal flavor, and the two-bite portion was small enough that Joelle could be counted on to finish it. Then, if anyone wanted more, Hanna would set out the rest on a plate.

Though her brain was elsewhere, her hand had turned the washes and lines of gray graphite into a rough, ugly portrait of her mother. Mommy wasn't ugly on the outside, but Hanna's inner self had summoned Suzette's inner self, and here she was, looking hateful and harried. Years ago, when Hanna had messed with her mother's medication, she'd done it in such a carefree way, unconcerned about consequences or miscalculations. But this time Hanna needed to be precise; she wanted to save Jo's life, not further complicate it with a half-done job.

The drawing was as dark and turbulent as the weather. Neither was helping Hanna's state of mind. Goose, she knew, wouldn't like this picture. No teenager thought their parents were perfect, but Goose loved his mom and dad; he'd had very different parents than Hanna had. She hadn't been jealous of that when they were younger, but as she got older and reflected on it more, she felt cheated. She'd been the "practice" child. Mommy made all her mistakes on Hanna, then got it right for Goose. Hanna was glad for Goose—glad he'd experienced a less complicated upbringing. But she couldn't help but wonder sometimes how the trajectory of her life would've been different if she'd had Goose-era Mommy.

Not quite sure if she wanted to keep or destroy the picture, she swiped the sketch off her table. It landed in the corner near the window.

That seemed right, banishing Mommy to the corner for a punishment. Hanna got a fresh sheet of paper and started again, this time letting herself imagine a bright, creative future for Joelle—a future without the burden of a baby.

———

Boyd had stayed for dinner. He followed Joelle and Jacob into the kitchen, where they took their regular places at the immense island. The three of them chatted about prom plans while Hanna plated the appetizers. With her back to everyone, she retrieved the small bowl with the crushed tablets and added a spoonful of hummus. Quickly, she mixed it all together and spread the bowl's entire contents on two of the little bread toasts. She was serving the crostini on individual small plates so they wouldn't look too out of proportion, and Jo was getting the one with the chipped rim. With the other plates ready to go, Hanna added a dollop of olives and tomatoes to Joelle's portion.

"We don't want to do anything too fancy," said Boyd, turning down Jacob's offer of a rented limo.

Of course Boyd Bland didn't want to do anything fancy. Hanna could already picture his idea of a wedding, with matching outfits from Old Navy, and grilled cheese sandwiches at the reception. Joelle wasn't a girl who demanded a lot, but Hanna thought she deserved someone who would make a little more effort. Someone with a little more vision. For a moment she pondered how Jo and Goose would get along. Joelle was only a little older—but Goose was probably several degrees more demented.

When all the appetizers were ready, Hanna stacked two plates on her left arm, restaurant style, and carried a third. The chipped plate was the last one she'd serve before going back to get her own.

Something was poking at Hanna from inside her intestines. She wasn't certain if it was her Other self, gleeful over Hanna's mischief, or her own misgivings. What if Joelle ate one piece—or one bite—and then pushed the plate away? Her preferences in food were becoming more unpredictable. What would happen if she only got a little bit of both medications? Or what if the doctor was wrong by a few days and Joelle was already past the ten-week mark? It didn't mean the pills wouldn't work, but they *might* not. And Hanna wasn't sure if that would put Joelle at a higher risk for complications.

The three of them grinned as Hanna-the-waitress approached the island.

"Everything smells delicious," said Jacob.

She'd made an entire meal inspired by Middle Eastern dishes, and the kitchen carried the aromas of garlic, lemon, parsley, and sautéed onions.

"Just a little taste to start," she said, serving Boyd's plate. "I didn't want to ruin everyone's appetites."

Next she set a plate in front of Jacob.

"Thank you," he said, so pleased with his little family and their little lives. Perhaps they *were* back on the path toward happily ever after, but Jacob didn't deserve any of the credit for that. If he had insisted to Jo that terminating the pregnancy was her best option, she would've listened. It remained beyond Hanna's comprehension that he blithely—or helplessly—accepted everything that came along. Was he really such a believer in inevitability? It seemed like an overly religious, or overly lazy, way to move through the world, and though Jacob identified as Jewish, he wasn't religious.

Hanna's mind barked out protests and warnings.

What if Jo gets really sick?

What if she eats just enough to fuck herself up?

What if she's allergic to the medication?

What if . . . ? What if . . . ? What if . . . ?

If anyone could see signs over Hanna's head, the way she sometimes did with other people, they'd see flashing alerts reading *Distressed!* and *Panicking!*

Joelle reached out to take the last plate. "Thank you!"

Hanna felt herself ripping in half as the two parts of her battled for control. One self screamed, "Do it!" and the other cried, "Hanna, no!" She felt everyone's eyes on her, saw in her peripheral vision their open mouths and gleaming teeth.

They would kill her, if they knew.

She realized in that moment that she'd miscalculated: she shouldn't have made the pills part of a family meal. She should've slipped them to Joelle when it was just the two of them. The audience had become like a table of wolves. Hanna withered in proximity to their fangs and claws.

As she turned toward Joelle, Hanna let the momentum carry her—and tilted her forearm ever so slightly. The chipped plate slid off her arm and onto the floor.

"Oh no!" she cried, secretly relieved to see that the plate had shattered in two—and the crostini had fallen face down on the kitchen floor.

"Oops," said Joelle.

"No worries." Hanna dashed to the counter and retrieved the portion she'd made for herself—and set it in front of Joelle. "Here, sorry. I'll just clean this up."

"Need help?" Jacob devoured the first of his crostini, and made no effort to get up and assist.

"I got it." Hanna scooped up the mess with the two halves of the plate. Wiped the floor with a paper towel.

When she returned to the island and took her seat, she brought the rest of the hummus hors d'oeuvres with her. Boyd and Jacob grabbed up extras.

"Yummy," said Jo, blissfully unaware.

Everyone but Hanna enjoyed the meal. They gushed over each dish while Hanna silently processed her failure. She didn't like failing. And her Other self was angry now and kept punching her in the ribs for being too soft, too weak. Too domesticated.

31

Hanna gazed into space, lulled into a half-aware stupor by the steady drone of rain on the attic windows. The meal had put Jacob in such a good mood that he'd asked her to pose for him. She lounged on the velvety antique settee wearing nothing but a voluminous cream-colored sweater that fell off her shoulders, exposed her legs. The gleam in Jacob's eye told her he thought she looked sexy. He moved around, adjusting his studio lights, in search of just the right ambient shadows. Hanna didn't feel sexy, in spite of the gothic mood. She felt like a stuffed doll as she followed Jacob's instructions:

"Look toward the window."

"Bend your right leg."

"Lean your head back."

She imagined he was a serial killer and this was his torture routine, posing a human doll into contrived boudoir pictures (before letting her die of exsanguination).

As she played the role of a drugged victim, something must have come over her face. Jacob said, "Nice, just like that."

Later he'd develop the pictures in his signature blurry style, and the end product would be less conventional. More opaque. Perhaps she would ultimately be unrecognizable, soft and ghostlike, the settee like a furry tamed beast, her hair the black of a bat's wing. As he moved around her, taking photos, her limbs responded like a marionette's, shifting at his command. *Whatever.* She didn't mind letting him pull the strings. The sweater was comfy, and the gloomy atmosphere soothed her; it made Jacob happy, and it gave her space to think.

Could she reorder the pills and try again?

No, she'd missed her opportunity. She stifled an annoyed sigh, well aware that there was still plenty of time for a surgical abortion, if Joelle could be persuaded. How could Hanna help her stepdaughter see that she was wrong about the future she was imagining—that it would be the dark sort of fairy tale? The grim sort, where promises came with an addendum written in microscopic print, spelling out the horrors to come.

Or perhaps this simply wasn't the role of the evil stepmother, whose motives might always be viewed with suspicion. Perhaps only Perfect Daddy could help the princess see the truth. So many conversations had already been had—except the one where Jacob spoke to Joelle alone, with all the gravitas of a patriarch.

———

"Jacob?"

"Hmm?" He fiddled with a setting on his camera.

"You know that if you spoke to Jo—if you told her you were okay with her ending the pregnancy—she'd listen to you."

He looked up, surprised. And didn't respond right away. For a moment they were trapped on a movie set, the actors well lit beneath the eaves, the rest of the room obscured in darkness. A flash of distant lightning strobed the sky and the rain started to peter off. The husband and wife gazed at each other like wax figurines, waiting for someone else to move them.

"Why are you so fixed on that?" he asked, curious not angry.

"Because it's so obvious to me it's the best option. She's young, she has dreams, she was on track for a completely different sort of life. Having a baby isn't what's best for her. How do you not see that?"

"It isn't the worst thing, and she's made up her mind."

"She made up her mind because you never counseled her. You can't really think it's okay if she settles—if she settles down with Boyd?"

He shrugged. "Boyd isn't the problem, really. He's a good kid. Responsible."

"Is he? Your sixteen-year-old daughter is pregnant."

Jacob's energy, and his formerly erotic mood, drained from his body. He slumped as he sat at the foot of the settee. "I'm just trying to do . . . It's already happened. We can't go back in time. I'm trying to do what Rachel would've done. What she would've wanted."

"And you think that's . . . ?" She asked it in a way that encouraged him to fill in the blank.

"Helping her. Being supportive. We've already talked about this." An edge of impatience came to his voice.

"You don't think it would be helpful and supportive to make ending the pregnancy an option for her? She's less than three months pregnant. There's still time." Hanna swung her feet onto the floor and clutched the sweater close to her neck. This wasn't a sexy conversation and she suddenly felt underdressed. "We're not in shock anymore. We can be calm and rational about this."

Jacob slowly nodded. Hanna had a glimmer of hope that now, under the bright lights, he could finally see the problem for what it was.

"I guess . . . after your miscarriage, it didn't seem right to . . . to lose another baby, intentionally."

"It isn't our baby, Jacob. It's not our life." *The hell it isn't.* In some form or another they would bear the responsibility of a baby in the house, and Hanna imagined herself bearing the ugly brunt of it: changing diapers, cleaning up vomit, doing laundry. And the dreaded babysitting.

She inched closer to him. But instead of meeting her in the middle, Jacob got up and started turning off the studio lights. She spoke to his back as he moved around the room. "Having a baby this young isn't in any girl's best interest. We owe her—at least make sure she knows she has your full support if she wants to change her mind."

He put the lens cap back on. Slipped the camera into its bag.

"I'm okay with her decision." The look he gave her now was undaunted. "Joelle is a smart, reasonable, loving person. It's not ideal—it wasn't my first choice for her—but I trust her to make this decision. At some point you have to accept that."

Do I? What if she didn't?

"But . . . school? And she's already talking about quitting her dance classes. Have you thought about how she's going to take care of the baby? Do you trust Boyd to . . . follow through?"

"Again, it's not ideal. But we're a family, we'll make it work. I know you don't like it when I bring her up, but Rachel wouldn't have pushed this hard for her to end the pregnancy."

"Are you sure?"

"Yes, Hanna. Unlike you, I actually *knew* my first wife." Now he sounded bitter. "She would've offered to do whatever she could to help Jo and care for the baby. Adopt it, take a leave from work—she would've made sure Jo knew she could have her baby *and* a life."

Hanna chewed the inside of her cheek, silenced by the cold fact that she couldn't compete with Dead Rachel. She remained skeptical that Rachel would so blithely accept less for both her own life and her daughter's, but Jacob knew where Hanna stood in regard to adopting Jo's baby. And it wasn't worth his asking if she'd be willing to stop working.

"I know you aren't going to quit your job," he said, halfway to the stairs, intuiting her thoughts. "I don't want you to give up what you love. But please just . . . This is happening. You have to be a little more adaptable."

He disappeared, the steps amputating his legs, and then his torso, as he descended. Hanna was left in the glow of a solitary lamp and the low-wattage bulb that hung above the stairs. She tucked her knees under the sweater, rankled yet again by the possibility of defeat, and unable to envision the compromise of adapting to Joelle's ascension to Mother.

Joelle, as Daughter, already outranked her; she would always be Jacob's first priority. Joelle as Mother . . . It was frighteningly easy to imagine her teenage stepdaughter surpassing her in maturity in the very near future. Hanna didn't want to take care of a baby. She didn't want to hear it crying and screaming. She didn't want to put it *first*, or see it gazing at her with trusting, dependent eyes. And she didn't want to become irrelevant in the household once Joelle emerged as her most "reasonable, loving" self. Hanna couldn't compete with reasonable and loving.

Her Other self agreed. And suggested that Hanna wasn't yet out of options. Perhaps she could make Joelle see that Boyd wasn't a prince—*show her the fine print!*—that sooner or later he would find a reason to leave Jo and the baby behind. He could say all the right words now while such words were easy. But eventually he'd be put to the test and his limitations would be revealed.

Might Jo change her mind about having the baby if Boyd was out of the picture?

Making the fetus go away was proving to be more ethically squishy than Hanna could manage. By comparison, it might be straightforward to get rid of Boyd. Could she make Joelle hate him? Reveal and exploit his flaws and weaknesses?

Back before she'd been sent away to the school for peculiar children, Hanna would probably have conjured an elaborate and ineffective way of murdering Boyd. But now she understood the real world better, and knew she didn't want to end up confined again—in a mental hospital, or worse.

She released her long legs from their sweater cocoon. They were well shaped from running, her calves nicely muscled. She posed for her own satisfaction, stretching her legs and pointing her toes, impressed with herself. Might her beauty be one of Boyd's weaknesses? Might she be able to lure him away from Joelle? She grinned.

It would be best if Joelle didn't want the baby, but as a backup option, Hanna could explore ways of making her not want *Boyd*.

32

Boyd. What a stupid name. If he'd been born a girl, would his parents, Ed and Ashley, have named her Girl? Hanna suppressed a snicker. She was having a hard time staying in the moment. Ashley had reached out to Jacob and suggested they all get together for coffee to "discuss the situation," and here they were on a Sunday afternoon, huddled around a corner table at Starbucks. It was some consolation that "the kids"—as Mr. and Mrs. Bland kept calling them—looked as miserable as Hanna felt.

After being in their company for sixty seconds, Hanna determined that Ed and Ashley were even more ridiculous than Boyd. Ed resembled an inflatable beach toy. His polo shirt stretched tight over his beer-and-hot-wings belly, while his biceps looked like he regularly infused them with growth hormones. Ashley was one of those women who tried to make herself look younger by wearing too much makeup. The gold chains layered like a lace ruff around her neck had the consequence of emphasizing her sagging, middle-aged skin. *Bet she's a smoker.* Hanna knew she was being crass and judgmental—but that didn't mean she was wrong.

As the organizer of this confab, Ashley made herself the keynote speaker. She found numerous ways to interject "since we'll be sharing a grandchild" into her remarks, and was full of ideas about who could look after the baby while Joelle was in school. Ashley volunteered to babysit on her days off from the hospital, and she'd also recruited her mother ("she was a nurse, too—and Millvale's not that far away") and Boyd's older sister ("a fellow teen mom").

"Blair's a stay-at-home mom, her oldest is seven, and then she has Skye, who's five, and Stone, the two-year-old. She's used to having lots of kids around and she got lucky with Chuck. Chuck's solid." Ashley looked to Ed to confirm Chuck's solidity, and Ed nodded.

"He's a good guy," Ed agreed.

"A good role model for Boyd," said Ashley.

Hanna tried not to grimace as she looked at Jacob. Was this what he wanted for Joelle? Stay-at-home teenagehood? A future son-in-law who was openly encouraged to rampantly procreate? Jacob gave Ed and Ashley a tight smile, and Hanna felt sorry for him. Surely he was imagining the same nightmare she was, where his smart, beautiful, capable daughter was lured away—invited into a world where it was okay for her to become a human incubator.

"I really appreciate that you've put so much thought into this," Jacob said diplomatically.

"Of course," Ashley replied with an oblivious grin. "And we're fine with having the kids stay with us. We turned Blair's old room into an office, but then it just became the catchall room for all the junk we couldn't find a home for. We started cleaning that out and they can use it as a nursery."

Hanna saw signs flashing over Ashley's head. *Hero! Saint!* This was Boyd's mother's way of manipulating the situation to her advantage, making herself helpful.

Boyd's cheeks went plummy, but Hanna couldn't quite interpret the glance he gave his parents. It wasn't gratitude. Resentment, perhaps? Did he hate having such an interfering mom? Joelle gripped his hand hard enough to make him sit up a little straighter. He opened his mouth but didn't say anything, so Jo turned to her dad, silently pleading with him to intercede.

"You guys are really being great about this," said Jacob. He beamed a smile at Jo. "But I'm not quite ready to have my baby girl leave the nest—she's only sixteen. We've got plenty of room—a finished basement with a guest suite. It would be like their own apartment."

Boyd and Joelle exchanged relieved grins.

"That's great." Ed took a swig of his manly black coffee and gave his wife a conspiratorial look. "We just don't want to be left out, you know."

"Of course," Jacob said.

Ashley leaned forward on the table, taking up more space, making herself appear larger. "Maybe if they're living with you, then our family can provide the babysitting—they'll never have to leave the baby with strangers. We've got three generations at the ready, eager to pitch in."

Ed nodded, agreeing. "That's a great solution for everyone."

"The kids will never have to pay for childcare, that's for sure," said Ashley.

When she'd agreed to this kaffeeklatsch, Hanna hadn't imagined it was for the purpose of prenegotiating custody and visitation for the shared grandfetus. (She really hadn't wanted to come at all, but did so for the opportunity to gather information to use against Boyd. Really, she knew so little about him; that he seemed embarrassed by his parents was potentially useful.) Now she couldn't help but reflect on Jacob's suggestion to adopt Jo's baby; at the time they hadn't factored in the other grandparents. A part of Hanna wanted to slip it into the discussion, just to see how hostile things would get—would Ashley and Ed fight them to the death to maintain control over their son's offspring? Jacob's passive acceptance of the teen pregnancy was starting to seem sane and wise when compared to Ed and Ashley's zeal.

"I want to take care of the baby too," Joelle said in a small voice.

"Don't worry, sweetheart—you will!" Ashley leaned over and gave Joelle's forearm a squeeze. "But you're gonna have your hands full. You kids are gonna need all kinds of help, at least until Boyd gets his GED and gets into a full-time position."

"Boyd knows he has to man up," Ed said to Jacob. "I can help him get a position in security when he turns eighteen. He doesn't have my background in law enforcement so it'll take some time for him to work his way up, but it's a foot in the door."

"Is that what you're interested in doing, Boyd?" Hanna was genuinely curious about his life ambitions, and she hadn't known his dad was an ex-cop. She filed that tidbit away under More Reasons Not to Risk Murdering Boyd.

Ashley answered for her son. "Security's his best option. And he kind of lost his right to choose a different path, at least for now. He has to work and support his family—those are the rules."

The signs flashed above her: *Noble! Dutiful!* Hanna saw through it to see a control freak who had lost control. *What if I'd tried this tactic? Taking charge of everything.* Maybe this was what Jacob believed Rachel would've done. Swept in like a mama bear—an eagle? A mother of dragons? Some sort of powerful animal—to take back the reins of authority, dictate how things would proceed.

His cheeks still blushing under their scrutiny, Boyd nodded, accepting his mother's verdict on his fate. He looked resigned to his parents' vision of the dogged-but-regal working class. But Boyd's essence was that of an unformed seventeen-year-old with pimples. Hanna didn't think it would go well if she asked Ashley why she was denying her son—and Joelle—their right to *choose*; she sensed something hot and feral just beneath the surface of everything Ashley and Ed had said. Hanna pictured them after a few too many drinks, brash and self-righteous. *Note to self: get them drunk; push their buttons.*

Jacob asked Ed about his job, and as the two of them talked, the conversation veered away from "the kids." Ed and Ashley had jobs that required guts and stamina; they worked on the boundary of danger, each saving people, in their own way—or so Hanna imagined. How did Jacob feel in the presence of such a puffed-up man? Jacob played house and toyed with magic potions in his little darkroom—and Hanna liked him that way. She would never have chosen a man like Ed. She had no interest in the real, gritty world.

Hanna turned toward Jo, making eye contact, wanting to reassure her that they'd never abandon her to these barbarians. And Hanna understood the greater threat now: it wasn't just Boyd. She didn't want the package deal that included his parents—and all the relatives waiting in the wings. Hanna would never be able to maintain herself as the nucleus of her small family if Ashley was in constant orbit.

"How long have you two been married?" Ashley asked with a dead smile.

"Four years."

"Wow. You must've been pretty young."

Hanna felt her competitiveness, the sharp cleats in Ashley's shoes as she climbed atop Hanna's shoulders and declared herself superior. A picture formed in her mind of a blazing fire, and Ashley within it, screaming as the flames blackened her skin. The Other self grinned. The Other self saw Ashley as a worthy competitor and wanted to annihilate her. But Hanna struggled with her confidence. She wasn't a parent like Jacob and Ed and Ashley. And she was closer in age to Boyd and Joelle. Who was she supposed to be in this merging—or warring—of households?

She put her arm around her stepdaughter, staking her claim, and was glad when Jo rested her head on her shoulder. The Other self smiled at Ashley—who must've seen something cold blooded and reptilian in Hanna's eyes.

I do not accept your dominance. You don't get to dictate how this works.

Ashley pulled away from the table, threading her arm through her husband's, as her own smile faltered. She flipped her phone over to check the time, and then reminded Ed that Blair was expecting them.

The men shook hands and said their goodbyes. Hanna and Ashley glowered at each other.

33

They walked home in strained silence. Boyd had gone with his family, and Joelle moped a few paces behind Hanna and Jacob.

"Go for a run?" Jacob asked. "Pop in and change real quick?"

Hanna looked at him, pleased that he was making an effort to include her, and then at the postcard-blue sky. The park would be crowded on such a nice day, but that wasn't what made her hesitate.

"That was weird, wasn't it?" As she voiced the question, she saw Jo lift her head, interested in her father's response.

"They're trying," he said halfheartedly. "I don't think anyone has the perfect blueprint for this scenario."

"Well, they did it once before. With Blair."

Jacob sighed. He seemed distracted and bothered. In theory they'd met with the intention of getting both families on the same page, but as far as Hanna could tell, everyone left feeling off kilter.

"It was like being at the principal's office," said Hanna. Joelle snorted and laughed. She had no idea just how much time Hanna had spent in such offices, under the glare of someone who had wanted to put her in her place.

"They weren't that bad." His defense of the Bland family lacked conviction.

"Now you know why we spend so much time at our place," Jo chimed in. "Boyd's parents are really . . . They're very black and white. They have very definite ideas about things."

Whereas the Altman family—Jacob, especially—was murky and casual. A bit gooey, even.

They turned up the walk toward their house. Jacob gave Hanna a questioning look: she still hadn't said if she wanted to go for a run.

"Need to clear your head?" she asked, unlocking the door.

"Something like that."

"I'd like to—thanks for suggesting it. But I've got some stuff to do here."

"Okay." Once inside he charged upstairs, eager to change into more comfortable clothes and flee.

"Want to sit on the deck?" Hanna asked Joelle, hoping she was interested in doing a postmortem of the family meetup. She grinned when Jo nodded.

———

They'd uncovered the patio furniture the previous day, in anticipation of the nice weekend. Fickle spring had become downright hot, at least for the day. Hanna and Jo sat side by side on lounge chairs, sipping herbal iced tea as they faced the yard. (Hanna would've preferred a whiskey sour, but the tea was more in the spirit of *we're in this together*.)

The border around the green grass was a landscaped swath of garden. Two sides of it were planted with hostas, deer-resistant perennials, and a few bushy viburnums, and the area that faced the deck on the other side of the yard was a bit wilder, with mature trees that made it too shady for much else to grow. They kept the bird feeders there, two on lower branches, one on a shepherd's hook. Sometimes a deer or two came by and ate sunflowers seeds from the lowest feeder. Now, they watched as a squirrel hung upside down from one of the tree-hung feeders, munching seeds with its front paws while its back paws clung to the rim.

"Oh! There's Molly!" Joelle whispered.

Molly was the name she'd given to the orphaned, three-legged groundhog. It hopped around in the sunflower seed detritus, feasting on the ones the squirrel knocked to the ground.

Last spring they'd spotted a mama groundhog and her young kit as they'd emerged from their maze of tunnels to nibble at the edge of the yard. But by late summer the kit was alone—and missing a back foot. Jacob had surmised that a fox had killed the mama. Whenever Hanna saw the three-legged kit, she pictured the fox going after it, clamping down on its back leg as the mama screamed, fighting (however it was that groundhogs fought), throwing herself at the fox's mercy. The natural world was brutal and predictable, but Hanna understood why Joelle had become so protective of the kit. Jo had maternal instincts. Since then, she'd taken charge of the bird feeders, filling them as needed with fresh sunflower seeds—and sprinkling some on the ground for the orphaned groundhog. As autumn approached, Joelle had also insisted on putting out peanuts and an occasional apple, hoping to help Molly fatten up for the winter.

Sometimes Hanna imagined the mama groundhog as her mother, Suzette. In real life a wild animal would never sit back and let its child be devoured; its instincts to procreate and protect were paramount. But in Hanna's fantasy, Suzette-the-groundhog didn't come to the kit's— Hanna's—rescue. Suzette-the-groundhog watched the kit get overpowered, and then devoured. She watched the fox eat her daughter, and then slipped away into her hole, relieved—doubly relieved: the mama was alive, and Hanna-the-kit was dead. That's what Hanna's mother would've done, if she'd been a groundhog.

Joelle looked so pleased as she watched Molly gobble up seeds. "Glad she made it through the winter okay."

In that moment Hanna wished for Joelle that all mothering could be so easy, so rewarding.

It wasn't until the three-legged rodent scampered away that Hanna felt like the moment was right to talk. She turned to Jo, ready to start the conversation, but was surprised when Joelle spoke first.

"I guess you didn't like his parents that much?"

"Was it that obvious?" Hanna tried to control the mask she wore in public, but she was never sure if she was entirely successful.

"Not while we were there, not really. But I could tell. And that crack about the principal's office." She smirked.

"They weren't what I was expecting." Hanna had thought they would be passive like Boyd. Hardworking bobbleheads, uninspiring and inoffensive. "It's a little confusing how they're so law and order, but neither of their kids could figure out how to use birth control."

Shouldn't Boyd have learned something from his big sister's mistake(s)?

"We really thought if we just timed it right . . . ," Joelle mumbled, probably referencing the pullout method, since it was unlikely they'd had the foresight to monitor her ovulation.

"Yeah, I get it. You're a kid." Hanna gave her what she hoped was a wise yet good-humored grin.

"Mm-hmm, lesson learned. The hard way. I'll be the poster girl for birth control after this, I promise. I am not going to follow in Blair's footsteps!"

"I'm glad to hear that. But speaking of Blair . . ." Now they were getting to what Hanna really wanted to say. "You know you'll be getting his entire family, right? Ashley, Ed, Blair, the nieces and nephews and grandma and God knows who else. It's a package deal if you have Boyd's baby. They'll be your family forever."

Hanna hoped it would be enough, while knowing it probably wasn't. But she was out of reasonable arguments. If it was her, she'd do anything to avoid joining an extended family of banal minions like Ed and Ashley. She almost wanted to lay out for Joelle why she'd chosen Jacob—that it was a plan, not an accident. She'd chosen someone with a background similar to her own. A man with a small household, who wasn't *too* family oriented. Financially stable, artistically compatible, with reliably normal behavior.

"I know it's hard to project yourself into the future. But someday you're going to want . . . other things." Hanna watched for her stepdaughter's reaction.

Jo's attention returned to the yard, perhaps looking for Molly. She nodded a little, pensive. On second thought, maybe she wasn't scanning the ground at all; maybe she was trying to force the future into focus. When Jo shrugged, Hanna assumed that the task had been too hard; most teens weren't as calculating as she had been, clear and dead set on conjuring the life she wanted for herself. Joelle didn't yet know enough about how adults slotted into types. While Boyd remained a bit nebulous in her mind, Ed and Ashley weren't.

"I can see them having a lot of cookouts," Hanna said with a grimace. "For Fourth of July and Father's Day and Labor Day . . ." She practically shuddered.

Joelle laughed. "I know that's not really your thing." The laughter fell away, and she grew more serious. "Yeah, I don't know. I've met Blair a few times and she seemed nice enough. It might be nice to have a bigger family. I mean, it's been great just the three of us. And when my mom was here. But . . . I don't know. That part doesn't bother me so much. I think Boyd's more eager to get away from them than I am. He wants us to get our own place when he turns eighteen—or when I turn eighteen, if Daddy won't let me move out when I'm seventeen." She looked at Hanna. "That's gonna be really weird, if I'm a mom and I'm not actually allowed to be an adult."

She appeared so innocent with the sunlight sparkling in her eyes. Hanna gave her a sad smile, understanding that Joelle wouldn't be swayed; she was determined to leave her current life behind. For reasons Hanna couldn't fathom, Joelle wanted to forgo her blessed, easy role as a pampered child and join the rank of Mothers. Was it because she'd lost her own mother so young? Was she trying to become the person she missed?

Hanna reached out and took Joelle's hand. "No matter what happens. We'll always be here for you."

"I know." She shut her eyes against the sun, beaming with a contentment—a maturity?—that was beyond Hanna's comprehension.

Yes, Hanna would be here for her stepdaughter. But she held out hope for the "no matter what happens." She wouldn't let Boyd—or worse, Ashley—dictate Joelle's life.

A pair of squirrels squabbled loudly, one chasing the other away from the bird feeders. Hanna was tempted to throw a rock at them. Greedy motherfuckers. Then again, she couldn't blame them for fighting to get what they wanted. Perhaps she needed to channel her inner wild animal. She didn't want to be like Suzette-the-groundhog, sitting idly by as her daughter was devoured by a fox.

Beside her, Jo looked to have fallen asleep. Hanna gazed at her, contemplating what the wily fox would do.

34

While she waited for a saucepan of water to boil, Hanna Swiffered the kitchen floor. She folded the laundry while she waited for the brown rice to cook. After dinner Jacob went to his office to do some paperwork, and they left Jo to load the dishwasher. As Hanna headed upstairs to her studio, she considered how hypocritical it was that she silently, but frequently, complained about how domestic her life had become. The truth was she valued the orderliness of it—and the ability she'd always had to keep things running smoothly. If she could bargain with a demon to do even more chores in exchange for the return of their regularly scheduled programming, she would. She didn't like not knowing what was going to happen, especially within the domain that was supposed to be her safe space.

Though she'd griped about the school for peculiar children while she was there, Marshes had been methodical and certain in a way that suited her. Her life with Jacob was like that, too, and it had been easy to envision their future in terms of Joelle growing up, going to college, moving out, establishing her own life. The future was supposed to have been Jacob and Hanna, doing their own thing—separately and together—in the quiet emptiness of their beautiful house. Now everything felt messy and convoluted. She no longer had a vision of freedom on the horizon, the child grown and gone.

What was her life going to look like?

Hanna sat at her drawing table, not because she intended to work but because her studio was the one place where she could expect to be left alone. The question from the afternoon echoed: *What would the wily fox do?*

She was self-aware enough to understand that she didn't evolve like other people. She was never going to be fundamentally different from who she'd been at seven, when she'd tried to kill her mother. In many ways her first attempt had been the most cunning, and least violent. But tampering with her mother's medication had only left her a little sick. For her next attempt, Hanna had intended to bash in her mother's skull—but she'd chickened out. The first half of the attack had gone according to plan: Mommy stepped on the thumbtacks, meant to cripple her. But the blood had been too gross, and Hanna had retreated without ever hitting Mommy in the head with the hammer.

Hanna's Other self, whom she'd called Marie-Anne at the time, had helped with the third attempt. But even together the spell they'd cast hadn't been strong enough. And at the bonfire Mommy had only gotten a *tiny* bit burned. Hanna had learned from her various attempts; she knew better than most that killing people took a lot more effort in real life than how it looked on TV: one smack in the head was never enough. But the most important lesson she'd learned was that she didn't want to get locked up again.

Her goal since leaving Marshes was to be less reckless, less impulsive. The therapists had worked with her for hours a week, for years on end, to help her manage her boiling stew of emotions, and get them to a safe simmer. But as she sat there on her stool, staring vacantly at her sketchbook, she felt her foundation crumbling. Someone like Hanna couldn't be groomed for adulthood as easily as a girl like Joelle. Too often now Hanna found her thoughts heading in crazy directions— up, down, sideways—as if Escher had put her brain on a carnival ride. Although, since talking with Jo in the backyard, Hanna found her thoughts returning again and again to a single matter: Jo's relationship with Boyd.

Understanding how they fit together might be the key to breaking them apart.

Whenever Hanna saw them, they were side by side, mute as their glazed-over eyes took in the giant TV screen. Or they were side by side with their heads bowed, separately fiddling with their phones. Yet, Hanna understood from her recent conversation that Joelle and Boyd must, at some point, discuss *real* things. When no one was around. Or when no one was looking. They evidently shared earnest information with each other—did they converse via text?

Perhaps, after so much time spent sitting fused together, they'd become telepathic. However it was they communicated, Hanna was now aware of another aspect of Joelle's secret life: she shared deep and secret things with Boyd, and he with her. And this led Hanna to think that perhaps she'd underestimated Boyd—or, more accurately, underestimated Joelle. Jo wouldn't handcuff herself to a lower life-form. *Would she?* Boyd must have some nonobvious quality that made him worthy of her affection. *Right?*

Given what Hanna now knew about the poor boy's authoritative mother, might he need—or want—the counsel of a less conventional adult? For a second Hanna had been on the brink of forming the words *less controlling adult*, but she had no need to lie to herself; she hoped to be less *obvious* than Ashley, but no less controlling.

What if Hanna extended herself to Boyd, made him aware that he could rely on her, talk to her? It was possible Ashley had already made the same move with Jo, though Hanna didn't sense they were close. Boyd's desire to wiggle out from his parents' clutches likely served as an effective wedge in his mother-son relationship—which probably kept Joelle at a distance from her too. For now, Boyd was dutifully biding his time until he could be his own man. Hanna could work with that; she could be the adult who helped him disengage from his mother's talons.

Jo and Boyd had been dating for several months, but until now Hanna hadn't been interested enough to learn more about him. The things she'd gleaned from seeing him in the company of his parents had been invaluable, but surely the internet had other riches to offer.

She pushed the sketchbook aside and reached for her laptop. Engaged, eager, she felt like a detective in search of clues. Who was this boy named Boyd? What fingerprints had he left in cyberspace? She started with Joelle's Instagram profile, knowing it would be the easiest way to start down Boyd's online rabbit hole. And there he was, tagged in the first photo. Down the rabbit hole she went—to Boyd's profile, and then his sister's. Hanna followed links, until she found the damning evidence she needed.

35

Hanna wasn't initially sure what she would do with the first pictures she'd saved: pics of Boyd vaping with his buddies. Some future day she might have a need to argue that Boyd had an addictive and/or unhealthy lifestyle. Did his parents know he vaped? Did they all smoke together? She imagined herself saying to Ashley, "I'm sorry, Grandfetus can't spend any time at your house unless you all stop smoking—it's bad for Grandfetus's little lungs."

Though Boyd was much more active on TikTok and Instagram, thanks to his relatives, Hanna found the most personal info about him on Facebook. There, she also found accounts for his parents; sister, Blair; brother-in-law, Chuck; and grandmother Diane—with all the photos they'd shared and tagged. They seemed to use Facebook as a family photo album, though none of them had bothered to make their profiles private.

On Blair's page Hanna saw pics of Boyd playing with Scout and Skye and Stone. It was a shock when Hanna realized that she and Blair were exactly the same age—which probably meant Ed and Ashley were close in age to her parents. Blair had opted for a different kind of domestic life, one that left her looking older than her twenty-four years. And there were, indeed, family barbeques, birthday parties, and holiday get-togethers with gaggles of small children. But the pictures that interested Hanna the most weren't the celebrations, but the woodsy outings with Ed and Chuck.

Perhaps she should've guessed that Ed was a hunter. He certainly looked at ease in full camo, unshaven, a rifle slung over his shoulder—very unlike the tight man in the polo shirt, squeezed into a table at Starbucks. However, it was something of a surprise to see Boyd the Blob at his side, similarly dressed and armed—and beaming an unabashed grin. And with them was the solid Chuck—chubby, cheerful, and heavily bearded and, judging by the flag bandanna and miscellaneous patches, a card-carrying patriot.

Hanna heard the high-pitched hum of alarm. It tingled across her skin. The men in these pictures—Ed, Boyd, Chuck—looked too at ease in these surroundings. Forest. Cabin. Crouching behind a tree. On camp chairs around a fire. Shooting beer cans with pistols. They'd documented everything, proving to friends and strangers that they were living the life, and Hanna scrolled through every album on Ed's and Chuck's pages. There were recent pictures, and ones that went back years; Boyd had been hunting with his dad since he was a freckled cherub with a gap-toothed smile.

Was this the real Boyd? Happy in the woods? Pink cheeked with victory as he stood with his dad and brother-in-law over the carcass of a buck? He didn't look shy in these pictures. He didn't look particularly bland, or like the blob who melted against his girlfriend and avoided making eye contact with adults. Hanna didn't like the gleam of confidence in his eyes, the smirk on his face, the mud and blood on his boots. And most of all she didn't like that within Boyd was a killer.

Was the placid Boyd a facade, masking this more savage side? Did Joelle the Vegetarian know about her boyfriend's hobby? Did she know how much he relished the slaughter?

There they were, dressing a deer. Chuck with a bucket of entrails. Boyd with a knife, cutting away the pelt. Ed holding up baggies of meat. And the buck, naked, its stippled body so red and vulnerable, spread eagle and held by ropes between two trees. Hanna was supposed to appreciate this as food, as primal, as survival. Here were men tending to their birthright, guaranteeing full bellies for their clan. But all

Hanna saw was something sinister, something far removed from her own life—from Joelle's life—of ready-to-eat treats from Trader Joe's, of culinary wonders delivered to her door.

These were people who could kill. That they used these skills on animals was little comfort. At least animals would run without thinking about it first, primed in their response to stay alive. Humans were weaker. Humans would ask, "Why?" And then beg for favors and time instead of taking a threat at face value. Hanna hated that these men were lurking in her stepdaughter's life, waiting for her to become one of them. Or, perhaps worse, was Joelle one of those girls who fantasized about "changing" her boyfriend? Did she cajole him—or think privately—that someday she could sway him toward being a vegetarian?

Hanna saw in these pictures a boy who would hold an animal's beating heart in his hand—a boy who would eat it raw if another man told him it would bring him wealth, courage, victory. Had Joelle seen any of these pictures? If so, what had she made of them? And if not, was Boyd intentionally keeping secrets from her?

No one is who they say they are. Words lie.

Hanna's mind raced, full of questions. How many guns did Ed keep in his house? Did he keep them locked up tight? Or maybe he displayed his favorites on the wall, in lieu of art. Boyd probably had guns of his own. Was he one of those teenage boys who loved the look and power of an AR-15? Firing a gun was easier than working through life's inevitable setbacks. Did he have the emotional maturity to cry instead of pulling a trigger?

Except as a surreal fantasy, Hanna couldn't picture Jo with a baby in her arms, rocking it to sleep in the shadows of Boyd the Bomb's gun collection. And he was a bomb, blowing up all their lives.

This might be just the ammunition Hanna needed.

For now she saved the pictures she deemed the most damning. Later she'd decide when and how to reveal them to Jacob and Joelle—but they needed to know about this side of Boyd. This side of his family.

The icing on the cake was the shot of Ed and Chuck and Boyd toasting the camera with their cans of Budweiser.

A boy with a beer wasn't the worst of crimes. Nor was a boy with a vape pen. But a boy with a beer and a gun? And the encouragement of his father? Hanna was convinced now: these weren't good people. *Takes one to know one.*

Needing to contemplate her next move, she set the laptop aside and opened a sketchbook. She couldn't wait to tell Goose about her discoveries. He would get it. He would understand the unbearable problem that Boyd & Family presented. A handgun emerged in the graphite lines on her page. It looked like the Glock 19 that Ed had been holding in the target practice photos. The gun came to life as Hanna added more detail. Boxy and sleek and lethal.

I want one, Hanna thought. And her Other self said, *I want one too.*

36

Dear Goose,

A rather strange thing happened. I was asleep in bed and I heard a voice. I awakened in a state of confusion, because at first I thought I'd heard *you*—as a little boy—crying out from a nightmare. But that was impossible, of course. And then I thought it must've been Joelle, but she hasn't cried in the night for the entire four years that I've lived here. I was ready to lie back down, thinking maybe I'd been jolted from sleep by a raccoon fight—have you ever heard raccoons fight? I was alarmed the first time I heard them shrieking out in the yard in the dead of night. It sounded like a creature in terror and agony, being eaten alive—apparently that's how they squabble over territory. Raccoons are such divas, even more dramatic than squirrels, affronted by everything, strident in their outrage.

Anyway, Jacob was still sound asleep beside me, and just as I laid my head back on the pillow, I heard the voice again. And it was whispering my name!

"Hanna . . . Hanna . . ."

Okay, now you're probably imagining a spooky ghost voice, calling out from the dark. But no, it was a happy, familiar voice. Like a friend, trying to get my attention.

I got out of bed and tiptoed out of the room. Everything feels so weird at night, when the house is dark and everyone is asleep. I made my way down the hallway without turning any lights on, but even though my feet knew the way, the atmosphere felt different—like the ceiling was higher. Like the walls weren't at right angles with the floor and the hallway behind me was getting narrower. I headed straight for my studio.

"Hanna, finally!" came a cheery voice.

I turned on my desk lamp. And there on the shelf, sitting upright in his velvet-lined box, was Skog. He yawned and stretched.

Needless to say, we had a warm reunion—I hadn't seen Skog awake for many years. I started to update him on my life and marriage and he quickly cut me off.

"I know all of that, silly. My dreams are all of your waking hours."

I was so excited to hear that. I thought it might take hours to fill him in on all the important milestones he'd missed, but he knew everything about me. I picked him up and we waltzed around the room a little, but just like old times, Skog had more on his mind than fun and games.

(And in case you're skeptical of this story: yes, I did wonder a couple of times if this was just an elaborate dream. But it wasn't. Skog came out of stasis because he'd sensed the turmoil that's been brewing in my life.)

Goose dear, take a moment to look at the selection of photos I printed, and you'll understand what I've come to learn about Boyd and his barbaric family. Seriously, stop reading now and look at the pictures.

I'll wait . . .

So you see how this situation is deteriorating? I can't have these people as members of my extended family! Who knew Boyd Bland would be such a parasite, planting himself in the framework of our lives, leaving a sticky trail for his flesh-burrowing kin to follow.

Suffice it to say, Skog was alarmed. He grasped my concern that Joelle might be vulnerable to Boyd's family's control. And that Boyd might not be the boring, safe boyfriend he pretends to be. Just like the old days, Skog was full of ideas and advice. I already feel better knowing he's here as a confidant—and I don't in any way mean that as a slight against you, dear brother. I just mean he's *here*, physically, in my house, able to talk with me whenever I need him (now that he's awakened). I hope you find some measure of comfort in that—he has been a stalwart friend. My oldest friend, really.

At one point as we were sitting at my desk talking, I burst out laughing—much to Skog's annoyance.

"I really don't think I'm being funny," he said, all huffy.

"No, but you're being so *Skog*."

"You mean on point? Practical?"

I swallowed my laughter then because I realized he was just trying to help me. In my defense, it just sounded so didactic to hear my little bean-stuffed weirdo warn me—out of nowhere!—that "the biggest mistake people make is not planning for the disposal of the body." I wasn't positive who he thought I might be thinking of killing—Boyd? Ashley? But he urgently wanted me to understand that this was why people got caught.

"The killing isn't the hard part, contrary to your past experiences," he said. "It's when the body is found that people get in trouble. So. Much. Evidence."

I admit, it gave me a lot to think about, even though I hadn't been considering murder as a viable option. I tried to reassure him of that—I don't want to make the kind of stupid mistakes I made when I was a kid. Especially since Boyd's father used to be a cop. Even if I succeeded in making a homicide look like an accident, Ed is probably the kind of guy who would poke and dig around and find someone to blame.

Okay, I'm suddenly a little self-conscious about how insane this letter sounds.

In an alternate universe I would be telling you how I helped Joelle do her hair for the prom, and how Jacob took a million photos of her (with and without Boyd). And *those* are the pictures I would've sent you. But this other stuff seems so much bigger—and yet the prom stuff *did* happen. After Jo left, Jacob and I joked, in a cringe kind of way, that at least we didn't have to worry about her losing her virginity at the after prom. The whole thing seemed kind of surreal, like it was the last hurrah, the final, fancy celebration before Joelle's life changes forever.

A darker reality is moving into our house. I feel its presence already, a wraithlike guest with a leather suitcase full of thumbscrews.

I better stop here. This letter has gone off the rails a bit, but I wanted to tell you everything that's been going on. I'm still debating what actions to take, though by outward appearances I *look* to be handling things better—at least I think that's what Jacob would say. But inside I'm a tropical storm spinning my way to hurricane strength. I'm glad Skog's here to help; I need all the help I can get.

Yours,

Hanna

37

Dear Hanna,

For fuck's sake . . . a *bit* off the rails? Sister dear, you sound like a train that jumped the tracks and is barreling down a mountainside toward a swiftly churning river. I am sputtering and spitting and trying not to set my hair on fire as I write this . . .

YOU CANNOT TAKE LIFE ADVICE FROM SKOG!!!

You cannot take ANY advice from Skog!

In your own words, Skog is a "bean-stuffed weirdo"—a beanbag toy from your childhood, Hanna! And for the love of holy vampire bats, if *you* weren't contemplating offing one of the Blands, don't let Skog talk you into it!

Gimme a second to calm down . . .

Okay, the truth is—and how could you not know this would happen?—I *am* jealous. I would totally brainstorm body disposal with you if that's what you really needed—for fuck's sake, I'm not going to be outdone by a BEANBAG.

I guess I'm okay with the general idea of you having a "friend" to talk to, and maybe Skog's been around since before I was born, but let's keep things in perspective: I have a bigger brain than he does. Like

MASSIVELY bigger. If you have some thinking that needs to be done, you should really come to ME. And frankly, I'm a little pissed that I even have to put these incredibly obvious facts into words.

I'm trying not to be mad at you. I know you're unsure how to handle the tangled path your once easy-to-navigate adulthood has taken. And I wish I was there, instead of Skog, as part of your daily support system. If you want, we can consider other forms of communication. Letters are great—we've gotten into a good rhythm and I know we both love how tactile they are. We're both purists in our own way, but you may need something faster at times. Email is an option: easy to type, quick to send. That could be in addition to letters, not instead of. And you can actually TALK to me if you need to. Okay?

Taking a deep breath . . . (You could probably use one too.)

I totally get why you're freaked out by the Blands. But I urge you to proceed with caution. Whatever you end up doing, there will be consequences. I'm not trying to be a dick, these are the simple laws of physics: every action will have a reaction. I don't want you to get hurt. I don't want you to do something that messes up your whole life. I know you pride yourself on not being as impulsive as you used to be—but that means you can't just *react*, you have to use your *brains*. And your brain is *almost* as big as mine. ;-)

Get what I'm saying?

And don't forget, we can talk anytime. I am always here for you! (Maybe tuck little Skog back into his coffin and nail the lid shut?)

Yours,

Goose

38

Hanna read her brother's letter multiple times over the following days. The act of reading it over and over helped her focus; she needed to decide what to do with the evidence she'd uncovered. *Use your brains.* And finally it came to her, the perfect idea.

She found herself home alone after work on Monday. She'd picked Jo up after school and taken her to her voice lesson, but afterward Jo planned to go to the library with her friends to study for finals. Jacob would be out for hours, showing houses to a client. Hanna changed out of her black scrubs and went to her studio to create a little project on her laptop. She wasn't that skilled with Photoshop, but that was okay—she wanted the graphic to look unpolished, crude even. Like the kind of thing a punk band would hang on a telephone pole to promote a gig.

It didn't take long to create the collage of images. She grinned at it, satisfied, then clicked Print and stood beside the printer as the page jutted out line by line. If she'd wanted the final product to appear slick and professional, she could've used Jacob's laser printer instead of her cheap ink-jet, but the half-assed quality made it look more feral. More dangerous.

Before removing the paper from the tray, Hanna put on a pair of rubber cleaning gloves. She folded the paper and scribbled a note on the back—with her left hand: *found this in computer lab*. Before leaving the room, she deleted the file off her computer.

Downstairs in Jacob's office she printed an envelope with a fake return address and found a stamp. Both were self-sticking, so she wouldn't have to lick them. She was probably being overly careful, but in case anyone decided to test for DNA or fingerprints, she didn't want to leave evidence that could lead back to her.

The post office was only a few blocks away, so she headed out on foot. She slipped the envelope into her purse and shoved her gloved hands into the kangaroo pocket of her hoodie. As she strolled, she took in people's houses, looking for details she hadn't noticed before. A large, glowing fish tank visible through a living room window. A stack of recycling—cardboard boxes plastered with product names, a telltale sign that the household shopped at Costco. When she reached Murray Avenue, she switched her attention to the people bustling along the sidewalk: she didn't want to be spotted by anyone she knew as she passed the teahouse, the supermarket, the state-run liquor store, the hair salon.

She stopped outside the post office and deposited her mail in one of the blue collection boxes beside the front door. The envelope didn't have far to travel, and she expected it would reach its destination tomorrow or the day after. With her back still turned to the street, she slipped off the rubber gloves and returned her hands to her kangaroo pocket.

So easy.

Easy, but well planned. She was proud of herself for acting with such measured deliberation. This was how a mature adult would handle the matter—well, a mature adult bent on anonymous destruction. She grinned as she walked home. In a day or two, she would reap the results of her carefully sown mayhem.

On Wednesday afternoon, Hanna arrived home from work and found Jacob in the kitchen, frozen in place, mesmerized by something on his phone.

"Hey," she said, grabbing the pitcher of iced tea from the fridge.

Jacob didn't answer. His face was tight with worry.

"Everything okay?" she asked, trying not to sound too eager or hopeful. She'd anticipated a chain of events that might include sending out messages to parents. Was Jacob engrossed in such a message?

The front door opened, and he sprang back to life.

"Joelle?" he called, summoning her.

"What's going on?" Hanna asked, all innocent curiosity.

Jo came as far as the entryway, her two-ton backpack dangling off her shoulder. "What?" she asked, weary and annoyed.

"School's canceled tomorrow." Jacob hurried to her, holding up his phone screen. "There's been a threat. Of a shooting."

"Oh my God!" Hanna arranged her face and voice to seem surprised and not delighted.

"I know," Jo said, disgusted. "Boyd was suspended, till they get it sorted out."

"What? What does Boyd have to do with this?" Jacob was in full-on Father Mode, revved up with concern.

Joelle dropped her backpack and trudged over to the island. She sat on her stool as if on the verge of collapse. "Nothing, but the principal got a picture. And it's all fake and it's just someone fuck—messing with him. But now Boyd's in trouble and everyone's pissed off and—"

"Wait, back up. What are we talking about?" Hanna looked to Jacob. "Is that what you were reading? An email from the school?"

"A text."

"About a school shooting?" She sounded appropriately alarmed.

"Mind telling us what you know about this?" Jacob demanded from his daughter. "The text only said they were canceling school and investigating a threat—and obviously you know more than that."

Joelle shook her head in disbelief. "Someone sent this picture of Boyd, holding a gun. And they made it look like he was standing in front of all these dead kids, covered in blood."

"Oh my God!" Hanna the Concerned Stepmother exclaimed.

"And it said"—Joelle changed her voice to a goofy, lower register—"'You with me, bro? Thursday. Lunch.' Like, who would even say that!"

"Where did the principal get the picture?" Hanna asked.

"Supposedly a 'concerned student' found it outside the computer lab and sent it to him." She rolled her eyes. "Please. It's *so fake*. But the school called his parents, and the *police!*"

"That's what they need to do," said Jacob, "for a threat like this."

"It wasn't a threat! Even the principal thinks it was just someone trying to get out of finals. But they have to *investigate* because they don't know who Boyd was 'talking to'—so maybe someone still plans to show up at lunch tomorrow with a gun."

"Better to be safe than sorry, Jo."

Joelle spun on her, enraged. "You aren't listening! No one's listening! Boyd didn't make a save-the-date reminder for a murder buddy! This is insane!"

Jacob went to his daughter and sat beside her. His efforts to soothe her by rubbing circles on her back were rebuked when Jo twitched and leaned away.

"I know it's unfair," he said, "but too many times warning signs go unheeded. The school has to check it out, they have to assume the worst."

"But they're not going to let Boyd return to school until they're sure he's innocent! How are they even going to prove that?"

Hanna took the stool on Jo's other side, secretly thrilled behind her mask of concern. It was going exactly as she'd hoped. "I'm pretty sure they can tell if it's a fake picture. Right? Can't they tell things like that?" She looked at Jacob for encouragement; he nodded.

Jo slumped over, dropping her head on her folded arms. "He won't even get to finish his junior year."

"If someone's pranking him," said Jacob, "they should be able to figure that part out, even if they don't know who did it."

"You don't understand," Jo whined, lifting her head. "The picture of him—just that part—is real. It's the rest of it that's fake."

Jacob froze again. "A real photo of him holding a gun?"

Joelle nodded.

"He has his own gun?"

"A rifle. He hunts with his dad."

Stunned, Jacob looked past his daughter to Hanna. Finally there was real doubt on his face. She didn't say anything, just watched as something came into focus for him.

"You knew he had a gun?" he asked Joelle. "That he hunted?"

"Yeah. Wasn't thrilled about it, obviously. But they eat everything they shoot."

"Still sounds a little at odds. I would've thought that was something you'd care about, being a vegetarian."

"Daddy, I don't need a lecture right now!"

Jacob glared at her. "I would've liked to know this *before*. That your boyfriend has a gun."

Hanna wished she could tack on the other things she knew—about the vaping, and the drinking. But she was happy to see him sufficiently riled up.

"Why? Lots of people have guns, this is America!" Seeming sick of the conversation, Joelle slid off her stool and went to the entryway to grab her backpack.

Jacob chased after her. "It is a big deal—it's exactly why we have so many school shootings! Volatile teenagers shouldn't have access—"

"You're freaking out over nothing! He wasn't going to shoot—I can't believe you're acting like this. Boyd's mad, his parents are pissed at everyone—Boyd said they're talking about suing the school for defamation of character."

Hanna scoffed, unable to stop herself. "I don't think that's a thing. He was going to take his GED anyway, Jo—he was almost done with school."

"But someone made him look like a *monster* and it isn't fair!" She stormed out of the room lopsided, lugging her pack of books.

They let the dust and intensity settle for a moment. Jacob dropped back onto his stool.

"Was I overreacting?" he asked.

"I don't think so." As he had tried with Joelle, Hanna moved beside him and rubbed his back. "School shootings are real, even if this was a false alarm."

"But about Boyd? Why does that freak me out that he has a gun? And knows how to use it?"

"Because he's dating your daughter? And she's pregnant with his child? I think you have every right to be protective."

Jacob nodded, relieved. "I mean, he's always been nice enough. But it's starting to hit home—we don't know that much about him. His family. I'd certainly never let him keep a gun *here*, under my roof. And I don't really want Joelle living alone with him if . . . What are we getting into?"

He looked to Hanna, desperate for an answer. She shook her head, pretending to be helpless, at a loss. Of course she knew the conclusion that needed to be reached, but it would be better if Jacob reached it himself (now that Hanna had made it so easy): Boyd wasn't a good match for his daughter; Joelle would be better off without him.

39

Hanna arranged to work only half a day on Thursday so she could be there with Jacob when Boyd came over for "a little talk." She didn't know exactly what he was going to say to Boyd, but there was no way she was going to miss it. And Jacob had seemed to appreciate it when she volunteered to be there with him, "a united front." Boyd wasn't coming over until noon or so, said he had an "appointment." Hanna wondered if it might be at a police station.

Jacob went out for a run shortly after Hanna got home at 11:15. She sensed he was starting to crumble under the pile on of recent worries. She better understood now how he'd been trying to make the best of the situation, but even a patient, even-keeled man could only take so much. On his way out the door, he'd asked if she wanted to join him—"Quick run around the block?"—but of late she was better managing her own frustrations by cleaning.

That morning she'd dusted the living room and vacuumed the area rug before going to work. Now the sunbeams pouring through the windows revealed the winter's grime on the panes, but she decided to take advantage of Jacob's absence and head to the attic. He never cleaned up there, and for Hanna it was often out of sight, out of mind. After a quick change into jeans and a T-shirt, she grabbed the Swiffer and the duster and the cordless hand vac and headed to the third floor.

She stood at the top of the steps and surveyed the attic. It had such a different atmosphere during the day, when its gothic vibe evaporated in the sunlight. Without the moon and shadows, the room seemed more like a rustic cabin, less refined than anywhere else in the house. The sitting area was relatively tidy, but she could practically smell the dust. Rotting skin particles and the carcasses of microscopic insects. For now she started with the sitting area, using the hand vac to suck up the dust from the settee, end tables, lamps.

As she ran the upholstery attachment over the old sofa's worn cushions, she thought about the sex she and Jacob had had there. They'd spent a lot of time up here when they were first dating. She'd been curious about the artistic side of him. Every time she'd posed for him then, they'd ended up having sex, feet dangling akimbo off the short sofa.

Working swiftly, she zeroed in on the floor's most obvious dust bunnies; she didn't have time to get the vacuum and do a proper cleaning—this was her "meditation" time, and she fantasized about how things would go with Boyd. Would Jacob (finally) get really angry, lose his temper? Scream that this boy had no place in his home, wasn't good enough to be with his daughter? She imagined Boyd blubbering, turning pink and puffy. Then stumbling away with his shrunken manhood and dashed dreams. But what if it wasn't Jacob who got angry, but Boyd? They hadn't seen the other side of him in person yet, the side who didn't see the pain and fear in an animal's eyes. The side who didn't care if a fawn was orphaned so he could have a freezer full of steaks.

She wasn't sure when she'd become so invested in the animal kingdom. *Am I becoming soft?*

Hanna found herself feeling grateful that she rarely cooked meat anymore. Some chicken now and then, and sometimes when they ate out she got a dish with shrimp. In more ways than this, Joelle had had a good effect on her. Hanna was a better person for having been her stepmother. She owed Joelle, didn't she? A good mother would make sure her daughter's life wasn't derailed. *Save her from the fox.* Hanna's simple mission for the noon talk was to amplify every aspect of Boyd's bad behavior. Where Jacob had been giving him the benefit of the doubt, Hanna now needed to zero in on every possible fault.

———

The darkroom door was closed; it was the one room in the house she never touched. In front of it was the large dining room table he used as a work surface, messy as always with discarded photos, materials for cutting mats, miscellaneous scribbles and notes. Well aware how there could be a method to another person's madness, she wouldn't dare tidy it, but she swiped the duster over the surfaces. A manila folder caught her eye, carelessly stuffed with eight-by-ten photos. The folder was dated—Jacob was meticulous in keeping track of the when and how of his creations—and the date corresponded to the last night Hanna had posed for him. The night she'd failed to give Joelle the abortion pills. The night she'd most plainly suggested to Jacob that Jo's life would be better without a baby.

Since Jacob showed her most of his finished work, Hanna assumed he hadn't yet developed a picture from her sitting that he really liked. But she was curious to see what direction they were taking. Upon opening the folder, she found a page of notes: negative numbers and exposures, cryptic annotations of the various things he'd tried in the darkroom. Beneath that was the stack of prints. As Hanna sifted through them, her mood darkened.

She'd always admired his artsy, somewhat abstract style. The way he deconstructed recognizable things into washes of gray. His pictures consistently had an interesting use of light, with a slightly off-kilter perspective. Many times she'd seen herself as a fuzzy form, elongated by a low angle, or otherworldly in a blowout of illumination where some part of her was overexposed. But these. These were grim pictures. Ugly pictures.

And she was ugly in them.

Either while shooting or developing, he'd brought out an imbalance of darkness. Hanna remembered wearing the loose sweater, posing on the settee. But alone in the darkroom, Jacob hadn't seen anything cozy or sexy. Instead he'd transformed her into a wraith. Black shadows turned her vampiric. Her body looked broken, her facial expressions demonic.

Was this an artistic experiment? Or was this how he'd seen her in that moment?

He'd never turned her into something grotesque before, and she didn't like it.

Hanna closed the folder and finished cleaning, wondering if she should say something to him. Ask about what he was trying to achieve in the photos? Alternately she could wait and see if later he showed her anything from the roll—and maybe the finished product would look different. It rattled her, this possibility that Jacob had seen and captured an element of her Other self. Was it a recent discovery for him? Or had he known for a while that this Other self lurked within her? Still, she didn't want him to see it, and she certainly didn't want him immortalizing it in his art.

She was tempted to destroy the pictures. Find the negatives and set them on fire. But that would only create more problems, more questions. *Hanna, how could you do such a thing?* She remembered her daddy saying to her once, "It's like . . . you're two different little girls." And later she understood what she'd seen on his face when he'd said it: fear. Sadness too. But it was the fear that ultimately made her daddy abandon her. Hanna didn't want to be abandoned again. She didn't want her husband to question who she was or fear what she might do.

Use your brains.

She heard a door slam downstairs and knew Jacob was home; she gathered up the cleaning products and hurried down. The curtain would rise soon—and this was the role she'd chosen for herself. Good wife. Good stepmother. It had been an easy facade to wear, until Boyd came along. Stumbling onto the stage with the wrong lines, leaving everyone around him unsure what to say or do. She trusted that Jacob had rehearsed his script and was finally ready to take center stage and confront the interloper. Hanna perceived that her part would require *reacting*: the concerned wife (for her husband), the compassionate adult (to keep on Boyd's good side)—with an undergirding of steely resolve. She needed to bolster Jacob's arguments, and poke at Boyd's shortcomings.

"Honey?" she called as she approached their bedroom.

"I'm gonna take a quick shower." Sweaty and naked, he slipped into the bathroom.

She almost wished he could meet with Boyd like that—like a god. Like an ancient Olympian, sweaty and naked and admired. The Altmans would be the stars of this show, and Bumbling Boyd, with his gummy mouth and cache of guns, needed to get the fuck off their stage.

40

Hanna stood in the kitchen, leaning against the counter, and snarfed down a yogurt. She imagined their gorgeous countertops dripping with blood. In her head it looked beautiful, not gory. The crimson-red accents breathing life into the arid browns.

But it would be a bitch to clean up.

She remembered Skog's advice about disposing of bodies. Any method that left a lot of evidence, liquid or otherwise, was a bad one. No, no one would be getting their jugular slit or their throat slashed today. She chastised herself (halfheartedly) for her violent thoughts: they were just going to *talk*. Yet her mind's eye continued to admire the flowing expanse of blood—the way it pooled across the smooth counters and trickled to the floor below. The Pollock-like splashes of cardinal droplets. The rich color was a comfort. She was blessed in that she didn't always have to *imagine* it; her job rewarded her with many calm moments to watch in silence as the tubes filled with warm, fresh—

Jacob bustled in, shattering her reverie. He whipped open the refrigerator, but couldn't figure out what he wanted. Hanna had hoped the run, the shower, would leave him centered and composed. She could still smell a hint of their calming lavender bodywash, but all he seemed was agitated. His hair was damp. Wet patches showed through his shirt where he hadn't toweled off well enough.

Joelle skated into the room in fuzzy socks and plopped herself at the island. "Boyd's on his way, be here in a few." She bent over her phone, tapping out a message.

Jacob spun around. "We'd like to talk to him alone, please."

"Why?" Jo glared at him, suspicious.

"Because we haven't had many opportunities to. Please." The word was a polite but insistent request for her to leave.

Scenarios seemed to play out behind Jo's eyes (all likely with less carnage than what Hanna let herself envision). "But . . . I want to be here for him, to support him."

"We're not gonna gang up on him, we just want to talk."

To mediate the standoff, Hanna joined them on the other side of the island. "I know you want to be there for your boyfriend, but he has to be able to stand on his own too. Just let us talk alone for a bit and then you can join us."

Joelle looked from her dad to Hanna, not quite ready to trust them. But she slid off her stool, sighing. "Please just don't be mean to him. Things are hard enough."

"I have no interest in being mean to him," said Jacob.

"Fine," Jo grumbled.

The doorbell rang. All three left the kitchen. While Jacob headed for the front door, Hanna stood in the foyer. She suddenly felt like she was there to be the stage manager, to make sure no one went rogue and abandoned their script. She watched as Jo marched up the stairs two at a time; Jacob didn't let their guest in until they heard her bedroom door slam shut.

"Oh," he said with surprise when the front door was only half-open. "I wasn't expecting you."

Hanna craned her neck to see who was on the porch.

As Jacob opened the door wider, Ashley stepped inside, with Boyd meekly in her wake.

"Oh, hi," said Hanna. Her heart was pounding, nervous in spite of her anger. This wasn't what they'd agreed to. This wasn't the person they wanted to talk with.

Jacob looked at Hanna, his face exploding with the same dismay she felt inside. She knew he was desperately trying to rewrite the lines he'd prepared, to accommodate a very different audience. They'd planned on talking with Boyd in the kitchen, but now that seemed too informal.

"Let's go sit in the living room," she said, leading the way.

"Thank you. Sorry to just bust in on you." Ashley carried with her a cloud of sweet perfume; she'd made some effort with her appearance. The roots of her hair had recently been dyed. Her nails were done. Hanna felt underdressed; she and Jacob had prepared to engage a teenage boy, an inferior in the social hierarchy.

"You have a beautiful house." Ashley's eyes darted around, appraising everything—the artwork, the furniture, the windows and their view of the backyard.

"Thank you." Jacob waited for his guests to pick their places on the couch.

"Can I get you anything to drink?" Hanna asked Ashley, obliged now to play the hostess.

"I don't want to take up too much of your time—but maybe a soda, something diet?"

"Sure." Hanna marched off to the kitchen, muttering inaudibly. "Presumptuous bitch."

They didn't keep a lot of soda in the house, but she found a can of Diet Pepsi at the back of the fridge. In spite of how tempted she was to serve just the can, she quickly put ice in a glass and fixed a proper beverage. She returned to the living room in time to hear Ashley say:

"But I know sometimes Boyd is . . ." She looked at her son, searching for the best word. *Bland?* "Not the best communicator. And I wanted to make sure we got this sorted." She accepted the drink and sipped it eagerly. "Thank you."

For a moment all four of them sat perched on their separate sofa cushions, glancing at one another, ready to start, but unsure who was supposed to talk first. Hanna hoped Jacob would jump in, barrel on with some version of what he'd rehearsed. But of course Ashley beat him to it.

"We wanted to reassure you—this is just a royally screwed-up mess. We're handling it, but I'm sure it freaked you out. We were pretty upset too." Ashley spoke only to Jacob, as if Hanna didn't matter. "But I can assure you Boyd would never do something like this—someone has a twisted, messed-up sense of humor. He swears he doesn't have any enemies." She looked at her son.

"I don't," he mumbled. "I don't know who would do this."

"And I know the school had to take it seriously," Ashley went on. "But they've really lost the plot here. Boyd doesn't fit the profile—he's not antisocial, he's not bullied."

At that, Boyd squirmed a little. Hanna could believe that Boyd the Blob *had* been bullied at some point in his school life. His mother's denial in that regard made Hanna wonder what other blind spots she had.

"He's just not the type who would go ballistic. He's about as far from a rampage killer—"

Jacob held out his hand to interrupt her. *Thank God.*

"That wasn't really . . . We were concerned, of course—but it wasn't really about the school, the threat."

Hanna wished her husband didn't look so nervous. It struck her that she could jump in and speak for him—but then there'd be a weird tableau of taciturn males letting their more assertive women do the talking.

"If this isn't about the threat . . . ?" Ashley blinked, confused. She gripped her glass in both hands; all that was left of her drink was brown-tinged ice cubes.

"I mean it is, that's how it started. But Jo told us the photograph, the picture of Boyd with the rifle—that part was real." He seemed like a plastic action figure, too inflexible to maneuver through any real combat.

Ashley gave a little nod, a little what's-the-problem shrug. "Someone stole a picture of him. It could happen to anyone."

Hanna had already checked, and the family's Facebook profiles had been reset to private.

Jacob glanced at her before plunging into the next part. She understood where he was headed, and why he was hesitating to confront their cultural differences.

"I know hunting is normal, a normal activity," he said, color rising in his cheeks. "But we're not comfortable with guns, with killing."

Again Ashley gave a what's-the-problem shrug. "That's fine."

"I don't want my daughter around guns. And I worry about teenagers—"

"There's no reason you or your daughter have to be around our guns. I'll let Ed know not to invite you hunting."

Ashley gave him a twisted smile, halfway polite and halfway an accusation: *You're not our kind.* Hanna saw her looking at them with new eyes. Whatever Ashley and Ed had thought of them before, now Jacob and Hanna were on the Other side. But Jacob wasn't finished making his point.

"I'm saying it worries me . . . I don't want Joelle or a—" He couldn't say *baby*, but Hanna saw it on his lips. "I don't want them living in a household with . . . It's too easy to lose your temper and reach for—even if Boyd isn't the type. I just don't think, in our troubled modern age, that teenagers are really mature enough to handle the implications of—I mean, look at Kyle Rittenhouse."

Hanna wanted to curse at him for invoking the name of the teenage vigilante: a hero in some circles, a murderer who got off scot-free in others. Ashley gawked at him. Hanna read an effort at self-control in her hesitation, an attempt to not blow things up.

"So . . . you're saying, what? I don't understand what we're doing here." She plunked her empty glass on the coffee table—was she getting ready to leave? Or did she expect Hanna to refill it?

Jacob glanced at Boyd. Hanna watched the tension flicker and stretch between the three of them. Ashley abruptly turned to her, ending Hanna's role as the passive observer.

"Where are you with this?" Ashley demanded.

"I'm . . ." Now it was her turn to stutter. "I support my husband."

And for the moment she could forget about the ugliness he'd seen in her, the ugliness he'd captured in his photos. Nothing Ashley did, with her hair or nails or perfume, could mask the foulness she was struggling to contain. An angry beast simmered inside this middle-aged mother. *Maybe it's in Boyd too.*

"Of course you do." Ashley's lips puckered like she'd tasted something sour. "But it's not like we're going to change our lifestyle for you."

"We aren't asking you to," said Hanna.

"We take our Second Amendment rights seriously."

"This isn't about that," Jacob insisted.

"Then what is it about? Exactly?"

Jacob took a beat, took a breath, readying himself. In spite of Ashley's antagonism, he seemed calmer. Hanna wasn't sure what else he wanted to say, but she admired his determination—especially given the doomed atmosphere, the feeling that the conversation was about to plunge off a cliff.

41

"What I'm trying to say . . ." Jacob sat up a little straighter, more confident now as he locked eyes with Ashley. "This has made me see our whole situation in a broader light."

Yes! Hanna silently cheered him on.

"Our whole situation?" Ashley asked, clearly playing dumb.

"Our kids . . . are *kids*. They're not ready to make decisions that are going to impact every aspect of the rest of their lives. Joelle had dreams of doing musical theater. Maybe going to New York City. She's been taking classes since she was little. You know that?" he asked Boyd.

He shrugged. "She's not totally sure."

"Things change," said Ashley. "Life changes. You roll with the punches."

"I've been reluctant to say too much—it seemed too hard to course correct." He glanced at Hanna. "But my wife's right. We're still the parents here. We're not powerless to influence what our kids do."

Boyd gaped at him, confused—and a touch worried? Hanna felt both pride and shock that Jacob had come to this conclusion, and was able to voice it in the presence of Boyd's mother.

"So what do you want us—them—to do?" Ashley's glare moved away from Jacob and settled on Hanna. "Are you really one to give advice? You couldn't have been much older than Boyd when you met your husband."

"I was an adult. With a career." She said it defiantly, but of course Ashley was right. Hanna had been only three years older than Boyd when she got married. Was it possible that Boyd had the same agenda she'd had, to live free of his parents? She spotted him nimbly dashing off a text.

Things could've easily gotten derailed, degenerated into a catfight, but Hanna held her tongue, and Jacob persisted in his earnest attempt to make his point. *Save his daughter.*

"We have to look at the bigger picture. Even if it's uncomfortable. Even if it makes some of us, all of us"—he looked at Boyd—"unhappy. None of us, except Hanna, has even suggested that maybe they shouldn't have this baby. But more and more I'm thinking about . . . Pregnancy is dangerous. More dangerous for someone who's only sixteen. And what if there was a choice to make—between Jo or the baby? And there's no question. I would choose Joelle."

"Daddy?" Jo burst in, phone in hand; Boyd must have summoned her. "What are you talking about?"

"Sit."

Jo responded to her dad's command by parking herself next to Boyd. Her wide eyes blazed with alarm.

"Hi, sweetie." Ashley smiled at her—*staking a claim*—before challenging Jacob. "She asked a fair question. What are you talking about?"

"I'm talking about the fact that there's no debate. That Joelle—her life—is more important to me than an unborn child, and if I had to choose—"

"Why would you have to choose?" Jo demanded.

"Because something could happen to you. Pregnancy is an intense, life-altering experience."

Ashley rolled her eyes. "Like you would know."

Jacob ignored her childish interruption. "You never got to talk with Mommy, really talk with her, about why we didn't have more children. You remember—how you used to ask for a little brother or sister? Mommy had a hard time after you were born. We got help quickly and her depression didn't last long . . . There was no question she loved you to death. But she decided then that one was enough. I know you think you can handle everything . . . But this is bigger than what you imagine it is. And I've been feeling less sure about this cascade of decisions. Maybe it's time to reconsider some things."

All around, open mouths of shock.

Hanna relaxed her leg so that her knee touched Jacob's. She gave his wrist a quick squeeze of support. And she forced herself not to grin. He'd finally come around. She'd gotten into his head, fed him the seeds of doubt.

"Are you saying . . ." Ashley shook her head, as if blinking away a mirage. "Are you trying to say you don't want your daughter to have this baby?"

"I'm saying"—he directed his answer at Joelle—"that we haven't talked about all the hard things. And before it's too late, we should do that. I don't think you ever really considered—"

"She's almost four months pregnant!" Ashley reared up like a cobra ready to strike. She oozed revulsion as she said, "Are you seriously encouraging your daughter to get rid of it?"

"It isn't too late," Hanna said to Jo. "But the pills aren't an option anymore."

"Wait—wait a minute." Ashley struggled to fish words out of her swamp of disgust. "You think there's something wrong about hunting animals. For food. But you're okay with your daughter killing her baby—my son's baby?"

"That's not what I believe. That's not what I'm saying." Giving up on Ashley, Jacob focused on Joelle. "Let's just *talk* about it. Make sure you fully understand the implications of whatever you choose—the big picture, about how all of this will affect your life."

Hadn't Hanna been encouraging Joelle—and Jacob—to do that from the beginning? Oh well, better late than never.

Jacob spoke to both Boyd and Jo now. "If you have a baby together, you'll need to coparent—forever. Regardless of what happens. Regardless of if you're a couple or not. It's easy to think now, when everything's fine, that you'll be together forever, that it'll all turn out exactly how you want. But you know life throws a few more curveballs than that. You both have good intentions, you want to do the best you can—but there are no guarantees. Every potential parent has to consider that, but you're both minors, and you really need to think about, talk about, with us"—he gestured toward Hanna—"what your lives might look like with or *without* each other. Single parents. A baby, a child to raise. What you'll have to give up. The compromises you'll have to make."

"People make it work." Ashley saw before her a creature from another world, a monster in human form whose actions and language she couldn't comprehend.

"Yes, people make it work," Jacob agreed. "But I want better for my child than just getting by." To the teens, he continued: "Are you ready for this? Really ready? Everything you feel at this age is so strong, so all consuming. But have you talked about what your lives will look like? Do you know each other's priorities, beliefs? You have a lot of adults around you, willing to help. But you'll have to set your childhoods aside and be ready to make a lifelong commitment—if not to each other, to a baby. A baby who can't wait for you to get your act together, can't wait for you to get a few more hours of sleep."

Jo had tears in her eyes. She looked young and overwhelmed—and surely that was her father's intention.

"I'm just asking you to talk about *everything*—and if not with us, then with each other."

Hanna wondered how many married couples prepared for a baby with the intentionality of what Jacob was asking "the kids" to do. But as a tactic, it was a good one. In his measured, ominous voice, he made the future sound like a black hole, a void that defied comprehension. What was Joelle supposed to imagine? The unknown terrors of adulthood, of parenthood, of being a monogamous couple? It seemed to be working.

The tears swelled beyond her capacity to hold them back. She let go of Boyd's hand and fled the room.

———

"You're a real piece of work," Ashley said to Jacob as she headed out.

"They need a dose of reality."

"Like you can predict the future."

Jacob, Hanna, and Boyd trailed behind her, stopping in an awkward huddle at the front door.

"I see what your game is," said Ashley. "You take all of life's most natural things and turn them into something horrible. We're real people. We live real, down-to-earth lives. Maybe that's not what you want, for yourselves or your kids. But we're not ashamed. Yeah, change is scary, but change is inevitable. Boyd knows we're here for him—and Joelle. We lead by example, not scare tactics."

As Ashley slipped out the door, Hanna took a parting shot.

"So they cleared up everything with Boyd? He'll be back at school?" She was fully confident now that she'd never be a suspect.

Ashley glared at her. "Probably not. Life has curveballs, like you said. But he can take his GED, and start working, and get ready to *support* his family." She turned to Boyd. "Wait for me in the car."

They all watched as he trudged down the walk. Ashley waited until he'd reached the car before she spoke again.

"You know, I wish my kid had found a 'better' family to marry into too," she said to Jacob and Hanna. "But it isn't Jo's fault, and we would never hold it against her. It would be nice if you could be as respectful toward my son. He's not a 'mistake' that ruined your lives. He's a smart, kind, quiet boy who knows what's right."

"I never said he was a mistake," Jacob protested.

"Not in so many words. But I heard you. Loud and clear. You think you're better than we are. I'd tell you to check your privilege at the door—but this is your house."

As Ashley stormed off, Hanna got a fat whiff of her perfume. It was too flowery for Ashley's personality. She needed a scent with a spiky undertone, something slightly rancid that made people wrinkle their noses.

Jacob shut the door as he and Hanna retreated. As the doubt crept in, his energy flagged. "Did I just make all of this worse?"

"No. You said what needed to be said." She draped her arms around her husband's neck. "I'm proud of you. I know that wasn't easy."

"Why do I feel like I'm the bad person now?"

"Because it's hard to say what people don't want to hear."

"I guess. I mean, I know for so many reasons that Joelle would be better off if all of this wasn't happening—not now, when she's so young. But the truth is . . ." Why did he sound like he was about to change his mind? "The truth is I'd feel terrible, endless guilt if Jo chose not to have the baby because of anything I said. It's one thing if she chose it for herself, but . . ."

Unlike her husband, Hanna wouldn't feel the least bit guilty if they succeeded in talking Joelle into ending the pregnancy. She secretly hoped they were halfway there. But for the sake of her husband's softness, she continued to play the comforting wife—it helped that the words she spoke were true. "Jo has a mind of her own. You said the things you'd regret not saying, but she's going to make her own decision."

He nodded. Gave her a tiny peck on the cheek. "I'm gonna go finish the photo I was working on."

"Okay. I'll check on Jo in a bit." Hanna watched her husband make his way up the stairs, his thoughts seemingly a burden as heavy as his worn-out legs. Did he intend to finish the ghastly picture of her? Would it help relieve his stress to make her the monster?

Something tickled the back of Hanna's throat. She coughed into her elbow.

When that didn't relieve it, she stepped into the powder room. Turned on the light and stood in front of the mirror. Leaning in close, she opened her mouth as wide as she could.

No eyeball peered back at her from the dark cavern of her throat. No bony fingers reached for daylight—nothing was trying to crawl its way out. No, she couldn't blame the thoughts she was having on her Other self. But the idea had come into sharp focus during their final minutes with Ashley. And now Hanna knew exactly what she needed to do. It was something she'd sworn to herself she'd never attempt again.

42

Dear Goose,

The good news is I have clarity about what needs to be done. The bad news is I'm unsure which method to choose. I was being hasty in my desire to remove Boyd from the picture. He was the obvious problem (for obvious reasons). But I see now how Ashley is the glue that holds that family together. Without her, the house of cards that is their extended household will crumble. Without the rudder that steers their ship, the family will flounder in the ocean. (Pardon me for the bad metaphors, but I'm on a roll.)

She is the one who needs to be disposed of.

Getting rid of Boyd isn't good enough, you see: Jacob's heart-to-heart forced Joelle to think about the possibility of being a single mom—and she was undaunted. Of course she was imagining a situation where she and Boyd broke up—*not* where he died—but it's clear to me now that Boyd's untimely death would have no impact on Jo's decision to become a teen mom. But Boyd is a mere guppy, inconsequential when compared to the shark that's swimming in the same tank. I have no doubt that Grandma Ashley wouldn't hesitate to come for Boyd's baby in his absence.

You see, Goose, flushing the guppy would accomplish nothing. But if Ashley were out of the picture, it would destabilize his family's entire foundation.

Should the kids break up, I can't see Boyd putting up much of a custody fight without his mama bear to do the growling. Without Ashley, Ed will be a basket case (though Blair may try to step in as some sort of young matriarch), and Boyd will be set free to do whatever was his instinct before his father demanded he "man up" and his mother dictated his life's path. Without Mama Bear, Boyd will be a seedling in the wind, flying off to find himself. (Again, apologies for the mixed and tragic metaphors—it's just that I literally see Boyd morphing into a happy whirligig upon his mother's untimely death.)

I wouldn't have needed to ponder these things if Joelle had reached another decision. But she is determined to have her baby, no matter what. Her resolve has grown stronger the more she's been asked to consider the downsides. I think on one level Jacob is relieved—the thought of a baby doesn't scare him (unlike me). But that isn't to say he isn't worried, and I know one of his biggest concerns is the lifelong attachment to the baby daddy's kin. My worries are quite a bit more existential and dire: I'm not sure I'll be able to survive with a baby in my house. My acceptance has come slowly, but I believe my days of married life may be numbered.

I cannot keep hammering at Jacob about my distress, my terror at the prospect of being responsible for a baby: even as a "step-grandparent," in this situation

the things I'd be responsible for would tentacle outward into infinity. To keep harping at Jacob makes
me sound unhinged. The parts I've told him, about
my mother and my childhood, are real. But for him,
these fractured anecdotes will never add up to a suffi-
cient reason to avoid cohabitating with his grandchild.
Nothing about what I've told him fully explains why
it terrifies me to even consider being an occasional
babysitter. But I don't want to tell him—I don't want
him to know—the damage I once caused. It was a
mistake, but I have not found the people in my life to
be very forgiving. And it was yet another thing that
Mommy and Daddy used as ammunition to fill me
with doubt.

Now I am suffocating in this doubt as Joelle's
abdomen starts to swell. It is a constant reminder. A
ticking clock that a baby is coming. At this point I
have to admire Jo's determination. She is not distrustful of her ability to be a mother. She is not worried
about her—or her child's—future. But what am I to
do, where am I to be, while she becomes something
beyond my own abilities? It's easy to say I could just
pack my bags and leave. But I can't do that while still
caring about what becomes of my little chosen family.

I know what would happen if I just walked away.

Jacob wouldn't have the backbone to manage his
household. And he certainly wouldn't be able to stand
up to Grandma Ashley. I am a worthy adversary for
her, but if I left, I fear how things would be for Jacob
and Joelle. They would slowly (or quickly) lose out on
being the custodial household—in my absence, Ashley
would see to that. In spite of her own child-rearing

mistakes, Ashley will want to dominate Boyd's child; she will consider it her duty.

So you see, there is no other choice. Jo is having a baby, and I anticipate needing to remove myself from their lives, as much as that may pain me. For any number of baby-related reasons, my sanity will be at risk and it will be better for all—especially the baby!—if I place myself at a safe distance. But I can't leave them vulnerable to Ashley's domination. When I imagine Jacob, Jo, and the baby living in the house without me, I picture Ashley as a hungry fiend, nibbling away at their willpower and autonomy. I see the newly configured Altman family becoming bite-size snacks that Ashley feeds on.

Which leaves me with one question—the thing I need your help with:

How shall I kill her?

It is a last resort—an option I thought I could avoid. But I must be strong for my family. It's a decision I'm making with love.

I've taken your advice and have not discussed this with Skog—though he is right in that killing is a two-part plan: the murder itself, and the disposal of the evidence. My mind is all over the place and I don't trust myself to think it all through.

Brainstorm with me, dear brother?

Yours,

Hanna

43

Dear Hanna,

Thank you for trusting me. I applaud you for how thorough you've been in your thinking. You are wise to recognize so many things about yourself, and the plan you propose is commendably selfless. I'm trying to think of alternatives—I wish you and Joelle weren't in such opposition. Her determination to be a mother has forced you to reach the conclusion that you can't cohabitate with a baby. In a way I feel like she's forcing you out of your own house. I hate to think of you giving up the life you've created—though I, better than anyone, understand your fear when it comes to child-rearing. But have you considered the possibility that this situation may be temporary?

Perhaps you just "separate" from Jacob (for an unrelated reason); surely he will understand why all this turmoil has given you a Lot To Think About. Joelle may end up marrying Boyd, but even if she doesn't, she'll probably want to move out in the near future anyway—right? (Maybe?) And at that point you could "reconcile" with Jacob and move back in. Possible? I'm sure you could make it convincing—playing up your youth, your troubled past. And then you could return to him, better than ever . . . and having conveniently ducked out of diaper-changing duty. Worth a try?

I just hate to think of you burning bridges. Of course, the most important bridge that must remain intact is the bridge to your future—which means whatever you decide to do with Ashley, DON'T GET CAUGHT! I've been giving Ashley's demise and disposal a great deal of thought. I, too, wish this was a path you could avoid, but you've argued admirably in support of your decision. I think it's in my best interest now, and yours, to be a calm and rational sounding board so you don't make any hasty mistakes. And toward that end, I think your best route is to keep it simple.

Here's an ideal scenario:

Learn her habits. Maybe she likes to go for an occasional jog or a power walk through the park. Roll up on her, shoot her in the head, and lead foot it out of there. It's perfect because there'd be no cleanup, no evidence left behind, and if you're careful, no witnesses.

If Ashley's not into fitness or nature, you could try plan B:

Learn her habits. Trail her in her car after dark. When she gets somewhere more remote, roll up on her, shoot her through her car window, and speed away with your headlights off. Same benefits as above, except you might need to take two shots because the first one, through the window, might not kill her.

Do either of those options sound doable? Being unfamiliar with her habits, I can't be super helpful in that regard—but I'm happy to brainstorm. Let's come up with something that will keep you SAFE!

Yours,

Goose

44

Dear Goose,

Hmm, a convenient separation from Jacob isn't a bad idea. It isn't without risk: if it pisses him off enough— if I seem like I'm just running away and shirking my wifely, adult responsibilities—he might not want to take me back. But it could potentially be an Exit Strategy that preserves the bridge to my life with Jacob. (It's also possible that Joelle will NOT "move out in the near future." I mean, she's super young and she's got a good set-up at home, so . . . ?)

And now, yes, let's brainstorm!

Here's the sad truth: I cannot legally purchase a gun.

I did a little research after seeing how well-armed the Blands are: I really wanted to have at least a hand-gun on hand, in case our war with them became less theoretical. But because of my "involuntary confine-ment"—even though I was a *child*, for God's sake—I would be flagged by Pennsylvania's Instant Check System. It seems more than a little unfair to me that my youthful actions should be held against me indef-initely, especially since I was released from Marshes as a functioning member of society.

It's not impossible that I could find a way to buy a gun illegally—I'm sure there are black market avenues for that. Or maybe I could cautiously query some of my acquaintances? An illegally purchased gun could be the safer route, less easy to track, since the gun wouldn't have official records. It's something to consider.

One possibility that really appeals to me, though it might not be practical, is antifreeze. I saw this true-crime show about a woman who killed her husband and two kids using antifreeze. If she'd just killed the husband, she would've gotten away with it. But she got ambitious and started poisoning her kids, who were young adults—and their deaths looked a lot more suspicious. And get this: one of her daughters was in on it, helping her! They were in the process of poisoning the youngest kid, who was only ten, when they were caught.

If I'd had access to antifreeze when I was young, I totally would've used it on Mommy. (Sorry Goose! The fact is, if I'd been more competent in my childish efforts, you never would've been born.) I guess antifreeze tastes sweet and mixes in well with soft drinks. That was how the woman killed off half her family—but she gave them small doses over a period of time. Initially they had flu-like symptoms, and then got sicker and sicker. I think it was kind of a Munchausen by proxy thing with her, as she "took care of" her bedridden kids for a while, though her intention all along was to kill them.

As easy as antifreeze sounds, I wouldn't have that kind of access with Ashley. Even if I invited her over to make amends for our last bungled conversation, I don't know if a large one-time dose would pose a threat to ME, in terms of getting caught. How quickly does a large dose kill? I certainly wouldn't want her dropping dead in my house! I need to do more research.

A couple of other methods have come to mind—but they're just as problematic. If I ever had reason to draw Ashley's blood, I could shove a syringe of oxygen into her vein instead. That would work great . . . except for the fact that I'd be an immediate suspect. Maybe I could find some other opportunity to pump a big air bubble into Ashley's bloodstream? It's a nice, clean method at any rate.

A similar approach would be an overdose of insulin. That's a nearly indetectable way to kill older people, as it looks just like a heart attack—which, in people of a certain age, wouldn't seem suspicious. That was how that serial-killer nurse killed so many patients: he contaminated random IV bags with insulin. Of course the big problem with insulin is I would need to procure it (which leaves a trail of evidence), and then administer it surreptitiously. It's ideal for it to look like the person died in their sleep, but how would I do that without living under the same roof as the intended victim?

Those are my ideas so far, though I realize they're flawed. Unless Ashley could die of natural-looking causes (which is my first choice), I think a public place—like the park you suggested—would make for a more challenging and confusing crime scene. (So less of a chance that I'd get caught!) I'd prefer to not be there at the moment of her death—like, if I poisoned her, I'd want her to go home, get sick, die in bed or her bathroom or whatever—but obviously that won't work for a shooting.

I also really don't want to have to worry about getting rid of the body, so I think my best approach is to let it be found easily. I can't see myself messing around with vats of acid, or schlepping a hundred and fifty pounds of deadweight off to some swamp to be eaten by alligators. I'll need to be careful with the other details, like being fully covered if I'm in contact with her (at least I have endless access to surgical gloves), making sure there are no witnesses (physical or digital), avoiding the use of objects that can be easily traced, etc. But I don't think it's feasible to attempt a bodyless crime, in spite of how alluring it would be for Ashley to simply disappear off the face of the earth.

After thinking about all this stuff, I totally get now why people hire hit men. There are a *lot* of logistics to think about! It's almost hilarious to me now that my seven-year-old self wanted to bludgeon Mommy in her bedroom. Or that I ever thought it at all probable that she would spontaneously combust (with the help of a few witchy spells). I didn't stand a chance of avoiding the school for peculiar children! Oh well, lessons learned.

Knowing you, you've probably been mulling over more methods, though I hope you haven't become as obsessed about it as I have. I know you hate it when I mention Skog, but he is right: there are a thousand ways to kill someone—but to kill someone without it pointing back to you . . . ? I think our best bet is to focus on opportunity and means—access and tools. And if Boyd's father has a lot of friends who are cops, I need to be extra, extra careful.

Could we stage an accident? Something that doesn't look suspicious enough for a serious investigation? Ugh, I can't stop thinking about this.

Thank you again, dear Goose, for sharing your time and thoughts with me. I'm sure you have things you'd rather be doing! I haven't been drawing much the last couple of weeks, but I've enclosed a sketch of Mommy as an UnderSlumberBumbleBeast—the adult, horror version—with buttons for eyes, forks where her arms and legs should be, and a cigar cutter for a mouth. Let's call her Insatiable Suzette. If this little monster lived under your bed, she'd climb out to slice off your toes and feed them to her friends.

Yours,

Hanna

45

Dear Hanna,

Girl, you need to give your brain a rest!

Thanks for the sketch. I always like to see the murky inner lining of your soul. That is your true self, not the pretty face you present to the public (no offense). I had different experiences with Mom and Dad, but her personality is always a bit villainy, isn't it? You may not want to hear this, or you may think it's unfair coming from me, but . . . she tried her best. If nothing else, she nurtured your considerable creativity and artistic skills. So perhaps, on occasion, you can think on that in an affectionate, or at least a positive, way? And not because Mom needs your fuzzy feelings, but surely it would benefit *you* to have something less painful from your childhood to dwell on?

Anyway . . . yes, of course, I've continued to ponder the fine art of murder. Where for you it's an obsession, for me it's a fun distraction. (Pathetic, but true.) So first, let's consider possibilities in the category of Unfortunate Accidents. (And I wholeheartedly agree, a well-staged accident would be *ideal*. We can also consider ideas that might look like a botched robbery.)

Once again, I'm going to ask you to learn Ashley's habits: Where does she go and when? And with whom? Does she take a lunch break outside of the hospital where she works? Does she have a regular schedule for doing errands or visiting with family? What routes does she usually drive? Is she ever walking—to and from a parking lot, locally in her neighborhood, elsewhere?

Let me know what you find out, and then we can weigh possibilities like pushing her in front of a bus (or a truck). Or, if she's predictably in an area without surveillance cameras, you could consider a hit-and-run (though that wouldn't be my first choice, because of the likelihood of damaging your car).

And speaking of cars . . . Can you get yourself educated on the mechanics of the automobile? People die in car accidents all the time—perhaps you could facilitate such an accident? A little problem with the brakes? Or something that would cause Ashley to lose control? (Sorry I don't know more about cars, but seeing how I'm not yet old enough to drive, I haven't made this knowledge a top priority.) There is the risk that a malfunction at a high rate of speed could injure innocent parties—how do you feel about collateral damage?

We have avoided this next category so far, but we really have to consider what I will call the Hands-On Approach—which will require you to get your hands dirty in a more direct way than anything else we've discussed.

You could stab her in the neck with a kitchen knife. Chef's knives are available everywhere, so the weapon provides some anonymity. Again, this will require knowing her habits, but you could approach her in her car, or somewhere where you won't be spotted. Perhaps you pretend you're having car trouble and Ashley stops to help you? A stabbing is a personal death and you can't half ass it. It's also a bloody death, so you have to anticipate some transference of evidence. The knife itself you could ditch in a river afterward (lots of big rivers in the Burgh to choose from).

While I'm not sure if you'd be strong enough to strangle someone to death with your bare hands, you could with the help of a garotte. This is the most time-intensive method we've discussed, as you'd have to physically participate for at least a few minutes. The big advantage it has over a stabbing death is it won't make such a mess. I'd recommend strangling her from behind so you wouldn't have to look her in the eye. Not that you'd be likely to chicken out or become overwhelmed by remorse, but still. I'm pretty sure you don't want Ashley gawking at you while you do the deed.

Does she park in a parking garage at work? (Don't you love the dangerous ambience of a parking garage?) I don't know why I'm so determined to involve her car in this, but maybe you could hide in her back seat. You could be there, ready and waiting, when she gets off of work. Stab (or garotte) her before she even starts the car, then slip away. I trust you'll come up with a good Murder Outfit if you decide to do this in public, something that keeps you covered and lets you vanish incognito.

I think you have enough to mull over for now. And you know your primary homework assignment:

Learn her habits! Know your "mark." And speaking of homework . . .

When you narrow down your options, we can fine-tune a plan. In the meantime let's pray hard that Ashley chokes on a chicken bone. Or has a brain aneurysm. Or slips on a banana peel in front of an oncoming herd of murderous clowns. Ooh, I could spend all day coming up with fun ways for Fate to strike her down! Alas, homework . . . though I've scribbled a quick rendering of the clown herd for your amusement.

Yours,
Goose

46

For five days Hanna had been keeping a compact rental car parked on a neighboring street, halfway between work and home. Her routine had become going straight to the rental car after work, where she put on a nondescript jacket and sunglasses. After driving for a few blocks, she'd tuck her hair under a dirty-blonde wig. She'd learned from Boyd that his mom usually started her shifts later in the day, so every afternoon Hanna parked near the Bland family's humble brick house in Greenfield, and waited for Ashley to venture out.

While Hanna waited, she attempted to look like she wasn't on a stakeout. She pretended to have a conversation on her phone, or studied something on Google Maps. Sometimes she ate a snack. Often she scrolled through TikTok, one eye on her target. Only once had anyone seemed to notice her, an older woman walking a tiny dog in a sweater. The woman gave Hanna the stink eye, at which point Hanna's fake phone conversation erupted into an argument. She watched in the rearview mirror as the dog walker moseyed away. Then Hanna took a moment to admire how good she looked as a blonde. It was a nice wig, shorter than her own hair and with more layers. It was unlikely she'd ever cut her hair in that style, or dye it, but it was fun to play dress-up.

On the first day of the stakeout, Ashley's car was in the driveway, but she never came out of the house. After almost three hours, Hanna had to abandon her post and go home to throw something together for supper.

On the second day, Ashley's car was already gone when Hanna got there. She waited around for a while, but none of the Blands went in or out.

On the third day, Hanna hit the jackpot. Soon after she arrived, Ashley left the house. Hanna followed her to UPMC Montefiore—and trailed her right into the parking garage. As Ashley turned in to the area reserved for employees, Hanna continued up the spiraling ramp as if heading for another level. She just needed to know Ashley's routine; it would be easy enough when she was ready to park nearby and approach Ashley's car on foot. She made a mental note of the time, guessing that Ashley would work a twelve-hour shift. Was this her usual shift, or did her schedule vary? While she was there, Hanna parked for a few minutes and got out to survey the area for security cameras. The garage definitely had the right ambience for committing a crime.

On the fourth day, Ashley left the house at the same time as the previous day and drove toward Oakland. Hanna made sure to stay several cars behind so she wouldn't be spotted. Once again, Ashley headed into the parking garage, but Hanna didn't follow her in.

On the fifth day, Hanna found herself gazing, bored, at the Blands' empty driveway. She was almost nodding off when Boyd came out the front door, headphones on, and walked toward Murray Avenue. His hair was rumpled and he looked slightly dazed, as if he'd just woken up. He hadn't gotten in any real trouble over the threatening photo incident, but his high school days were over. Now he was juggling two part-time jobs, at Giant Eagle and Starbucks, trying to save enough to buy a car. Based on his slobby appearance, Hanna guessed he was on his way to *her* house, to see Joelle, though she didn't follow him to see if he walked the whole way or grabbed a bus. Hanna left soon after he faded into the distance: it was time to return the rental car.

It had been a tedious week, but she'd have to rent another car in the near future. So far she'd only tracked Ashley during the week, late afternoons and early evenings, and she wanted to get a feel for the Bland family's comings and goings on the weekends and later and earlier in the day. And it would be helpful to know Ashley's exact routine when she got off work. Unfortunately, if Hanna wanted to observe the Blands at other times, she'd have to call in sick or take a personal day, and she wasn't quite ready to do that. It was bad enough that she'd been disappearing all week during the afternoons, and even at work she was often distracted. She didn't want to jeopardize her job, but it was weighing on her, the things she was risking to regain control of her life.

She stuffed her disguise in her bag before dropping off the car keys, then summoned an Uber to get back home.

———

Hanna was roused from her uncomfortable position by a rapping on her door. She'd fallen asleep in the corner of her studio, her legs thrown over the arm of her semiplush chair. Her midsection was accordioned, and her head flopped at an odd angle on the armrest. Jacob opened the door before Hanna was fully alert. As she sat up, swinging her legs to the floor, the items on her lap scattered at her feet. She quickly bent over to grab them, reaching for the loose papers first.

"Is that a letter from your brother?" Jacob asked, coming over to help her.

"Yes." She grabbed up the pages and stuffed them in the keepsake box as quickly as she could. Her husband had no real idea what they communicated about, and when he asked after Goose, Hanna gave him the basic updates on school and little else.

Jacob retrieved her dropped book, a battered copy of *My UnderSlumberBumbleBeast*, a tale that explained the strange noises that came from beneath a young girl's bed. Hanna had cherished it since she was a child, even after her daddy stopped reading it to her. The book had inspired the creation of Skog (who bore a slight resemblance to the story's main nonhuman character, Lollipop Hand). As Hanna guiltily pushed the keepsake box out of the way and clutched the book to her chest, she noted Jacob's icy expression.

"You still read that book?" he asked.

"It inspires me," she mumbled. A nonanswer for a question she didn't want to explain.

The book was full of weirdos, freaks, creatures that everyone—except the young protagonist—would see as misshapen and broken. They rattled and squeaked in their foreign tongue, understood only by the girl who cherished them. Young Hanna, herself misunderstood, always felt in alignment with the ugly yet adorable little monsters. Perhaps as an adult it was harder to justify her attachment to them, but to her they still spoke of impossible yet better things. The ability to dream something into existence.

She got up and set the book on the shelf next to Skog. As she stood in front of her drawing table with her back to Jacob, she flipped over anything she didn't want him to see. *A doodle of a garotte.* He wasn't supposed to be in here; this was her private space. *Everything* in here was private. Jacob stood with his arms crossed in the center of her room, taking up too much air.

"It's a mess in here," he said.

Hanna shrugged.

"The whole house is a mess," he continued.

"I've been busy." She couldn't actually remember how many days it had been since she'd cleaned anything.

"With what?" he challenged.

"Did you come in here just to pick a fight with me? Because if you're mad that the house is a mess, you could do some of the cleaning yourself."

"As a matter of fact, I did come in here to pick a fight with you. You've been holed up in here for weeks—or else you're out . . . doing whatever it is you've been doing. You're never around. I just got home and Jo and Boyd are asking about supper—"

"Shit." Hanna hadn't planned on falling asleep after she returned the car. "I meant to order from Dumpling House. They're usually pretty fast, it won't take long." She reached for her phone.

"You missed her doctor's appointment."

"I didn't miss it," she said, unlocking her phone. "I asked you to take her."

"Which would be fine if I knew why. So are you going to tell me? What's going on?"

Instead of calling the Chinese restaurant, Hanna met her husband in the middle of the room. She stood too close, hoping he'd take a step back—or retreat all the way into the hall.

"There's no reason you can't take her once in a while—she has monthly appointments set up. And Jo and Boyd are at no risk of starving," she said.

"That's not the point."

"What is the point? That I haven't been here at everyone's beck and call? Like you're all used to?"

"No," he said, his tone belittling, "the point is you're being secretive. And distant."

She shrugged, unimpressed. As far as she was concerned, she hadn't done anything wrong (yet), and she didn't appreciate him barging in with his bad attitude. "There's a lot going on. I needed some time to myself."

"Okay." He glared at her, waiting, as if expecting more of an explanation.

"What do you want me to say?"

He softened, but in the way of giving up, not with forgiveness. "Sometimes I forget how young you are."

"What's that supposed to mean?"

"It's the most basic of courtesies, the minimal level of respect, to let the people you live with know where you are. We expect it of Joelle."

"I'm not a child. You're being incredibly condescending."

He gestured toward her desk. "This place is a pigsty, you're reading kids' books, and God only knows what you're feverishly working on in here. Something you clearly don't want me to see."

"They're *unfinished*. You don't like people seeing your unfinished work either." A truth, about a lie: she wasn't hiding incomplete drawings from her husband, but he'd never understand what she'd really been doing. "This is my private space, I can do what I want in here."

"Not if it means shutting out your family and your responsibilities." Finally, he headed out, calling over his shoulder: "Are we having Chinese?"

"Yes, I'll call them now." She placed the call as he shut the door. It only took a minute to order; they always got the same dishes.

Before going downstairs, she went to her bedroom to put on comfy pants. It was getting dark outside. The house was shadowed in hostility. It wasn't quite her intention, but maybe she was building a plausible case for requesting a short separation from Jacob. Still, she needed to be careful. And she needed to manage her time better. There weren't enough hours in the day to work full time, handle all her domestic duties, create art and TikToks, and do all the investigative work that Goose had suggested. For the first time she questioned if it was wise to rely so heavily on her fifteen-year-old brother. But then she told herself it was better than relying on Skog.

Jacob, Jo, and Boyd were in the living room, watching TV while they waited for the food to arrive. Hanna bypassed them and went into the kitchen, hesitant to be in everyone's company. She felt a little slimy inside, like a chastised schoolchild. Were they all thinking that she'd done something wrong? That she was bad? Lazy? Forgetful? Selfish? She hoped someday they'd all appreciate what she was willing to do to make their lives better, to protect the family unit from Authoritarian Ashley. But it was possible they'd reap the rewards of her efforts while still thinking of her as defective. A slightly broken monster.

Hanna shrugged to herself as she got out the dinner plates. *At least I don't let people push me around.*

47

They ate dinner in front of the television, silently consuming their moo shu chicken, homestyle bean curd, mixed vegetables, and chicken with black bean sauce. Hanna was more interested in Joelle's baby bump than she was in the TV show. Seemingly overnight, Jo now had a small, swollen mound visible beneath her T-shirt. Hanna tried to picture what was in there. A shell-less lobster in a bath of precious fluids. As Jo ate her bean curd, the tiny shell-less lobster had dinner, too, siphoning up the nutrients through its umbilical straw. Imagining its alien-like hunger nauseated Hanna.

It was impossible for her now to believe that she'd ever pondered, even briefly, having a baby of her own. How could Joelle just sit there, gazing at the television, picking up tofu with her chopsticks, oblivious to the foreign matter congealing in her uterus?

When the episode they were watching came to an end, Jacob stood and put the show on pause. "Seconds? Food, another episode?"

"Both," Jo said. She and her father hurried off to the kitchen to reload their plates.

For a moment it was just Hanna and Boyd.

"You don't want more?" she asked.

"I took a lot the first time around," he said, concentrating on his fork as he shoveled up more bites of chicken and vegetables.

"How are your jobs going?"

He looked at her, nodding. "Good. Busy—I'm studying for my GED too. But I like working. Jo says I smell like coffee all the time."

Hanna gave him a little smile, glad she wasn't close enough to inhale his skin.

Jacob and Joelle returned with their second helpings. Boyd met her eyes as she sat back down, and they communicated in their telepathic way. Just as Jacob was about to hit play on the remote, Jo spoke up.

"Daddy? Can we ask you something for a sec?"

"Sure." He left the television screen frozen in place. Jacob didn't seem worried about whatever Jo and Boyd wanted to discuss, but Hanna felt a sliver of unease. These two had a knack for plunking stones in the calm surface of the family pond.

After another exchange of their secret, inaudible language, Boyd set his plate down. Something dark, probably black bean sauce, stained the corners of his mouth.

"I wanted to ask you if it would be all right . . . I know it's five months before the baby comes, but we were wondering . . ." In spite of his hesitations, it was the most Hanna had ever heard him utter at once. Boyd looked to Joelle before continuing. "We were wondering if it would be okay if we started sharing the room downstairs."

Jo gave him a good-job grin before turning her expectant face toward her dad.

Hanna's unease curdled into a lump of disappointment. The household of three would now become four. And soon enough five. Everything was changing, and she couldn't stop it.

"Are your parents okay with that?" Jacob asked.

"My mom wants us to live there."

"Is she going to be mad if you're here?" Hanna asked. Things were already awkward, bordering on tense, between their two families. What would happen if they pissed Ashley off even more? That Jo and Boyd had chosen her and Jacob over Ashley and Ed was a positive sign—it at least signaled that "the kids" had picked their side. But Boyd's parents wouldn't like it.

"I mean, she's not gonna say no. I don't think."

"It just makes sense," Joelle chimed in. "We can get some practice living together. And get stuff ready before the baby comes."

"Were you still thinking of working this summer?" Jacob asked her.

"I'd rather get my driver's license."

"You can do both," he said.

"I need to practice driving."

"It's not like you've never been behind the wheel," said Jacob. "It won't take that long, you're almost ready. And it would be good to get a little job experience, earn a little money, before . . . right?"

Jo turned to Boyd and gave him a wounded, slightly panicked look.

"What about the babysitting?" he whispered to her.

Hanna could almost see the summer Joelle had envisioned for herself: passing the milestone of becoming a driver, going to the pool with her friends, hanging out—doing whatever it was they did when they were together. All in the spirit of it being her last free summer as an irresponsible teen. Hanna couldn't blame her for wanting that, but Jo was the one who'd insisted on joining the clan of Motherhood. Jo didn't know that her father had talked about buying her a car; now Jacob was waiting to see if Boyd would pull his weight. He was off to an okay start, but it was inevitable that Jacob would be providing a *lot*, and it remained to be seen if Boyd and his fellow Blands walked the walk.

"Babysitting sounds like a good compromise," Hanna said. It was the mature thing to say in the moment, but Hanna imagined her own head spontaneously combusting. Babysitting had become her worst nightmare. But in all likelihood Joelle would be good at it.

"Get a little practice taking care of kids, that sounds like a plan, right?" said Jacob.

"Yeah." Jo sounded more doomed than excited.

"I'm sure you can find someone who needs a few hours here and there, it's not like you have to work full time." Jacob was being patient with his daughter's reluctance, but Hanna knew him well enough to see the strain beneath the surface, the effort he was making not to succumb to his own frustrations.

"My sister is looking for a sitter," said Boyd. "Just a couple times a week."

He announced this for Jacob and Hanna's benefit, as Joelle was obviously already in the loop. Hanna felt less good about the babysitting option, knowing it would put Jo in the grips of Boyd's family. By the clenched look on Jacob's face, he wasn't thrilled with it either. It was too late to walk back his enthusiasm for a part-time babysitting gig, but he was probably concerned that brother-in-law Chuck owned an arsenal—and that one of the kids would pull out a gun and playfully bang-bang Joelle in the heart.

"There you go, problem solved," he said in a tight voice.

"Why are we even talking about this?" Joelle shot back. "We asked about Boyd moving in!"

"Because I don't want you just lounging around in the basement all summer. Boyd has a plan, I want you to have a plan too."

Jo looked to Hanna, as if maybe she could change her father's verdict. She gave her stepdaughter a sounds-reasonable shrug.

With an enormous sigh, Joelle relented. "Fine. I'll babysit. And get my license. And grow a baby."

"Good. Then yes—if Boyd's parents agree, he can move in."

Boyd grinned, showing off his dingy picket fence of square teeth and evenly spaced gaps. He turned to Joelle, but she didn't beam in reply. Instead she leaned back into the couch and resumed eating.

Hanna tried to give her husband a conciliatory smile; he'd handled that well. But apparently he was still irked at her, or irked in general. He pressed play, and the living room filled with television noise. Her appetite gone, she set her plate on the coffee table. She didn't care about the show, but for the sake of performing her role in the family, she remained on the sofa, and mentally worked on her shopping list. She wanted to have some Diet Pepsi on hand, and antifreeze, just in case.

48

Mindful now of how much time she was spending alone in her studio, Hanna made sure to head to bed at a reasonable hour. Most of the things she'd been sketching recently could best be described as two-dimensional mayhem. The working frenzy of her unsettled mind. She'd abandoned precision and nuance in favor of nonrepresentational bursts of emotion, created with the disregard of a toddler defiling every corner of the paper. It had been weeks since she'd had new work to post on TikTok, but she couldn't show her followers—or Jacob, or anyone—the lawless scribbles that were consuming her time.

She left her work face down on her desk before turning off the light and leaving. As she closed the door behind her, she noticed the side of her hand, silver with graphite. Before she'd never worried about anyone snooping in her private space, but now the thought of it bothered her. Her childhood therapists might have understood the benefits of such unfocused expression, but Hanna moved through the world with a self-consciousness about her ability to seem abnormal; other people would see her scribbles as unhinged.

When she got to her bedroom, Jacob was just finishing in the bathroom, heading for bed.

"Hey," she said.

"Hey."

She slipped into the en suite and quickly scrubbed her hands, brushed her teeth. Unsure if he was still irritated with her, she'd expected to come out and find him curled up on his side, eyes shut, pretending to be asleep. But his lamp was on, and he was lounging against the headboard, scowling at his phone.

"Everything okay?" she asked, changing into her pajamas—a cute shorts set, because Jacob liked to see her legs.

"Yeah," he said, distracted. "I have a young couple who are getting cold feet. Not sure they can 'commit to such a major expense, given the uncertainty of our situation'—yadda yadda yadda."

"I'm sorry."

"It happens. They might change their minds." He sighed, and continued to scroll through his phone.

Hanna slid under the sheet, aware of the distance she was keeping from her husband. She felt something inside her that she struggled to name, a sensation that was part emptiness and part jagged teeth. If she'd had a pencil and paper on hand, she could've drawn it, a crevasse-like thing that divided the easy territory she and Jacob had once shared. She wondered if she'd accidentally dug the abyss herself—a side effect of weighing if she should leave him, temporarily, to escape unwanted exposure to Joelle's baby.

Joelle's baby. The words almost made her shudder. The more real it was becoming, the more toxic it felt. The initial announcement of Jo's pregnancy had triggered a slow poison, and now it had had time to accumulate; it was getting harder and harder for Hanna to breathe.

"I guess it's time to tell my parents."

Jacob's words startled her. Lost in her own thoughts, she wasn't at first sure what he was talking about.

"About Jo's situation," he said, responding to her confusion.

"Oh. You haven't told them?"

"I was waiting. In case she changed her mind. No point in them freaking out unnecessarily."

"Are they going to freak out?"

His parents had retired to Arizona soon after she and Jacob had married. Hanna had sensed their disapproval the couple of times they'd gotten together for dinner—their clamped smiles and dubious stares—but she didn't know them well enough to predict their behavior. They sent Jo money for Hanukkah and her birthday, and talked to her on the phone. But if Jacob communicated with them with any real frequency, Hanna was unaware of it. Her in-laws had come to town only twice since resettling in Arizona, for Joelle's bat mitzvah, and for the funeral of Jacob's uncle.

"My mom's always concerned about what the neighbors will think," he said with scorn. "Never mind that their current neighbors don't know me, and *our* neighbors couldn't care less. It's just her lame way of being judgmental."

"They love Joelle. Maybe they'll surprise you?"

He frowned, his thoughts somewhere far away. "They're going to say this wouldn't have happened if Rachel had been here."

"You said that too."

For a moment he looked at her without speaking. "I did. I'm sorry. Look . . ." But then he hesitated before finishing his thought. "I won't let them blame you, but I suspect they'll try. I don't think . . . They were never super supportive of our marriage, but it's easier for them to hold it against you rather than me. I know it isn't fair."

"I'm the scapegoat."

Jacob rolled his eyes. "My family *loves* scapegoats, loves to pick someone to be the center of their disapproval. Most of the time it's just gossipy bullshit. But I don't want you to be hurt by it."

"Thank you. I appreciate that." And she did. Sometimes she was amazed by her husband's maturity. The way he lived with his swirling mass of emotions but rarely let them surface in an unreasonable way. Hanna wondered if she was supposed to be doing more for him—being more understanding, making herself more available for him to share things with. But she genuinely didn't know how to do more than she was already doing. She pulled the sheet up to her chin, feeling suddenly vulnerable and sleepy.

Jacob scrunched down beside her and Hanna was tempted to turn away, not wanting any sort of intimacy. But she forced herself to maintain eye contact with him.

"Are you going to tell your parents?" he asked.

"Why . . . ?" The question confused her on so many levels.

"You're going to be a grandmother—it's a little weird, I know. But a big life event."

I am not *going to be a grandmother.*

He left space for her to reply, and when she didn't, he asked: "Do you ever . . . tell them anything?"

"No." Didn't he know that? Why was he bringing it up?

"No emails? Texts? The occasional photo?"

"Daddy follows me on TikTok." Her father never posted anything, but he frequently liked her videos. Sometimes he included a comment, usually about how her mother "really loved this one." She'd made videos inside the house, on the deck, in her studio; her parents had a window into her life. She could've looked for them on Instagram or Facebook or whatever, but she didn't need or want their performative updates.

"Right, but . . . nothing personal?"

"Why?" she asked again. "What would I say to them?"

"Time has passed." He shrugged. "One of the positive things about something like this—a new baby—it's a good chance to reach out to people. Share good news."

Was this good news? That Hanna, by way of marriage, was going to be a grandmother just shy of her twenty-fifth birthday? Her parents would not clap their hands with joy. Even if they didn't blab all the gory details, they'd want to warn Jacob and Jo about who Hanna had been. They'd warn them to keep Hanna away from the baby. So she couldn't do it any harm.

"I don't think they'd be that interested," she said diplomatically. "No offense."

"You might be surprised. Babies have a way . . . In the end everyone loves to gush and coo, you can't help but smile at a baby." He smiled, imagining it.

Hanna's body felt like a board, stiff and barbed with splinters. She wanted Jacob to shut up. Her tone, though soft, edged on the boundary of hostility: "You can tell *your* parents if you want to."

Jacob tried to caress her fist as she clutched the sheet. "I just don't want you to regret it later. They'll find out, they'll know—even if you're not the one to tell them. Letting them know is an easy excuse, and it could really be a chance to try and reconcile."

"There's nothing to reconcile. They hate me. What don't you understand about that?" She rolled the plank of her body onto her side, giving him a view of her back.

Finally he got the hint and moved away from her. Turned off his lamp. Hanna was grateful for the darkness. The room—her husband, her life—vanished for an instant as everything recognizable disappeared. Then her eyes started to adjust.

"They don't hate you, Hanna," Jacob said softly.

"You don't know them," she whispered back. *You don't know* me.

"Parents, even imperfect ones, don't hate their kids."

I might have given them good reason. But she said nothing, and pretended she was asleep.

49

Hanna vacuumed around and under the Ping-Pong table. She started toward the card table, then stopped and shut off the vacuum. In his early days as a widower, Jacob had played poker down here with his buddies. But that was years ago, and Hanna folded up the table and chairs and lugged them to the storage room.

The subterranean rooms had a slight chill and smelled faintly of mildew. The ceiling was a little low and the floor, though carpeted, a little hard, and the sunlight barely made its way through the short windows. But it was a great rent-free apartment for two teenagers. Joelle and Boyd wouldn't have a full kitchen of their own, but the bar had a sink and a minifridge. The former game room would now be their living room, complete with a sectional sofa (smaller and less comfortable than the one upstairs), and a television (also smaller than the one upstairs). And there was a three-quarter bathroom and a decent-size bedroom—large enough for a queen bed, and, eventually, a crib.

Hanna spritzed Febreze everywhere—in the air, on the furniture—until the basement reeked of Linen & Sky. Just as she was finishing up, she heard Jacob and Boyd on the stairs, carrying down Jo's dresser.

"Mine's gonna go in the bedroom," came Jo's voice from behind them, "and Boyd's will go just outside our door."

Hanna stepped out of the way to let them carry the dresser through. Joelle trailed them, carrying two laundry totes full of clothes. And behind her came Ashley, lugging a huge duffel bag.

"Hi," said Hanna. Ashley must have just arrived. Hanna had never seen her so dressed down before, in distressed jeans and a Steelers T-shirt, makeup-free and ready to work.

"Should I leave this out here?" Ashley called to Boyd, dropping the duffel.

"Yeah," Boyd answered from the bedroom.

Now Ashley turned to acknowledge Hanna, her demeanor cordial but stiff. "This is a nice setup. I see why the kids like it."

"It gives them a little space. So they can figure things out."

Ashley nodded, and Hanna watched her glance around. Was the basement nicer than the Blands' living room? They hadn't seen each other since the day Ashley had turned up unannounced. To keep things running smoothly, Hanna intended to kill her with kindness.

Jacob and Boyd emerged from the bedroom. "Your dresser next?" Jacob asked him.

"I pulled the pickup as close to the door as I could," said Ashley. "Will that work? Do you need help?"

"No, that's perfect," Jacob replied.

"We got this, Mom."

Maybe it was the excitement of doing something out of the ordinary, but everyone seemed to be in a buoyant mood. Jacob and Boyd jogged upstairs to get the next piece of furniture, and Joelle bounded out of her new bedroom.

"Need help putting everything away?" Ashley asked her.

"Sure!"

"Can I get you something to drink?" Hanna said to Ashley. "I stocked up on Diet Pepsi and diet root beer, just in case . . ."

Just in case the perfect moment arose. And Hanna was ready with more than soft drinks.

Ashley considered her in a more appraising way. Her chilly efficiency softened. "Thank you, I appreciate that. How about a root beer?"

"No problem, back in a sec. Need anything Jo?"

"I'm good!"

Hanna heard the shuffle and squeak of Jacob and Boyd easing a heavy object along the hallway above her head. She hurried up the stairs so she'd be out of their way before they headed down. She felt a tingling sensation in her stomach as she entered the kitchen.

Am I really going to do this?

But in spite of the nerves, the answer was yes. She'd gone shopping the day before, so she'd have what she needed if and when Ashley came to the house again. And here she was. Helping her son move into the basement. It was a sign—and an opportunity—that Hanna couldn't ignore.

———

Hanna filled a glass with a bit of diet root beer, a few drops of antifreeze, some more soda, and another drop of antifreeze. She mixed it together with a chopstick, then dumped in a handful of ice cubes. She was glad Ashley had requested the root beer: it was sickeningly sweet and better suited to masking other flavors. Hanna really wasn't sure if antifreeze tasted like anything other than *sweet*—all she knew was a woman had used it successfully to kill half her family. And she would've gotten away with murder if she'd been less greedy and poisoned only *one* person.

From the research Hanna had done online, she knew a fatal dose was barely four fluid ounces, but she didn't want to administer a single dose: the resulting death would be way too suspicious, and an autopsy would be done. If they figured out it was a poisoning, it might lead right back to Hanna. Doing it this way, it would take more than one glass—more than one visit—to build up the toxicity levels in Ashley's system. But perhaps she'd come over regularly now to visit her son and grandfetus.

I'll host a baby shower.

It was the perfect excuse for a prolonged visit, here in her house. And Ashley would probably come over more frequently as Jo's due date approached. And maybe she'd be a constant presence in the days and weeks after the baby was born. *This might really work.*

The glass of root beer in her right hand, she gripped two bottles of Diet Pepsi in her left, and headed back downstairs. She heard her husband say:

"Is there anything else you wanted to bring over?"

"That's it for now," Boyd replied.

His dresser was now in place just beyond the bedroom door, and everyone was huddled in a little group.

"We borrowed Chuck's truck for the furniture," said Ashley, "but anything else should fit in the SUV, if he changes his mind later." Hanna handed her the glass. "Thank you."

"I brought a couple Diet Pepsis? If anyone's thirsty?"

Boyd reached for one.

"I saw there was some root beer?" Jacob asked.

"I can run up and get you one," said Hanna.

"You can have mine. I don't mind having a Pepsi." To Hanna's horror, Ashley extended the glass toward Jacob.

For a second Hanna's heart drummed in her chest and she frantically tried to think of a better reaction than knocking the glass from Ashley's hand. But then Jacob reached for the Diet Pepsi, twisting off the cap as he stepped sideways toward the sofa.

"Glasses are for guests," he said with a laugh before sitting down. "Might as well take a load off for a sec."

The adults sat, while Boyd and Jo stood in the doorway to their new bedroom, sipping from the same bottle and giggling at each other.

"It's nice and cool down here," said Ashley.

"Yeah, one of the advantages to being belowground," Jacob replied.

Indeed, summer was starting with a blaze of heat. Hanna scanned the gathered group, noticing the various ways they sweated. Boyd's shirt was damp at the armpits. The hair touching the back of Jacob's neck was wet. Joelle had a sheen of sweat on her forehead. She hadn't carried anything heavy, but she'd been complaining of being hot and cold, hormonally off balance. When Hanna's eyes fell on Ashley, the only thing she could focus on was the glass at her lips.

Ashley gulp-gulp-gulped before coming up for air.

Hanna half expected to see her give the glass a quizzical look with her brows knit together. But Ashley gave no indication that anything was amiss.

"Thank you for this." She spoke without looking at anyone, and Hanna wasn't sure if Ashley meant the cold drink or Boyd's new home.

A moment of silence oozed too long and began to feel awkward. Hanna considered bringing up the baby shower, to fill in the conversation, but Jacob spoke up before she got a chance.

"Did they ever find out about that photo? Who did it?" he asked.

From the corner, Boyd and Jo turned to listen. Hanna leaned forward, invested—for her own reasons—in Ashley's answer.

Ashley shook her head and shrugged. "Ed really wanted them to pursue it, get to the bottom of it. But once the school was satisfied that Boyd wasn't involved, they dropped it. Everyone said it would be too expensive and time consuming, but that's a shitty prank to play on someone. Could really mess up their lives."

Jacob nodded. "Well, I'm glad they cleared him at least."

"It sounds like he's got a lot of good things going on," Hanna said, giving Boyd a nod of support.

"Kid's a hard worker." Ashley downed the last of her soda with a satisfied *Aahhh!*

"Right. Speaking of work . . ." Jacob stood. "Guess we should get back to it."

"What's next?" Ashley asked. "Unpacking? Need help rearranging anything?"

Hanna took Ashley's empty glass and headed upstairs, leaving them to do the rest. Her part was done. The basement was clean, and Ashley had finished her drink.

50

A week later Hanna found herself facing one of her worst nightmares. A cookout. At Ashley's house. She invited them to their annual Father's Day get-together, and while Hanna argued to Jacob that it had been a *polite* invitation—that Ed and Ashley probably didn't expect them to actually show up—Jacob thought it was an important olive branch and insisted they go.

Hanna had tried to conjure a minor emergency as a last-minute excuse, claiming that Goose was in the midst of a teenage crisis and she needed to spend some virtual time with him. But Jacob shot that down on the grounds that she could talk to him before the cookout, or after they got home.

"We won't be there all day. And it's not like he's asking you to come see him at school, right?"

Hanna had no choice but to quickly concede; the last thing she wanted was for Jacob to ask questions about Goose that she'd be forced to make up lies for. It was stupid of her to have used her brother as an excuse, but he'd been on her mind a lot recently. Certain memories were haunting her with greater frequency and intensity, like how Goose had been a shining beacon—for the whole family—in the years after she returned home from the school for peculiar children.

It had probably been unfair that they'd all been so invested in him, so hopeful and expectant of the better homelife his presence could bring. It put an unfair burden on his small shoulders, and created a painful juxtaposition for Hanna. Her parents sought to build a buffer around little Goose, all in the name of protecting him—from the dangers of the world, and from her. They couldn't believe that Hanna's love for him was genuine. They doubted her capacity to love at all.

One of her favorite recollections was holding his sweaty, eager hand whenever they went to the zoo. The zoo was one of the few places where Mommy or Daddy didn't hover between them every second; they trusted in Hanna's public Good Girl behavior. Mommy and Daddy would stroll along behind Hanna and Goose, letting her guide him to the exhibits to ooh and aah at the sea turtles and elephants. It wasn't that she was a Bad Girl—or even a particularly moody teenager—at home, but obsessive Mommy wanted to do it all *perfectly* the second time around. Hanna had accepted being pushed to the side as her punishment, her penance, for the misguided things she'd done when she was younger. Mommy didn't care what the therapists said; she always gave Hanna the skeptical eye, not trusting that she'd been cured of her capacity to commit bodily harm.

In a way, Mommy always knew her a bit too well.

There were other memories, darker ones that lived half-smothered beneath a heavy blanket so Hanna wouldn't have to think about them. She still didn't want to think about them, but the months of talk about having (or not having) children had set them free. It had all fallen apart years ago, but she wished more than ever that she could go back in time and change it.

She'd do it all perfectly if *she* had a second chance.

If she hadn't messed everything up she might—*might*—even still have a relationship with her parents. With Daddy, at least. Now all she had was her special correspondence with Goose, which she cherished— but she wished she could be a better big sister to him.

Thinking about the past made her angry that she couldn't stay home and work on a letter or draw Goose a goofy picture. But Jacob and Joelle were ready to go. Hanna got the fruit salad she'd made out of the refrigerator. It wasn't the most creative dish to take to a cookout, but it was what she could manage on short notice. She wished she could bring some bottles of Diet Pepsi, spiked with antifreeze. But she didn't want to risk poisoning anyone other than Ashley.

———

Hanna had to pretend that she wasn't familiar with the neighborhood of compact but well-kept homes with their tiny patches of lawn. It was much more crowded than when she'd done her stakeout, and they had to park on the next street over. The scent of flaming charcoal and hamburgers hovered in the air, and she felt as if she'd been transported into a sitcom world of cloned houses and cloned families. Normal people had holiday cookouts—not bonfires with questionable pagan origins (though Daddy had stopped celebrating Walpurgis after Hanna attempted to set Mommy on fire).

Multiple vehicles were parked in the Blands' driveway. Jo led them past the cars and around to the backyard. The flowered sundress she'd chosen to wear effectively hid her baby bump, but Hanna wasn't sure if that had been the intent. She, too, wore a sundress, though hers was black, in soft jersey. It was comfy, but Hanna couldn't shake the sense that she'd come in disguise. Typically she'd wear shorts on such a nice day, but she didn't want Boyd's family staring at her legs. Funny (not funny) how the mere existence of her long, shapely legs could make people sneer at her, their thought bubbles condemning her as *stuck up*, a *slut*, a *gold digger*.

As the Altmans stood at the fringes of the party, Hanna wondered if she and Jacob were thinking the same thing—that their own yard was infinitely better suited for a gathering of this sort. There weren't even that many people—a half dozen-ish adults and an equal number of young kids—but Hanna felt like she was crammed in an elevator, not outside on a lawn.

Ed stood at the grill, stainless steel spatula in hand, beside a bearded dude who Hanna recognized from Facebook as Chuck. With them was a skinny bald man in a Penguins jersey who looked vaguely familiar, but hadn't been tagged in the family photos. Blair, with a crop top that showed off her stretch marks, and a trendier haircut than she'd had in her pics, was gabbing with a pregnant woman as they set paper plates and condiments on the picnic table. Kids galloped in serpentine paths around clusters of folding chairs. Half of them were Blair's, but Hanna wasn't sure who the rest were. The kids' friends? The pregnant woman's offspring?

Boyd spotted Joelle and loped over with a lopsided grin on his face. The two of them slunk away, leaving Hanna and Jacob to stand like the outsiders they were.

"I'll put this on the table." Hanna gestured with the fruit bowl and left Jacob behind. Served him right to stand there like a fish out of water; he was the one who'd wanted to come.

Hanna greeted Blair and the pregnant woman as she placed her bowl on the table with the other salads. "Hi, I'm Hanna."

"Oh, hi! I'm Boyd's sister, Blair—so glad we can all finally meet. My husband's over there with my dad, and my kids are out there running around. This is our cousin Mel."

"Melanie, but everyone calls me Mel. Nice to meet you," said Mel. Up close, Hanna could see that Mel was a few years older than Blair, maybe closer to thirty. "My kids are out there too. And that's my husband, Ryan." Mel pointed toward the bald man at the grill. Jacob was with them now, a proper sausage fest.

"Do you want something to drink?" Blair asked.

Hanna immediately thought of her own hostessing, and the anti-freeze she'd added to Blair's mother's drink. Beside the picnic table was an ice-filled tub overflowing with soft drinks and beer. Hanna grabbed a can of ginger ale, confident that it was tamperproof.

"Thanks so much for having us," said Hanna, trying to seem socially normal in spite of her absent gratitude.

She followed Blair and Mel to the nearest cluster of chairs, where Ashley was sitting beside an older woman who held a short-legged, overweight dog on her lap. Thanks to Facebook, Hanna knew this was Diane, Ashley's mother.

"Hi, glad you could come," Ashley said with a tired smile as Hanna sat beside her.

For a moment all Hanna could do was stare. Ashley's complexion was gray, in spite of the makeup she'd tried to use to cover it. Her bejeweled T-shirt slipped off her shoulder; she looked as if she'd lost at least five pounds in the last week, and her skin appeared oddly saggy.

"Are you okay?" Hanna asked with genuine concern.

"Almost. Don't worry 'bout me. I had some kind of nasty flu. Sickest I've been in ages, but I'm on the mend. Hanna, this is my mom, Diane. Mom, this is Joelle's stepmom."

"Heard a lot about you. Jo's such a sweet girl." Diane seemed to be missing most of her bottom teeth; it made her lower jaw look disproportionately small. With one arm she lifted the dog's upper half, bouncing him a little. "And this is Porky. And yes, his name was Porky before he got fat, 'cause he looked like a piglet when he was a pup."

The dog barked at Hanna. The ladies started chatting, but she couldn't concentrate on what they were saying. All she could think about was Ashley—the "nasty flu" and her unwell appearance. Had Hanna done that? She'd been unsure exactly how large a dose Ashley had ingested, and had wondered off and on all week what the effect had been. Now she knew. If this was all the result of a single poisoning . . . *Damn, antifreeze can fuck you up.*

51

With her knees clenched together, Hanna balanced the paper plate on her lap. Ed's hamburgers looked unappetizing, so she nibbled on salads: potato salad, three-bean salad, cucumbers in sour cream, and her own fruit salad. The liquid from all of them was pooling and mixing on her plate, making it soggy in the middle.

She didn't like eating with plastic forks. Or surrounded by chaos. Stupid Porky trotted from person to person, begging—but every time he neared Hanna, he bared his teeth and growled at her. Jo and Boyd were sitting in a circle on the grass with the kids, who beamed at the two teenagers with wide-eyed adoration. Only one stray toddler was immune to their charms—Blair's youngest, who gaped at Hanna as he leaned against his grandmother's chair.

Hanna found it unnerving, the way the kid stared at her with his crystal ball eyes. His lips were stained purple; he chewed on a Popsicle stick, sharpening it into a weapon. She wanted to shoo him away. She wanted Porky to grab onto his calf with his tiny vicious teeth and drag him off. What was the kid's name? It started with an S—Snotface? Shithead? When no one was looking, Hanna gave him a snarl of disgust. Shithead's expression went from neutral to savage, and he drooled a little as he took the Popsicle stick from his mouth. He was like the human version of Porky the Foul Dog.

Christ. Hanna hadn't been around children since Goose was young. She remembered now that he had in fact, on occasion, gotten on her nerves. Grabbing onto her with his sticky, demanding hands. Poking his nose into everything she was doing. Had she actually liked Goose when he was little? Or had she reframed the memories based on her love for him now? Teenagers seemed like real people, with fully developed personalities and interesting thoughts, but the same couldn't be said for these fledgling aliens with their searching eyes and silent judgments. *Is that how I was as a child?*

Based on how repelled she felt by Shithead, maybe she didn't like kids. At all. Not until they had a few more birthdays and became less creepy and needy. As Shithead continued gawking at her, Hanna got a whiff of something that almost made her gag. True to the name she'd given him, he smelled like shit. *Bet he took a dump on purpose.* Someone needed to change this kid's diaper ASAP. But the women around her seemed unbothered by his stench. They gobbled and gabbed and gulped and belched—and laughed laughed laughed.

Hanna looked to the men's cluster, which had conveniently moved to within arm's reach of the food table, and tried to make eye contact with Jacob. She sent him a telepathic message. *Get me out of here.* But when he met her gaze, all he did was raise his beer bottle in greeting. He looked content and victorious. She wondered what the Guys were talking about. Guns? Politics? Sports? Some sort of testosterone-laden subject—which would be better than the conversation Hanna had to endure. After initially swapping recipes, the Gals had moved on to favorite brands of moisturizer, and were now talking about a reality dating show that sounded utterly degrading. Why did people humiliate themselves just to be on TV? It wasn't that hard to get laid, or snag a spouse.

"Do you ever watch it?" Mel asked, trying to loop her in.

"No, I mostly watch movies," said Hanna.

"Have you seen the new *Spider-Man*?" Blair asked.

"Wait, which one is this?" Ashley asked.

Why are there so many fucking Spider-Man *movies?* "No. I usually watch foreign films."

They wrinkled their noses at her like she smelled worse than Shithead.

"I hate subtitles," said Diane. "I don't wanna *read* a movie, I wanna *watch* it."

"There's usually a dubbed version," Mel offered.

Diane rolled her rheumy eyes.

The backs of Hanna's thighs were getting sweaty. She glanced at Joelle in time to see her wipe ketchup off a little girl's mouth. Jo had balked at the prospect of babysitting, but she was obviously good with kids. *Unlike me.* This was her stepdaughter's destiny, sitting on lawn chairs with generations of other mommies, swapping banal advice and engaging in tiresome chitchat. Hanna couldn't understand why Joelle wanted that. And equally couldn't understand why, the longer Hanna sat in this circle of women, the more it troubled her that she didn't fit in. She wasn't maternal, or neighborly, or family oriented. She didn't think anyone would even consider her their best friend. The one thing she could boast about was her relationship with Jo, even if it was more sisterly. *I'm a good stepmom.* It suddenly bothered her that these mommies, young and old, didn't know that about her.

"I wanted to let you know," she said, interrupting a frivolous exchange between Ashley and her toothless mom. It was the first time Hanna had initiated a topic of conversation, and the women all looked at her. "I'm going to host a baby shower for Joelle. I'd like you all to come, of course. I'm not sure when it's going to be yet. When do they usually do the baby shower? A few weeks before the due date?"

A series of looks went around the circle. Hanna tried to interpret them, but no clear words appeared above their heads. She saw a hazy *clueless* floating beside her, but Hanna wasn't sure if it was Ashley's thought or her own. It accurately described how she felt. Wasn't inviting them all to Jo's baby shower a nice thing? Didn't it show that Hanna could be supportive and hospitable?

Why was everyone around her acting so puzzled?

52

"I thought Mom was hosting the shower?" Blair said. A neon *confused* burst into life above her.

"Doesn't the girl's family usually do it?" Hanna asked. "Her mom?"

The women nodded. Shrugged. Except for Ashley—who shook her head and said:

"A female relative or friend. There isn't a hard-and-fast rule. We were thinking of a Saturday in early October."

Hanna wished she had some sort of superpower, one that allowed her to Taser people by blinking at them. Ashley was being unforgivably presumptuous—especially since she hadn't discussed this hijacking of the baby shower with Joelle's family.

For the sake of her stepdaughter, Hanna tried not to sound (too) angry. "Jo and I are really close. It's something I'd really like to do for her."

Blair winced at her buddy Mel.

"Jo doesn't have a lot of other family here," Ashley countered. "So it just makes sense if it's going to be mostly Boyd's relatives for his side of the family to host it. This is far from everyone." She gestured around at the people in her yard. "For a big milestone like a new baby—a first baby—all the aunts and uncles and cousins will come."

"We've had a lot of practice with this sort of thing," Diane chipped in.

"Not that that means . . ." Blair was flustered, but she kept trying. "Of course we want you to be there, and help with the planning. We weren't going to decide anything without talking to you first."

"But . . ." But they already had made plans without talking to her. Hanna grappled with an explosion of wounded feelings. She was simultaneously hurt, enraged, jealous—but she also still believed she could win this battle. "I'm sure Joelle will want to have her shower at home. She'll have friends she wants to invite."

Hanna couldn't picture Joelle surrounded by exponentially more of the bossy and boring Blands. (Though she almost laughed at the possibility of a crew of geriatric versions of Shithead.) Rather, she saw Jo with a gaggle of teenagers eating cake and playing Ping-Pong and video games in the basement. Perhaps in her mind it looked more like a birthday party than a baby shower, but given the age of the mother-to-be, that probably wasn't off base.

"Her friends are welcome here—Jo knows she can invite whoever she'd like." Ashley might have been weakened by her recent illness, but the look she gave Hanna was pure don't-fuck-with-me.

"Are you guys talking about me?" Joelle appeared between Ashley's and Hanna's chairs.

"Just your baby shower," said Diane.

"I thought we'd have it at home," said Hanna. "I want to throw you a really nice party."

"Oh." Joelle looked stricken. "That's so nice."

Her tone didn't match her words. A gust of wind pressed the fabric of Jo's dress against her body, revealing the outline of her baby bump.

"And you're going to need a lot of things," Hanna continued. "Baby furniture, car seat, stroller, plus all the little stuff. It'll be too cold then to have it outside, but we have lots of room inside."

It made so much sense to Hanna that the gifts should be opened near the room where they would be used. But Jo still didn't look happy or excited; she gave Blair a what-do-I-do look.

"*We* have room inside," Ashley said, bristling.

Hanna hadn't intentionally insulted her, but also didn't care that she felt slighted.

"I'm sorry—thank you, Hanna. That's so nice." Jo glanced over at her oblivious father. No help there, for her or Hanna. "But Ashley asked me and . . . I didn't think you'd want to."

"Why wouldn't I want to?" Hanna felt her skin turning red with shame and fury. Reality was sinking in; she was losing. Was Ashley feeding Joelle lies about how Hanna couldn't, or wouldn't, live up to her responsibilities? "Why wouldn't I want to do something nice for you?"

Aware that she was putting her stepdaughter on the spot, making her squirm, Hanna whirled on Ashley. "Did you say something to her?"

"About what?"

"Why would she think I wouldn't want to have a baby shower for her?"

"I don't know—maybe because you made it clear you thought she should have an abortion?" Ashley's tone was icy and mocking. Hanna wanted to punch the smug look off her face.

"Just because I gave her reasonable advice about her options—" Hanna clenched her jaw to keep from screaming. She burst out of her chair to fling her plate in the garbage can. With her back to the circle, she grabbed a paper napkin and scrubbed at the wet patch the leaking plate had left on her dress. She could feel their eyes boring into her back, see their open mouths of disapproval and shock.

Jacob came over, touched her arm. "Everything okay?"

Hanna made a show of getting herself under control. "Sorry." She smiled at Ashley, at Joelle. "You should have your baby shower wherever you want. I overreacted—it just caught me by surprise. That you'd already made plans."

"We should have talked to you first," Blair conceded.

"It's okay. It's not about me, it's about Jo. We all just want her to be happy, and have everything she needs." Hanna thought she'd recovered well and delivered a good performance, but she couldn't stop herself from shooting an I'm-the-bigger-person smirk at Ashley.

"Wherever you want to have it," Jacob told the women. "We're happy to pitch in."

So much for her hopes that he'd get offended, territorial, about the Blands making plans for his daughter without his consent. He dumped more potato salad onto his plate and returned to the men. Hanna didn't think he was oblivious to the tension, rather that he was choosing to ignore it—escape it.

"Don't worry, it'll all work out," Blair said lightheartedly, smiling at Joelle.

"Sorry," Jo whispered to Hanna, "guess I'm not used to this kind of big family stuff."

Hanna gave her a squeeze and a kiss on the cheek. "We'll get the hang of it."

Jo sighed and returned to her spot on the grass with Boyd and the children.

Hanna wasn't sure what to do with herself. She felt embarrassed, as if a group of mean girls had told her her wet bathing suit was transparent. She didn't want to eat anything else, and she didn't want to sit back down beside Ashley, who was still giving her the stink eye.

Spotting a couple of empty serving dishes on the table, Hanna scooped them up. "Shall I take these inside?"

Ashley shrugged. "Suit yourself."

"Does anyone need me to get anything?"

"Thank you, I'm good." At least Cousin Mel seemed like a decent person.

Blair gave her what was probably meant as a sympathetic smile. But all Hanna saw in it was that Blair thought she was pathetic, a sorry misfit, outmatched. Before she said or did anything else that she'd regret, Hanna fled toward the back door.

53

As a stranger to the house, Hanna barely had the right to let herself into Ashley's kitchen, but she was glad to be away from everyone. She rinsed off the plate and bowl. Through the window over the sink, she saw them all out there—the circle of children, the circle of men, and the circle of women. The queen bullies, Ashley and Diane, were watching her.

Hanna stepped back so they couldn't see her.

Fuck. Fuck fuck fuck. She'd literally let them chase her away. And here she was in *their* house, doing *their* dishes.

Something jostled the screen door. When she went over to investigate, she saw Shithead twisting the handle, trying to get in. The door fit too tightly and wouldn't budge.

Once again Hanna stepped away so she wouldn't be seen. Was the little brat following her? Spying on her? She hated feeling so stupid, so out of her element, but she was certain about one thing: she sure as hell didn't want to babysit the smelly toddler, and if she was alone with him, he would become *her* responsibility.

This is Joelle's fault.

The thought struck her like a sword blow.

It *was* Joelle's fault. Everything of late was, in truth, her stepdaughter's fault. It was her fault that Hanna was here, being humiliated. It was her fault that Boyd was now living in their basement. It was her fault that Hanna was at her wit's end. It was *for* Joelle that Hanna was trying to remove Ashley from the picture—and Jo should rightly bear some of the responsibility if Hanna got caught.

She tiptoed backward, deeper into the house, as Shithead kept banging on the door.

"In! In!" he cried.

If that kid got in, Hanna did *not* want to be held accountable for what she might (or might not) do.

"Stone!" Blair called. *So that was his name.* "Stone, come here buddy!"

It wasn't unlike the way a person would summon a dog. As Shithead let out a protesting wail, Hanna left the kitchen, looking for a bathroom in which she could hide. The first door she opened was a closet; the second was a tiny powder room.

Tucked inside, she pressed her ear to the closed door. She heard the squeal of the back door opening, and Blair's voice cooing at the toddler.

"Hanna?"

She flipped on the light switch, as if that made it official that she was using the bathroom (not hiding in it).

"Hanna?" Blair's voice was closer now.

"In the bathroom."

"Okay."

Hanna rolled her eyes. She didn't need them checking up on her. What did Blair think she would do, steal something from the house? Blair's footsteps retreated. After a brief clattering in the kitchen, the screen door yawned open and slammed shut. Hanna sighed, and stood in front of the sink.

She felt out of sorts. Not sick exactly, but disjointed, like a robot that had been put together wrong. Toes for ears. Hands for feet. Intestines for arms. She leaned toward the mirror and opened her mouth, needing to reassure herself that the demon inside her wasn't on the verge of crawling its way out.

But she saw it.

Fingers in her throat. Reaching for her rope of tongue. Ready to start climbing.

Hanna shut her mouth hard and fast; her teeth clacked together. Was it real? Was it happening—was she finally about to come face to face with the Other self?

She swallowed. And swallowed again. Would that keep it inside? She didn't feel a lump. Her throat wasn't full, like it was when she didn't chew well and a chunk of food escaped down her gullet. She wasn't sure how she felt about losing a part of herself if the Other emerged and walked away. While her presence had sometimes felt like a burden, it had also been a source of strength. Who would Hanna be without her?

Should she help her come to the surface; would that be the generous thing to do? Set the Other self free?

Resolved to do her duty, Hanna looked in the mirror and parted her lips, ready to grab hold of a finger. She opened wider.

Wider.

There was nothing there but her tonsils, her uvula, her impeccably cared-for teeth.

With a sharp intake of breath, Hanna turned away. She pressed herself against the wall beside the towel rack and slid to the floor. Hugged her knees. Had the Other self changed its mind, or was Hanna losing hers? Everything had become so unpredictable; she didn't understand the what or why of anything that was happening.

The salads churned in her gut. Mayonnaise and cucumbers, vinegar and cantaloupe, kidney beans and pineapple and red-skinned potatoes. She pressed her hand over her mouth, hoping to strangle the urge to vomit.

———

"Hanna?" Jacob knocked at the door.

How long had she been sitting there?

He knocked again. "Are you okay?"

Her legs wobbled as they hoisted her upright. She opened the door. "I'm not feeling well."

"You don't look good." His brow crinkled with concern. "Ready to head home?"

She nodded, pressing her hands against her stomach, trying to stop it from bubbling. When they reached the kitchen, Ashley and Diane were putting the leftovers away.

"We're gonna head out," said Jacob. "Hanna isn't feeling well."

"Thanks so much for having us," she murmured, still determined to seem polite—to seem superior on some sort of measurable scale.

"You look a little green," Diane said, lowering herself into a kitchen chair. Porky wagged his tail against her ankles—until he spotted Hanna; then he started barking. "Hope Ashley wasn't contagious—Ash, are you contagious?"

"Don't think so, no one else has gotten it. But there might be something going around. Thanks again for coming." Ashley gave them a dark little smile.

Jacob exchanged hearty goodbyes with the Guys as he and Hanna crossed the backyard, heading around toward the street. Jo, opting to stay a bit longer, waved and said she'd see them later. As they walked to the car, Jacob babbled about the nicey-niceness of everything, but all Hanna could think about was poison.

Had Ashley somehow poisoned her? It didn't make sense—either how she could've traced her "flu" to Hanna, or how she could've made only Hanna ill from communal dishes. But she'd seen the way Ashley hid her nastiness behind an amused facade. Was that the real reason Hanna and Jacob had been invited? So Ashley could take a stab at revenge?

The bitch was a formidable opponent, but Hanna was all the more determined now not to lose another round.

54

Dear Goose,

Yesterday was one of the worst days of my life. On Sunday we made the terrible blunder of going to Ashley's house for a Father's Day cookout. (Next time you want to see a picture of a demon, I'm just going to draw a lifelike portrait of Boyd's mom. She doesn't even need fangs or claws or mismatched putrefying body parts.) I left there feeling sick as a dog and was *highly* suspicious that she'd found a way to slip a little oleander (or some such garden toxin) into my food. It was probably a big mistake that I was sitting beside her as we ate.

I was feeling somewhat, but not totally, better come Monday morning and I didn't want to miss work . . . but in hindsight I should've stayed home. I'm good at my job, as you know—I could do a blood draw with my eyes closed if need be—but I made a serious miscalculation. Are there poisons that delude you into thinking your brain is working just fine even if it's not? That's my only explanation as to why I picked Elise, third patient of the day, as my target to vent a little stress. Lord knows Monday mornings are busy—I could've picked someone else!

I had Elise pegged as a weak, entitled, sniveling tosspot. Her manicure was extra fancy and she spoke in a squeaky voice about all the bargains she finds at Marshalls (I got to hear all about it after complimenting her purse; it wasn't even that nice, I was just being friendly). I did my usual routine as I tied the tourniquet around her arm, speaking to her with gentle and positive words. And then I shot the needle through her vein and she yelped. I said, "oops" and softly apologized, making it look like I was concentrating as I "tried again."

I really shouldn't have "tried again," but as I said, I'd underestimated Elise. I took another jab—missed, clicked my tongue in faux vexation . . . And that was when Elise erupted. She yanked her arm away and started screaming that I wasn't supposed to "dig around" with the needle.

"Any trained phlebotomist knows that! You pull the needle out and redo it, not wiggle it around like you're trying to find a buttonhole!"

I was totally caught off guard—no one has ever attacked my competency. I tried to apologize and start again but she wouldn't let it go.

"How old are you? How long have you been doing this?"

"It was just a mistake, I'm sorry, I thought I could find the vein—"

"Have *you* ever had your blood drawn, little miss? Bet you wouldn't like it if someone dug around in *your* arm with a needle. It hurts like hell!"

By this point I was downright flustered. And then Raven poked her head in through the privacy curtain.

"Everything okay?"

I discreetly rolled my eyes at her, so she'd think my patient was one of the dramatic types that we often see. "Missed it on the first try," I said mildly, trying to seem cool and collected.

"Let me know if you need any help." Raven disappeared back into her own cubicle.

I wanted to spit at her. Since when have I ever needed help? And I didn't appreciate her planting the thought in Elise's head that maybe someone else could do it better—which is exactly what happened.

Elise got to her feet and pushed aside the curtain, barging into Raven's stall. "Actually, would you mind? I've had my blood drawn enough times to know when someone just doesn't care about what they're doing. I'm sorry if you hate your job," she sneered at me. "But I'm a real person who feels real pain and if you hate your job you should find something else to do."

"I love my job!" I know it was a lame comeback, but it was true and I couldn't think what else to say in the moment. I've never lost control of a situation like this. And Raven may be two years older than me, but I have more experience than she does and it was humiliating to see her standing there, ready to fix my not-even-a-real-problem problem.

"I'm sorry," I said again. "Let me try your other arm, I'll find a better vein."

"My veins are fine, little miss." The condescending bitch seriously kept calling me *little miss*. And then she turned her pinched face to Raven and said very politely: "Please, I'd like you to do it."

"Of course," Raven replied—it wasn't like she could really refuse. And then Elise walked out of my cubicle and left me sitting there like a complete asshole.

Needless to say, none of my frustrations were vented from this attempt to alleviate my frustrations. And I was left feeling shaky and annoyed. But guess what, little brother? This wasn't even the worst thing that happened yesterday.

I legit strove to be my most professional self after that, even though I felt like I was going to explode. After lunch I had a frail, half-senile man in my chair. Norman is something of a regular and I've drawn his blood many times. But he acted like he didn't remember me, and unfortunately I really struggled to find a good vein. His veins were rolling, and he was somewhat dehydrated. I really tried my best *not* to hurt him, but after my third attempt—dude, I *never* need three attempts!—Norman became the second person who blew up at me.

"You're doing it on purpose! You're trying to hurt me!"

I couldn't believe those words came out of his mouth! It was all the more upsetting because I was going out of my way to *not* hurt him. I feel sorry for the old people, they have enough problems, so I always try to be gentle with them—and usually I succeed. But Norman flipped out and started getting hysterical.

"This bitch is torturing me! Help!"

This time it was Andrea who burst into my cubicle. She's the most senior phlebotomist on staff—both in terms of experience and managerial duties. I've always looked up to her because she's as good a Vein Whisperer as I am, and it's meant a lot that she respects me. I didn't mind when she stepped in to draw Norman's blood—have I mentioned how I really wasn't trying to hurt him? But later she called me into the empty break room for a private chat.

This, dear brother, became the low point of my already no good, very bad day.

Andrea sat me down to discuss the "problems" I was having at work.

"What problems?" I innocently blurted.

I like Andrea; she's a straight shooter. But I wasn't expecting her to say, "It's come to my attention that you've been struggling with a lot of patients."

What?

I must have looked confused (or appalled), because Andrea proceeded to elaborate.

"I know you—you've always been on top of things, a fellow perfectionist. I could count on you for even the trickiest draws, but you've been off your game. For a while now."

It was the "for a while now" that made my skin prickle with worry.

I stared at her, unsure what to say. Had I been venting in ways that were less subtle than I'd thought? Did Andrea know more than she was letting on? I was genuinely afraid that someone (other than Elise and Norman) had complained about me. Finally I composed myself and managed to say: "My job is very important to me."

"I know it is. So I can only guess . . . Is something else going on? Personal problems?"

Again I was in shock. I had been so certain until that moment that I had successfully compartmentalized my life. I mean, I'd been quick to dash out on the days when I was spying on Ashley, and maybe I had more than usual on my mind. But I've always used my needle skills to relieve a little stress, and I thought I'd seemed Normal at work. I was unaware that anyone might suspect that my domestic life was bleeding into my work life.

I hate being put on the spot. And I hate being criticized or feeling humiliated. But I had the good sense in that moment not to get defensive—or go on the attack. (Which I could've done, seeing how the universe has conspired to make everyone act annoyingly condescending.) I've really never been "in trouble" at work; Andrea was right, the perfectionist in me wouldn't allow it. But in my *one* great victory of the day, I understood what Andrea wanted me to tell her.

I allowed my body to deflate, so I looked defeated, and I put on a sad-miserable-woe-is-me face.

"I haven't wanted to talk about it at work," I said mournfully. "But my stepdaughter is pregnant."

Andrea frowned, looking appropriately surprised and empathetic. "How old is she now, fifteen?"

"Sixteen. Just finished her sophomore year."

"Daughters are hard. Even when we give them all the love and support and info—"

"Exactly. Jo's a smart girl, but needless to say her dad and I had a different future in mind for her. There's been a lot going on—I'm sorry, I didn't realize how preoccupied I've been."

"I understand." There was a "but" coming—I heard it in Andrea's voice and the look she gave me made me want to crawl in a hole. "But you need to pay more attention. This isn't the kind of job where you can have off days."

I nodded, because I needed to acknowledge her and I knew lunging for her throat wasn't appropriate. To be reprimanded by Andrea, of all people, made me feel as if my spine was being ripped out through the top of my head. I felt useless and on fire. God knows what I would've done if the moment had gone on much longer, but fortunately Andrea was called away.

Goose, what am I going to do? My homelife feels like a fraying chunk of rope. All the strands of my carefully plotted existence, so strong when they're twisted together, are unraveling. My job is supposed to be the steady, predictable thing that keeps me centered. It's the thing I'm supposed to always be good at! I'm bungling everything and I don't know what to do. I don't like people seeing me this way, but I don't know how I'm going to fix all the things that need to be fixed.

Blunderingly yours,

Hanna

55

Dear Hanna,

In spite of your best intentions and your determination to fix everything yourself, maybe that's not realistic? I applaud the efforts you've taken thus far, and am truly sorry to hear about the difficulties you've been having. I also really wish that Jacob could be the true partner in crime (ha ha) that you need. But I'm here to remind you that you are not alone!

Hello? Lil bro here, waving frantically from the sidelines!

After a lot of consideration, I think I have a solution. You're not going to like it, but hear me out: let me help you.

Specifically, let me be your hit man.

This is a simple and brilliant solution (and when solutions are simple and brilliant, they usually work). It won't matter what method we choose if I'm the one wielding the weapon—gun, knife, garotte, whatever—because no one would ever suspect *me*. I'm not part of this equation so no one would think I have motive (or opportunity). And I've never met Ashley, I'm invisible to her. Which means I could roll up on her (metaphorically) without causing her alarm. She would never see me as a threat, so I could get as close as was necessary. And then slip away.

If anyone remembered seeing a "teenage boy" in the vicinity, the first person the authorities would think of would be the teenage boy in Ashley's life: BOYD. (How great would it be if we could frame Boyd? Two birds with one stone!) And if the very worst thing happened and I got caught? Well, I'm fifteen—and a reasonable case could be made for my insanity.

I know you're reading this and shaking your head, ready to declare that you don't want me involved, that you don't want me taking the risk. But *think* about it, okay? I know we established the rules of our unique relationship, but as we created this special correspondence for our own creative purposes, we could change the rules this once. I want to help you. This is important. And I don't have as much to lose as you do.

So yes, by all means send me that lifelike sketch of Ashley! I'm sure anything you draw will be accurate enough for me to identify my target—though you could just send some photos, like a Normal Person. If you choose not to be a Normal Person, perhaps you should draw her from different angles so I can be absolutely positive it's her, regardless of how I approach her. It would suck if I clocked her in profile walking out of her house—and it turned out to be her sister or something. (Does she have any sisters?)

I shouldn't admit this, but . . . I find this possibility very exciting. Mom and Dad would, of course, chalk it all up to you having a negative influence on me. They never liked how connected we were—but maybe they always understood, deep down, that we were more alike than they wanted to admit? Treated differently, perhaps, but more similar than we were dissimilar.

I AM HERE FOR YOU.

Goose

56

Dear Goose,

No. Absolutely not. I don't even want to consider getting you involved. You are my sanctuary, my one safe place and person in all the world. I do not want you—your reputation, your existence—damaged in any way.

But thank you . . . thank you! You make me feel less alone in the world—and that is enough.

You did have a brilliant idea though: let's brainstorm ways of framing Boyd! As it happens, I've already tarnished his reputation somewhat. The police didn't take "his" threat to shoot up the school seriously, but I'm sure they'd reconsider his character if he was suspected of killing his mother.

On a related note, here's something I've been wondering: Maybe Ashley carries a handgun in her purse. You know, for "protection." (Can you hear my sarcasm? I'd love to see some statistics on how many people successfully "protected" themselves with a firearm versus how many people killed themselves or shot someone accidentally—or on purpose.) But I digress . . .

I could believe Ashley would conceal carry. And maybe I could find an opportunity to check her purse—and steal her little deadly friend. Then we could stage some sort of shooting—perhaps "Boyd" kills his mom and tries to make it look like suicide! (I have to admit: a scenario that involves Ashley dying via one of her family's guns is especially appealing.)

I feel like, the more ideas we explore, the closer we're getting to a viable plan. It's important that we/I work out the logistics in a methodical way—I'm not trying to just blow up my life. I want feasible, proactive solutions, and I appreciate your input—I welcome it!—but that is where your involvement ends.

The anatomical sketch I've included of the human heart is more technical than it is creative, but what it represents is meaningful—because truly, my heart beats for you.

Yours,

Hanna

57

Hanna should've been at work, not lounging around doing nothing, but she'd called in sick. She wasn't sick, not physically, but her no good, very bad day had turned into a no good, very bad week. It pissed her off that Andrea had sounded skeptical on the phone. Hanna never called in sick, and she'd expected her colleague to be supportive and not question her reasons. She hadn't come right out and said, "Are you sure you aren't just hiding at home?" but Hanna heard the suspicion in her voice. When had Hanna become so transparent? If anyone else had called in sick on a Friday morning, Andrea would've assumed they were trying to finagle a long weekend.

"I hope you're better by Monday," Andrea had said.

It wasn't Hanna's imagination (probably) that she'd heard a warning in those words. They seemingly both knew that Hanna wasn't ill; come Monday, Andrea was expecting her to be the reliable, top-of-her-game phlebotomist Hanna had always been.

What if I've lost my touch?

More likely it wasn't her *touch* that was in jeopardy but her mind. She'd tried to keep things light in her letters to Goose. Maybe *light* wasn't exactly the right word, but she'd tried to sound confident, and hide how fractured her thinking had become. She didn't understand what was happening to her, why she felt so disconnected or why everything had become such a struggle. Not so long ago she'd been moving through her life one assured step at a time. Now reality itself was blinking in and out, like a strip of film stuttering through the projector's gate. Things she saw clearly one minute could easily scorch and melt a moment later. Everything felt out of reach. Strategies that had seemed viable while she was engaged in Goose's letters lost their substance before she could take action. She'd never been so indecisive or unsure of herself—unsure of the solidity of the ground beneath her feet.

She saw in her peripheral vision as Jacob came out the back door and headed across the grass. He was in his trying-to-make-a-good-impression clothes: pressed khaki pants and crisp shirt and tie. He must've been showing one of his higher-end listings. Once upon a time Hanna had known about his current clients and inventory of properties; somewhere along the line she'd lost track.

The shirt she was wearing was thin but long sleeved. She gathered the sleeves over her fists as he approached. Her eyes darted around, abruptly aware of where she was and how odd it must look.

"What are you doing here?" he asked.

"It's shady here. Nice and cool." She'd dragged a camp chair to the other side of the lawn, to sit among the trees.

"Why aren't you at work? Are you sick?"

"If I sit really still, the birds and squirrels don't notice me and come to the bird feeders," she said, ignoring his questions. She was only a couple of feet away from the bird feeders, though now that Jacob had invaded her strip of forest, the wildlife was nowhere to be seen.

He studied her, his features twisted in a question mark. "Are you okay?"

She wasn't sure how to answer that. No longer was she capable enough to pass off an easy lie. Since she hadn't gone to work, she hadn't bothered to shower that morning. For that matter, she might have forgotten to shower the previous day, and maybe the day before that. She felt comfortable in her leggings and top, but to the casual observer, she probably looked like a fitness junkie on the skids.

"I'm not feeling great," she mumbled, the simplest half truth she could come up with.

"Hanna . . . what's going on with you?" He sounded bewildered. "We've tried to talk about this before, but seriously—I don't understand what's happening. Or why. For weeks you haven't been out running, or posting on TikTok, or doing any of your usual things. I feel like I barely see you, even when we're both home. Where are you?"

Great. Now it was as obvious at home as at work that she wasn't fully present, that she was coming unglued. Had her online followers noticed her absence? Had she dropped other balls that a live audience would see rolling away?

She shrugged, her only answer to his question.

"We haven't had a conversation, a real one, in . . ." He thought about it, but couldn't land on a date. "And we haven't . . ."

This time when his words faltered, she knew exactly what he was declining to say: sex. She'd stopped initiating sex with him—and maybe she seemed too unapproachable. Or too withdrawn. Too dirty, in a bad way. *I'm in my head. Stuck in my head.*

"What are you doing?" Where before he'd been concerned, if perplexed, now his anger rose to the surface. "And why can't you answer that, or even try? You're not going to work now—is this going to be a regular thing?"

"No. I told you," she said lamely. "I'm a little under the weather." She pondered the origins of feeling "under the weather." Couldn't it be a good thing to be under the weather, like an airplane flying beneath a thunderstorm? Her mind was wandering, and she felt like a teenager answering to an unpleasant parent. She resented that her *husband* was making her feel that way, even as she tried to give him something to grab hold of. *So he leaves me alone.* "I've been writing to Goose more, we have some stuff to work out."

"Okay. Great." He made it sound neither okay nor great. "But it can't take that long to write your brother a letter or talk to him or whatever it is the two of you do—that can't explain what you've been preoccupied with. Every day."

Couldn't it?

"What about the stuff here? In your home?" He threw his arm behind him, gesturing toward the house. It looked lovely from this angle. Like something from a magazine. "Don't you care about that?"

She glowered at him. "That's all I care about." Everything she was doing was for them, their family. To keep their lives as close to the normal they'd always enjoyed.

"Are you sure that's what you care about? Because it doesn't seem that way. It seems like you're engrossed in your own . . ." He shrugged, shook his head. "I don't know, I don't know where your head is."

She slumped down in her chair, her eyes unfocused. "I'm trying . . . to do something. It isn't easy."

"*Some*thing? What are you talking about?"

For a second she considered confiding in him, telling him the truth. But Jacob wouldn't get it. He'd deny, out of misplaced kindness, that Ashley could or would torpedo their family dynamic. He only wanted to see the good things in her, just as he did with Boyd—and everyone. He'd made his borders permeable, but wasn't prepared to deal with the darkness that everyone held. *I wear my darkness like a sweater; it keeps me warm.* His mercy left him unable to defend even his daughter's life.

"You aren't behaving normally, you know that don't you?" It was an accusation, not a question.

Yes, she knew that, because of late everyone wanted to point it out. She looked to the bird feeder, wishing to see a black-capped chickadee, or the pair of cardinals—the male in his garish reds, his mate the more pragmatic one, toned down in brown. The sunflower seeds beckoned, but the creatures wouldn't come, not with the man of the house standing so near, dressed to impress—repelling all life-forms.

"Are you depressed?" With a shift of the wind, now he sounded tender. Her husband came with a lot of emotions—so many that she sometimes struggled to sort them all out. But she liked the tender side of him.

"I don't know. Maybe." Were her own emotions so erratic because she was depressed? It *did* depress her to think about Jo ballooning into a mom. It was so depressing that she endeavored to keep it away from her conscious mind. If only it could be undone. The embryo. Jo's exodus from childhood. Her traitorous ascension to motherhood—where Hanna could never follow.

Was depression the root of her problem?

She looked to Jacob, seeing a new possibility. "Maybe I am."

He stood there breathing as if he'd just won a race. "If you don't feel comfortable talking to me . . . maybe there's someone else, more neutral, who might be more knowledgeable."

"You mean a therapist?"

"Sure. Why not?"

He didn't know how many hours of her life had been spent in the presence of mental health professionals. The local therapist her family had gone to, and the battalion of psychiatrists and counselors at the "boarding school" she'd attended for three years. It hadn't just been "therapy"; they'd tried to fundamentally alter her way of being. For going on fifteen years, she'd played the game well enough to blend in, keeping at arm's length the demons with the most unhelpful suggestions. But they were back, and she'd lost the willpower to stop listening to their stories. Were they muses or guardians or tricksters? Or were they her true self, unbridled?

She didn't want to lose the life she'd made for herself.

"Yes, that's a good idea," she whispered.

Jacob's relief flashed around him like fireworks. "We could probably get a referral from our doctor."

Hanna shook her head. "I know someone."

Before she was sent away to school, she'd loved Dr. Yamamoto—so wise and perceptive. Later, she'd blamed Dr. Yamamoto for betraying her and banishing her to Marshes. But over time she came to appreciate her first therapist who, if nothing else, understood her better than anyone ever had. When Hanna was ten she came home and started seeing her again—"Beatrix, call me Beatrix." And Beatrix had helped her adjust to living with her parents, and having a baby brother.

"I'll find out if she's still here, and taking new patients," she told her husband.

He nodded. Smiled. "Want me to bring some lunch out? We can have a quick picnic before I get back to work."

She nodded. Smiled. Because having a picnic with her husband was an appropriate thing to do. With his back to her as he headed toward the house, Hanna imagined how angry Skog would be that she wanted to see Dr. Yamamoto again (in his mind, all therapists would forever be The Enemy). Would Goose understand? Or would he feel let down if she didn't follow through with their plans after so many letters back and forth?

I'll track down Dr. Yamamoto. She decided that was a top priority. Of all the things she owed her brother, her reason for needing a therapist wasn't one of them.

58

She put on a T-shirt and clean leggings. Her hair already in a ponytail, she pushed the flyaways back from her face with an elastic headband. For her husband's sake, Hanna had taken a shower the previous night. It felt so good that she'd taken another one that morning, and planned to shower again when she got back from her run. *The water is like amniotic fluid.*

Naked and wet, she'd felt herself readying for a rebirth. She wasn't sure when her new self would be born, but she'd take as many showers as necessary to help facilitate the process. Her new self would have her shit together. Her new self would know better ways of navigating the tricky stuff that Hanna was struggling to manage. Or so she hoped.

Jacob had just left for work, but not before Hanna made sure he saw her getting ready to go for a run. *So he knows I'm fine.* She was no more fine than she had been the previous day, but she was acutely aware that she needed to do a better job of faking it.

She tied the laces on her shoes as she leaned against the kitchen counter, then slipped her phone into her hip pocket and took a final gulp of water. Joelle still liked to sleep in on Saturday mornings—though now that she lived in the basement, sometimes Hanna almost forgot she was there. It helped that Boyd was doing a good job of being invisible; he worked a lot, and generally tried to make himself scarce. Hanna had yet to make sense of Jo choosing Ashley to host her baby shower. She tried not to hold it against her stepdaughter and instead believed it was Ashley's fault; the woman was a parasite, a worm with teeth.

Hanna went out the back door, curious to see if she could spy on Jo and Boyd through the basement windows. She wasn't sure why she wanted to catch them in the act of their domesticity (she certainly didn't want to catch them doing anything sexual), but a part of her really wanted to see them making the bed together, or arguing with expansive gestures, or canoodling with each other as they talked about their plans for the day. Joelle had always been more capable of cohabitating, of living like an ordinary person and following through with life's milestones, than Hanna had ever been.

She had to bend down to see into the basement. Boyd, fully dressed, was asleep on the couch; Jo was nowhere in sight. If they were sleeping apart, did that mean there was trouble in adolescent paradise? When she saw Jo later, she'd ask her. More than ever, Hanna had to make sure she kept doing all the things a stepmother—a functioning adult—would do. And if "the kids" were struggling to live together . . . Her mind immediately went to devious places. *Maybe it's not too late to get rid of Boyd.*

If he and Jo weren't getting along, maybe he'd leave willingly—and Ashley's side of the baby's family would officially be estranged. Jacob, Hanna, and Joelle could become coordinated allies again. She smirked, moving along toward the sidewalk to start her run, hopeful that Ashley would return soon to haul Boyd's stuff out of her house. Had Jacob been right all this time? He'd never been worried about "the kids" getting married because he was sure they'd break up long before Jo turned eighteen. Was there a chance still that reality would hit and she'd chicken out about having the baby?

As Hanna started doing the math, trying to figure out exactly how far along Jo was in her pregnancy (*too far*), she guillotined her thoughts. She was getting carried away, and such fantasies weren't helpful. But the Other self wasn't done: if Jo ended up alone, maybe she'd be more inclined to consider putting the baby up for adoption. *Shut up.*

Hanna had made a mental map of the route she would run long before she left the house. Usually she headed for one of the parks, but today she stuck to the residential streets. The run itself had been a decoy; her real mission was to go by Dr. Yamamoto's house on Wightman Street. When she was a kid, there'd been a copper sign next to the side door that Beatrix used for her private therapy business. If it was still there, that would mean Dr. Yamamoto was still in business.

As she ran, Hanna thought back to her first visit to the therapist's house. She'd liked the room full of toys, unaware then that the big mirror had allowed Dr. Yamamoto to study her while Hanna was in the room by herself. In her own way Beatrix was a master of deception and manipulation, but Hanna appreciated her skill. The good doctor was a worthy opponent, which meant Hanna respected her enough to accept her guidance. And if Hanna was being honest with herself, Beatrix had been a helpful bridge between Hanna's institutional life at Marshes and her dysfunctional life with her family. She might have ended up back at Marshes—or worse—if Beatrix hadn't helped her cope with the strangeness of Mommy-and-Daddy 2.0.

She remembered how they smiled too much, their skin like a rubbery mask as worry slithered beneath it. She remembered they were always holding out their hands, protective gestures to keep her from getting too close to baby Gustav. It was Beatrix who explained to them, multiple times, that she had no intention of pinching him (or stabbing him) or shoving small toys up his nose. Hanna also remembered her parents with their hands hidden behind their backs, or standing cross-armed in front of her, not quite able to hug or comfort her.

Her pace slowed as the street got steeper, and soon she was approaching the corner with the large, familiar house. The house's painted trim looked different from the color in Hanna's memory. The plants in the yard, though tended, seemed wilder somehow. There was an electric car in the driveway and a pair of wicker chairs on the porch.

Hanna had no idea if Beatrix was married or had a family; such things had been of no interest to her when she was a child.

It was the right place, but Hanna wouldn't know if it was still Dr. Yamamoto's unless she got closer: she had no choice but to trespass onto the property. If she'd been smarter she would've dressed like a Normal Person on the way to see their therapist, in case a neighbor spotted her snooping around. As it was, she looked like someone out for a jog who'd stumbled upon an uncanny mirage and had to stop and investigate; she felt like a character in a bad movie. *You could've just looked her up online.* But Hanna had been afraid of finding outdated information.

This will be proof.

And there it was. As she rounded the corner, she saw the side entryway and the patinaed plaque with Dr. Yamamoto's name. She was sure now; Beatrix was still here.

Hanna took a step backward, unsure what she should do next. Return to the sidewalk and head home? Continue on her run? In her planning she'd only gotten as far as verifying the existence of the plaque beside the door. As she hesitated, the door started to open. *Oh shit.* Hanna fled across the grass and hid behind a tree.

A hippie in a colorful batik dress emerged, followed by a wildhaired young boy. Hanna pressed herself into the tree's scabby bark, wishing she were home in the shower, warm water pouring over her, washing away her shame. She was eager to be reborn, to shed this cumbersome version of herself. Prior to Jo announcing her pregnancy, Hanna had been a lithe panther, a sleek and beautiful predator. Now she was a creature weighed down by barnacles, caught in a riptide, doomed to drown. *Hiding behind a fucking tree.*

She watched as the woman and her son reached the sidewalk and crossed the street, heading for their car. Now what? Feeling foolish, Hanna inched around the tree—she had to get out of there.

"Hello?"

Shit. Hanna didn't want to turn toward the voice. Didn't want Beatrix to recognize her. She hadn't realized there'd been someone standing on the other side of the door. Had Dr. Yamamoto seen her dash for the tree? *I look like a lunatic.*

She heard soft footfalls on the grass as Beatrix approached.

"Can I help you?" Dr. Yamamoto asked.

No. Yes. I'm unfixable. Hanna was no longer an apex predator; her instinct now was to pretend she was moss (*slime*) stuck to the tree. *If I don't move she won't be able to see me. Ha!*

"Can I help you?" Dr. Yamamoto asked again when she was facing Hanna, now just a few feet away.

Hanna stared at the ground, aware that she was being studied. "No, I'm . . . Sorry, just catching my breath." She sprinted away from her hiding place, her back to Beatrix, quickly putting distance between them.

"Hanna?"

For a moment she thought she'd gotten away, but hearing her name made her stop. It had been twelve years since Beatrix had seen her on a regular basis, and eight years since they'd seen each other at all. For some reason Hanna imagined her adult self was different enough from the amorphous teenager Dr. Yamamoto had last seen that she might escape unrecognized.

She could barrel on, keep running. Or turn to acknowledge her old therapist. It was too late to "act normal."

As she inched around she saw a warm smile on Dr. Yamamoto's face, though her crossed arms suggested that she was also a little on guard. Hanna expected to see accusations hovering above her, mocking words confirming her belief that Hanna had always been a hopeless case. But all she saw in Dr. Yamamoto's appearance was a hint of surprise, and a searching gaze.

"I have another client coming in a bit. But I have twenty minutes or so. Would you like to come in?"

Hanna didn't acknowledge Beatrix's questions, or even say hello. But she followed Dr. Yamamoto around to the side door.

59

It felt weird sitting on the sofa across from her old therapist. As a child she was rarely in Dr. Yamamoto's office. Even as a teen Hanna had preferred the more spacious toy-filled room. She couldn't remember the office well enough to tell how much it had changed. Looking around she saw a jungle of plants. A bookcase with art books and little ceramic pots. Watercolors on the walls. That's right . . . Beatrix painted landscapes as a hobby. The oak coffee table in front of her was ready with its box of tissues, in case she burst into tears.

"How have you been?" Beatrix asked with a smile, as if they were just two old friends meeting up for lunch.

"Good," Hanna lied, because that was how everyone answered such a question. As an afterthought she added, "And you?"

"Really good. My daughter just graduated from medical school."

"That's great." So Beatrix had at least one child, and she was well educated. Had the comment been an opening for Hanna to provide info about her own education? The last time they'd seen each other, Hanna had been in high school. "I didn't go to university."

"It's not for everyone. Clementine wanted to be a pediatrician, so it was kind of necessary. With your creativity, I imagine you pursued something in the arts?"

"I draw. Sometimes."

The conversation was stilted, and it was entirely Hanna's fault. Beatrix, warm and open, wasn't judging her, but Hanna felt inadequate.

Of all the people Hanna had ever known, Beatrix was the one person who might have believed in Hanna's ability to accomplish something meaningful. Now Hanna was afraid her therapist would see that the faith she'd had in her had been misplaced. Just being here, caught on her lawn like a Peeping Tom, was probably evidence that Hanna hadn't danced happily ever after into adulthood.

"How are your parents?"

Hanna shrugged. "I don't see them."

"At all?"

"No, not really. Not for a couple of years."

"Sometimes a little space is healthy."

Hanna nodded. "I always thought I'd move away, but then . . ."

Beatrix looked at her, waiting for her to finish the sentence. Hanna had never been embarrassed about marrying young—at least not when talking with people she didn't really like or respect. She was paranoid that Dr. Yamamoto was reading deeper histories into every sparse bit of info she revealed.

Hanna abruptly stood. "I should go. You're busy. I didn't mean to bother you."

But instead of escorting her out, Dr. Yamamoto crossed one leg over the other, getting more comfortable. "You came here for a reason, Hanna. It's okay. My next client will buzz me when she gets here, we have some time."

"Okay." She sat back down. Now that she was in Dr. Yamamoto's presence, Hanna remembered how good the therapist was at creating a safe space, like a circle of energy. Queenlike in her chair, she emitted a benevolent surety that made her patients want to trust her. *I want to trust her.*

"I got married a few years ago," Hanna said.

Beatrix's eyebrows flagged her surprise, but only for an instant. "Were you in love?"

Hanna smirked at how well the good doctor knew her. "Not exactly. But close enough."

"It's been a good relationship then?"

"It has. We've had a nice life together." And she meant that sincerely. "Nothing exciting. But stable. Compatible."

Hanna nodded as she thought about it. Jacob hadn't been an accident. She hadn't let her fate be decided by the quirk of lust or a fickle bout of romance. Her marriage had been an intentional product of her good judgment. She'd known what she was looking for, and if he hadn't appeared in her chair at work, she would've gone in search of someone like him. And for years she'd been *right*: her judgment had proved to be sound; her decisions were unassailable.

"Is something happening now in your marriage?" Beatrix gently prodded.

"We've always been good partners. We both like our jobs, and we like to go running. Jacob has his photography and I have my drawing. We used to like watching movies together."

"*Used* to?"

"His interests changed a little when his daughter started changing."

"How old is his daughter?"

"Sixteen."

If Beatrix was shocked that Hanna was so close in age to her stepdaughter, she didn't show it. "Does his daughter live with you full time?"

"Yes, Jacob's a widower. Joelle's mom died."

"You get along well with her?"

"Yes, always have, right from the start." Hanna inhaled, like she might say more. The breath dissipated, wordless.

Dr. Yamamoto picked up on her hesitation. "But . . . ? But she's a teenager, and she's changing now?"

Hanna nodded.

"Being a mother is hard," Beatrix said softly.

It hadn't been hard for Hanna, until recently. She turned her gaze to one of the watercolors hanging across from her, a mountainscape with a fjord of azure water. *I could be reborn there.* The world Beatrix had created looked so peaceful, so unlike the craggy turmoil of Hanna's inner life. They sat quietly as Hanna studied the picture.

"Joelle is pregnant."

Beatrix nodded in slow motion, a gesture that revealed some understanding of Hanna's dilemma. "You're afraid to be around a baby."

Hanna abruptly returned her attention to the therapist. "No! That's not it at all. Why would you say that?"

Dr. Yamamoto answered with an I'm-too-smart-for-your-bullshit look.

"That's not the only reason," Hanna said, her outrage deflating.

"I know how your mom made you feel. Untrustworthy. Unreliable. Bad?"

"I was bad though, wasn't I?"

"I think you know what I think," Beatrix said in her calm way. "Too many emotions and not enough ways to explain them. Too many desires and not enough ways to make yourself understood."

"But then . . ." Okay, so maybe as a young child, Hanna hadn't known better. But shouldn't she have wised up by the time she was a teen?

"You still think about what happened?" the therapist asked.

What a stupid question. How could I ever forget?

"I try not to." That was true. Hanna had creative ways of not thinking about the worst time in her life.

"Is that why you don't have a relationship with your parents? I know things never felt quite right."

"Maybe. It's just easier, for everyone. I was a constant reminder of all the bad things—"

"You weren't bad, Hanna," Beatrix insisted.

"Not so sure about that." Hanna sniffled. When had she started to cry? She wanted to believe Beatrix—had always wanted to—but she still wasn't sure she could.

Dr. Yamamoto surreptitiously checked her watch. "Are you ready to tell me why you needed to see me today?"

Hanna felt her spine start to detonate, like a building collapsing on itself. She slumped down; she shouldn't have come. Her old therapist knew her too well and wouldn't let Hanna deliver anything but the truth. *I can't tell her.* If she knew Hanna had poisoned someone, that once again she was fantasizing about solving her problems with murder, the good doctor would make a few phone calls and Hanna would be locked up again. *This time they'd probably throw away the key.* Her husband would find out everything. Her life would implode.

"I really shouldn't have come." Hanna jumped to her feet. "I just wanted to see if you were still here, so I could make an appointment. But you know I can't do anything the normal way."

Beatrix stood, smiling. "Let's set up a time then?"

"I'll call you." She was already in the hallway.

"Why don't we set it up now?" Beatrix followed her.

The door to the children's room was open. Hanna stopped. There she was, seven years old, sitting at the little table drawing a picture. *Give me the child at seven and I'll show you the grown-up.* The real quote had the word *man* in it, but Hanna had the gist of it. She turned to face Dr. Yamamoto.

"Are you afraid I won't follow through?" Hanna asked.

"Are *you* afraid of that?"

"I don't think I can tell you. Now, or later."

"I work mostly evenings and weekends now, to accommodate people's work schedules. Monday at seven?"

"I can't promise I'll be back." It felt good, and right, to be honest.

"Okay. Well, I'll be here Monday at seven, if you want to talk. It was good to see you, Hanna."

"Good to see you," she automumbled.

She felt Beatrix's eyes on her back as she went down the hallway and out the door.

A part of Hanna wanted to return on Monday. After just a few minutes, she was back under the good doctor's spell, wanting to please her with an offering of the sharp puzzle pieces of her life. *Maybe she can put me together, without getting hurt.* But what Hanna wanted was also what she didn't want, and she wasn't sure she could risk Dr. Yamamoto getting the truth out of her. When she reached the sidewalk she started running, and sprinted all the way home.

60

Hanna burst through the back door. Startled, Joelle choked on the water she was drinking and started coughing.

"Sorry." Hanna stood with her hands on her knees, sweaty and panting. The kitchen smelled like burnt toast.

"Were you racing somebody?" Jo asked.

"Myself. I won."

They both grinned. When Hanna caught her breath, she got herself a glass of water. Jo watched her, arms crossed, one foot perched atop the other.

"I was hoping I could practice driving?"

"Sure." Hanna hadn't been prepared to be face to face with someone so soon after returning home. She still felt weird about her encounter with Dr. Yamamoto—like she'd done something wrong, and then did something right, and then spoiled it by being awkward. She'd become a wine stain on everyone's white tablecloth, unsure how to remove herself. Someone else would know if they should laugh or make a fuss or apologize or pretend nothing had happened. Hanna never knew what to do.

"Since Daddy's not here I have to use your car," Joelle explained. "And you kind of have to be in it, because I have to be with a licensed driver?"

"Right. So you're asking me to take you driving?" She tried not to sound short tempered, but she really didn't appreciate Joelle's vague approach to expressing herself, especially when Hanna was struggling to navigate even basic interactions.

"Yeah. I'd like to just drive around for a while, maybe practice getting on and off the parkway. And then maybe I can pick Boyd up from work?"

"That would be *we* picking him up from work?"

"Yeah. He hasn't gotten a car yet."

Hanna had the sense now that Joelle had been waiting for her to get home—and was expecting her to drop everything and make Jo's plans a top priority.

"Okay," Hanna conceded. She didn't really feel like doing anything, so this was as good a thing to occupy herself with as any. "I have to take a shower first."

"How long's that going to take?" Jo sounded more panicky than was necessary.

"And then I need a quick bite to eat."

Jo opened her mouth like she was about to protest, but Hanna cut her off. She used her adulting voice to say, "Thirty minutes. You can survive waiting for another thirty minutes."

She left before Joelle could say something that would *really* annoy her. How absurd to see her stepdaughter sporting a baby bump while acting like a spoiled brat. *A child carrying a child.*

———

Hanna stood with her face in the spray, arms at her sides, nearly comatose in the warm comfort of the shower. She prayed to the void that it would engulf her. *Let me disappear.* Joelle deserved a stepmother capable of being an actual mother (*grandmother*). And Jacob deserved a wife who didn't mismanage life's hiccups. *Please please please.* She fantasized about emerging from the shower as a more capable woman.

Ha! It dawned on her that maybe Jo and Jacob—and everyone—had the right idea in watching so many superhero movies. If they were going to be influenced by the people they watched for entertainment, better to emulate superheroes than the lost and downtrodden characters in Hanna's frugal indie films. All this time she'd been trying to learn through films how humanity worked—what people had in common, what made individuals tick. But suddenly she understood the appeal of the superhero: they didn't hesitate and wallow in uncertainty. She'd watched so many protagonists bungle through their lives, dealing with misfortune and making mistakes; no wonder she hadn't absorbed any valuable lessons on how to take action, how to fight back.

Perhaps the cascade of amniotic fluid was working and her transformation was truly underway. Maybe that night she could sit with her family and enjoy a grandiose movie through the eyes of a conqueror.

———

As promised, thirty minutes later she was heading into the garage with Jo. She wasn't used to getting in on the passenger side of her own car, and maybe that was why, with a different point of view, the jug of antifreeze caught her attention from its place on the shelf. It appeared to be glowing—and not in a toxic, radioactive way, but as if the gods were spotlighting it to convey a message. Was there more she could do with the household poison?

Jo wanted to start by driving through Squirrel Hill's residential streets, which were narrow but lacking in traffic. She drove just below the speed limit, her eyes flicking to the mirrors and the frequent side streets, always on the lookout for cars and bikes and pedestrians. She'd been practicing with Jacob, though he'd mentioned that Jo had taken a lesson with Boyd's father, who'd proved to be an adept instructor.

They drove in silence until Hanna was confident that their conversation wouldn't be a distraction.

"How are you and Boyd doing, living together?" Hanna was proud of herself for remembering to follow up on what she'd observed through the basement window.

"Good, it's definitely more convenient."

It wasn't the answer Hanna was expecting. She fished a little more. "When I was heading out before, I saw Boyd sleeping on the sofa?"

"Oh, yeah. He does that sometimes if I'm already asleep and he's afraid of waking me up."

"That's very considerate of him." Apparently Boyd had learned that Jo was a light sleeper, easily awakened.

"He's the best." She cast a glance at Hanna. "He really is, if you get to know him."

"I'd like to get to know him," Hanna lied. She had no idea what to do around teenage boys, which was part of why she'd avoided dating when she was Jo's age.

"I know he's not the easiest. He only opens up, really acts like himself, when we're alone."

"I get it. Sometimes people are better one on one."

Joelle nodded enthusiastically. "Exactly."

They returned to silence as Jo carefully made her way through the business district on Forbes Avenue, crowded with cars and shoppers. Hanna understood that her presence was necessary, per the rules of Jo's learner's permit, but she felt weird and useless. Was she supposed to be providing tips? Or commenting on Joelle's execution of certain maneuvers? Driving seemed to be another thing that Jo took to without any real difficulty. It would look bad if Hanna started scrolling through TikTok instead of paying attention to her student driver—but could she get away with listening to an audiobook? The transformative moment she'd had earlier was reversing itself as her idle muscles atrophied, turning her into a fungus.

"Want to make the right on Beechwood?" Hanna asked, fighting to stay alert. "Head back around?"

"Sure." Joelle flipped on her turn signal. Her grip on the wheel loosened after she turned; the road widened and the traffic abated. "Are you okay?"

"What?" *Oh God, what was I doing?* She wanted to slump down in the seat and hide. Everyone kept noticing things about her, things she was unaware of projecting. Had Jo been studying her while Hanna had spaced out?

"I mean, I feel like you've been a little distant lately?" Jo tried to explain.

Oh. That. The girl wasn't wrong. "Yeah, sorry. I've just been struggling with some things."

"Daddy said something was going on with your brother? Is he okay?"

Hanna fought to temper the igniting flare of panic. It was bad enough that Jacob and Joelle had been talking about her. But worse that Jacob—needing some kind of excuse for her behavior—had reiterated her fabricated alibi. Hanna had made an error, long ago, in positioning her brother in a semisecretive way; she should've never mentioned him at all—Goose should be an *actual* secret. Every time her acquired family mentioned her birth family, Hanna got queasy. It inevitably felt like a TV episode with a time loop, where one character's storyline threatened to annihilate the possibility that everyone else was ever born.

"He's okay," she said, trying to brush it off. "Just teenage stuff."

"I know about teenage stuff, if you ever need any help?"

Hanna smiled at her, and the warmth inside her now felt appropriate and comforting, radiating from her heart. "That's very sweet. Thank you, Jo. You know, I was thinking we could watch a movie tonight? I need to learn about the superhero universe, I'm so out of touch."

"Sure!" Joelle grinned. "You know how I never used to like to rewatch movies?"

"Same."

"Right? I thought all the surprises were gone, there's nothing new. But Boyd likes to watch things over and over and I'm starting to get it now—like, seeing all the stuff I missed, and appreciating it in a different way. We'll see what he recommends—see if we can make a convert of you." She gave Hanna a conspiratorial grin.

"Okay." For a moment they were peers again, and it didn't even bother Hanna that Jo planned to consult with Boyd on what they should watch. "Do you want to make the right on Monitor Street and head for 376? Get onto the parkway?"

"Not really, but yes. I'll need you to keep an eye out when I need to merge 'n' stuff."

"Okay." Hanna sat a little straighter, on a mission now to be attentive.

"Should I head for Monroeville or downtown?"

"The Monroeville entrance is the absolute worst—how confident are you?"

"Let's head downtown then. Before I get too preoccupied, I wanted to ask you . . . Were you hurt about the baby shower thing?"

"Honestly? Yes." Hanna hadn't thought this drive would be productive, but it felt genuinely good to be together. Joelle gave her a guilt-ridden glance. "I'm not your mom, Jo—and I'm sorry if I've been weird lately. I've never tried to replace Rachel, but I've only ever wanted the best for you. I love you and I really value our relationship."

"I know, I do too. That's not why I said yes to Boyd's mom. It's just . . . it seems important to stay on her good side. Like, she has a way of making me feel like I'm going to do something wrong. She always seems really nice, but I know how it's been for Boyd. She acts like she trusts him but she really doesn't. She wants to have a say in everything, so when she offered with the baby shower, I just thought it was easiest to say yes."

"I get that, but I don't think you—or Boyd—are doing yourselves any favors by taking the easy route with her. She'll take over your whole life, your baby's life, if you don't push back. You know that, right?"

Joelle winced. "Kind of? We thought it would be easier if Boyd was living with us. But maybe it's worse 'cause she doesn't get to be in the middle of everything."

"She's a tricky one, I admit." Hanna didn't know a reasonable way of handling a person like Ashley.

Jo slowed down as she neared the end of the entrance ramp onto 376 W.

Hanna turned around to help gauge the onslaught of speeding cars. "You can go after the white SUV."

Joelle looked scared, but she got into the lane without any problems.

"Good job. You're a good driver."

"Thanks. But I don't want to go downtown, I changed my mind." She sounded nervous. "Can we get off?"

"You can take the next exit, but you're doing fine." Hanna stayed calm, hoping to be a soothing presence.

———

Ten minutes later Joelle pulled into a parking lot so Hanna could take over the driving.

"You did well—that's a lot for one day." Back in the driver's seat like she was used to, Hanna headed toward Squirrel Hill.

"I get nervous when there are cars all around me." In the passenger seat, Jo fiddled with the doodads hanging off her coin purse.

Compared to navigating interpersonal relationships, driving a car was easy. Joelle would probably master both, but Hanna wanted to help put distance between her stepdaughter and Ashley. In hindsight, perhaps Hanna's efforts with the antifreeze had been misguided: they all had to stop giving Boyd's mother so much attention and divert their efforts elsewhere. Joelle needed to stay focused on her own family, and learn to tune out the noise the Blands made from the sidelines.

As Hanna turned onto Beacon Street, nearly home, she had an idea about how to get Jacob and Jo united in a common cause—but it would involve some sacrifices. Earlier the gods had been trying to inspire her, and only now was the message clear:

Hanna had used the antifreeze on the wrong person.

61

This was how to have a normal evening with her family: play the role. It felt as easy as slipping on a pair of pajamas after weeks of wrangling with a sticky wet suit. She didn't need a second skin; she simply needed to say the lines and follow the direction of least resistance. Were they all feigning? Everyone was in a good mood, acting as if all was right with the world. Hanna had ordered pizza. Boyd picked the movie. He briefly explained about the various characters in the superhero universe as they slid gooey slices onto their plates.

"Carry this in for me?" Hanna asked Jacob, handing him her plate. "I'll get the drinks?"

"Sure." He'd changed into shorts and a T-shirt after getting home from work; the outfit made him look young, carefree.

"Jo, wanna grab the napkins? Everyone want soda?"

They bobbed and buzzed as they headed for the living room, leaving Hanna alone in the kitchen. She'd stashed the antifreeze within easy reach, and now quickly poured a small amount into one of the four glasses lined up in front of her. Her plan was to administer small doses—even less than what she'd put in Ashley's glass. Here at home, she'd have regular access to casual poisoning, and her mission now wasn't to kill anyone but to generate an illness that they could all rally behind. *We'll work together, be a family.*

It was a strange way of circling the wagons, but Hanna thought of it as a bonding exercise. They could nurture and fuss over their own, and forget about everyone else.

She added ice and soda, and carried the glasses in two at a time so she could hand them off directly—so there wouldn't be any mistakes. The right person would get the intended cocktail.

They ate their pizza and drank their drinks and watched the loud chaos on the screen.

Hanna forced herself to see the film through the nonsnobby lens of someone who simply wanted to be entertained. She told herself it was a good excuse to take a night off from trying to decipher the whys and hows of human behavior. The movie was as subtle as a peal of thunder, as nuanced as a checkerboard sunset. It hurt her ears and threatened to give her a headache. But it kept her attention. The overall impact of the story and the collision of imagery and sounds tugged at her emotions. *Like a fishhook ensnared in a hunk of flesh.* Whatever her expectations had been, she hadn't thought it would involve *feeling* so many things. The sensation would've been unpleasant if the film hadn't concluded in a victorious way.

"What did you think?" Joelle asked when the credits started to roll.

"It was like absorbing a powerful drug, through your senses."

When the three of them grinned in approval of her answer, Hanna felt as if she'd gained acceptance into a club (*a cult?*). Boyd asked if she was ready to watch the sequel, but Hanna begged off to tidy the kitchen and take a shower.

———

The warm water no longer seemed like amniotic fluid; she had no sense of the shower as a womb or herself in the act of transitioning. *Am I done?* That seemed impossible, but perhaps the actions she'd taken had been enough to launch the next part of the process.

A few minutes into her shower, Jacob slipped in behind her. Had she given him a cue of some sort before heading upstairs? Perhaps the mere appearance of Normal Behavior was sexy enough for him. His hands were like sea creatures grazing plankton off her wet skin. She closed her eyes and let him do whatever he wanted. The gasps she uttered were spontaneous, though they sounded rehearsed. Jacob didn't notice or care. He took her from behind, and Hanna wondered what he imagined with his eyes shut—did he ever fantasize about Rachel?

———

Hanna prepared a second small dose of the poison on Sunday morning. She hadn't really felt anything after Saturday's dose, and she pondered whether she might have miscalculated: Was she being too cautious in doling out her portions? She understood the chemicals needed time to interact inside her, but she was much larger than a rat: a lot of the info she'd found online had been about using antifreeze to kill rodents. Then on Sunday evening, as she was cleaning up after supper, everything around her started to wobble—or maybe she was wobbling? The first effects had begun, a sensation not unlike being drunk.

"I'm gonna go lie down for a while," she told Jacob as he lounged on the sofa. Per usual Boyd was at work, and she'd lost track of Joelle's plans. She tried to carefully articulate her words, but they slurred anyway. "Not feeling so great."

"Are you all right?"

Hanna almost giggled with glee at the concern in his voice. *Already?* Her staged pregnancy and miscarriage had been disappointing in the end, but this time around she might summon real sympathy from him. It helped that she didn't have to rely only on her acting skills, as the chemicals she'd ingested were genuinely making her sick—and could make her irreversibly sick if she wasn't careful. Her illness would be a test of Jacob's caretaking skills—and, to a lesser extent, Joelle's—and

Hanna hoped he'd be up to the task. None of this would be worth it if, in the end, he treated her indifferently or left her to look after herself.

"I'm feeling a little woozy," she admitted.

"Want me to bring you anything?"

She suppressed the urge to cheer. He was already volunteering to wait on her! But then the look on his face fully registered: there was something unfamiliar about the intensity of his worry.

Do I look that sick? She felt terrible, and it was getting worse the longer she remained in the living room entryway, using the wall to steady herself.

"I'll take a glass of water up with me."

The water would help, she told herself, if her kidneys were already affected.

"Do you need help getting upstairs?"

"No no." She stood straighter, determined to look stronger than she felt, not yet ready to seem like an invalid.

The kitchen rocked like a boat on rough waves as she retrieved her glass of water. She climbed the stairs slowly, gripping the handrail. Once in bed she exhaled, relieved she didn't have to move around anymore. Even with her eyes shut, lying still, Hanna felt the undulations as the room warped and bobbed around her.

She'd intended to spend part of the evening working on a letter to Goose, but there was no way she could sit upright, even in bed, and write coherently. For most of her life, she'd been healthy, a few colds and stomach bugs notwithstanding. It sucked to feel this unwell, but she endured it stoically, telling herself it was for a good cause.

62

On Monday morning Hanna awakened with a headache. Beside her, Jacob was still asleep, but he'd refilled her glass of water sometime in the night. She gulped it down. *It's like a hangover.* If that proved to be true, she expected to feel better with a little coffee, more fluids, and a couple of ibuprofen.

By the time she got to the kitchen, dressed in her scrubs, she realized it was worse than a hangover. Unfazed, she gathered the snacks and drinks she'd need for the day and headed to work. It didn't matter if she showed up sick; in fact, she hoped it would make Andrea feel guilty about doubting her reasons for calling off on Friday.

Hanna managed to keep it together for her first few patients. She took a little longer than usual, being careful to do the blood draws as painlessly perfect as she could. Never again did she want to be accused of being bad at her job. The previous week she'd allowed herself to be preoccupied, and her work had suffered; today she legitimately felt like roadkill, but she was determined not to let it impact her abilities. When the ibuprofen failed to kick in, she took two more. *My liver's gonna hate me.* She tried to picture what was happening inside her as the chemicals in the antifreeze metabolized in her body, becoming increasingly toxic. Was the ibuprofen actually making her sicker, given the impaired functioning of her organs?

After her fourth patient she stepped into the break room for another sip of water. As she sat at the little table, head in her hands, fighting a wave of nausea, she heard Andrea calling for her from the hallway.

"Hanna?"

"In here."

"Hey . . . oh." She dropped into the chair across from her. "I wanted to see if you were feeling better since last week, but obviously not. You look terrible."

Perhaps it was her medical background, or a habit as a mother, but Andrea reached out and placed the back of her hand on Hanna's forehead.

"You don't feel feverish."

Hanna shook her head. She already knew that antifreeze poisoning might lower her body temperature, but that wasn't something she could explain to her boss. "I really thought I'd be better by today," she said. "I didn't want to call in sick again."

"You should go home. Maybe go to urgent care or make an appointment with your doctor?" Like Jacob, Andrea sounded unusually concerned.

Hanna nodded. Stood. She'd driven to work, but now she wasn't sure if she could safely drive herself home. The room teetered and she stumbled. And collapsed back into her chair.

"Whoa!" Andrea jumped up and rushed to her side. She pressed two fingers to Hanna's wrist to take her pulse. "Your pulse is fast."

Yup, that could be one of the symptoms.

"This might be something serious. Do you want me to call an ambulance?"

Hanna hoped it wasn't that serious, but she was regretting that second dose of antifreeze. "Can you call my husband to come get me?"

"Of course."

After making the call, Andrea helped Hanna into the one room with a padded exam table, which they used for the most stressed or frail patients. She lay curled on her side, the table's paper covering crinkling beneath her. Andrea had to get back to work—and pick up the slack caused by Hanna's infirmity. But after a few minutes, Raven popped in.

"Hey, heard you looked like death."

Hanna tried to grin; it might have looked more like a grimace. "Do I?"

"You sure do. What the fuck? What's going on?"

"I dunno." Her tainted organs shuddered in protest of her sabotage, but Hanna was secretly delighted. It wasn't like Raven was her best friend, so there'd never been any reason for her to fuss over Hanna. Now she found herself loving the attention and seeing all her coworkers so worried on her behalf.

"Bubonic plague?" Raven asked with a playful wink.

"More likely a shitty virus. Or food poisoning." Hanna remembered that Ashley had claimed the very same explanation for why she looked like death at the cookout. For the first time she was grateful that Ashley was still alive, as it meant Hanna wouldn't die from this, in spite of how she felt.

"Well, I hope you feel better."

"Thanks." Hanna shut her eyes.

Raven was gone for only a moment before she returned. "Hey, your husband's here."

When Hanna opened her eyes, she couldn't focus; Raven and Jacob were in multiple places at once, trailed by ghostly versions of themselves. She wanted to yell at them to stop moving. Then Jacob was in her face, filling her field of vision, breathing hard.

"Honey?" He grabbed her hand.

"You run here?" she mumbled. He was slimy with sweat, unshaven, gross.

"Yeah, I'll drive you and your car home. You ready?"

"'Kay." She swung her legs over the edge of the exam table, ready to stand up. Jacob grabbed her around the waist.

"Andrea said maybe I should take you to urgent care, what do you think?"

"Nah. Let's just go home."

The people in the waiting room stared as Jacob helped her out. Hanna hoped they didn't think she was some wimp who'd passed out while getting her blood drawn. Needles weren't worthy of anyone's fear, given the daily horrors that came with being sentient, constant witnesses to human cruelty. And blood was beautiful, nothing to be afraid of. Though she now imagined hers bubbling, like the acidic pools of an active volcano.

Once on the sidewalk, she pointed to where she'd parked, wishing she'd made more of an effort to park closer. She had little memory of it later, but Jacob got her home and up the stairs and into bed. It crossed her mind as she sank into sleep that she might have really fucked up. She shouldn't have taken that second dose of antifreeze in a fit of impatience. What would happen now, if she'd taken just a smidge too much?

63

For two days Hanna was so sick that she had to pretend she was better than she was—which meant making sure she didn't complain about how wretched she actually felt; the last thing she wanted was to be rushed to a hospital and have her blood drawn.

In the documentary about the woman who'd poisoned her family, they'd guessed—without checking—that her husband had died of a heart attack, and the doctors had been at a loss to find a diagnosis for her first sick child. It was only after the first child died and the second child developed the same symptoms that people grew suspicious about the possibility of poisoning. Hanna was pretty sure the antifreeze itself couldn't be detected in her system, since its main effect was causing a toxic reaction, but the doctors might wonder why certain lab results were so wonky. She didn't want to undergo a battery of tests, and she certainly didn't want anyone to know the source of her illness.

On Wednesday she finally felt well enough to get out of bed. She was able to shower without fear of the slip-and-fall death of urban legends, and go downstairs to fetch her own bagel and beverage. Dr. Yamamoto had left her a message, disappointed that Hanna hadn't returned for the appointment they'd scheduled for Monday. Hanna finally called her back, relieved to get her voicemail, and explained that she'd been sick and would reschedule when she was feeling better. At least that would buy her some time, as she wasn't sure yet if she wanted to see Dr. Yamamoto again. On some level would the good doctor be proud of her that she'd evolved and instead of hurting other people, she was now hurting herself?

Probably not.

Though she still felt like a pickled piece of meat, she knew she was on the mend—and didn't want to let her recovery show *too* much. The previous two days had been a rehearsal of sorts; now she could proceed with a Method actor's approach to how to authentically portray feeling unwell. She planned to use what she'd learned to prolong the drama— safely this time, without ingesting more poison.

She was bored of being alone and didn't want to spend any more time in her bedroom, so Hanna dragged a blankie downstairs and made a nest on the couch. It was perfect: everyone who came through—Jacob, Jo, even Boyd—asked her how she was doing and if there was anything they could get for her. In between their brief visits, she watched TV and scrolled through TikTok and tried to think how she would explain this to Goose—he would not be happy to hear about her change of tactics with the antifreeze.

That evening Joelle the Vegetarian made her chicken noodle soup, and Jacob brought home Taiwanese desserts from Pink Box Bakery, just as she'd requested. Hanna delighted in their attention. She loved being waited on. She hadn't realized just how tired she was of the *Jo & Boyd Show*, and the *Ashley Hour*; it felt good to be the star of her own home. Though it was midweek and not officially a family dinner day, they joined Hanna on the couch to eat supper and watch a movie. Jacob was about to hit play when Boyd spoke up.

"Oh, I was supposed to tell you," he said to Hanna, "that you might want to get checked out by a doctor."

"I think I'm past the worst of it," she reassured him.

"Yeah, it's just, we saw my mom"—with a quick glance, he included Joelle—"and told her you were sick and she thought it sounded like what she had a couple weeks ago."

Hanna's hand, with its spoonful of soup, froze on its way to her mouth. She didn't like where this conversation was going, and especially didn't like that he and Joelle had been swapping stories about her symptoms with Boyd's mom.

"Ashley was getting better," Jo explained, "but then she started having weird problems with her pee."

"Yeah, my dad made her see a doctor—'cause she always thinks she can just fix everything herself. And I don't know the details, but something was up with her kidneys."

"They talked about dialysis," Jo chipped in.

"Well, Mom said it wasn't that extreme, but yeah—"

"That was before the results of the tests I guess."

"Yeah. So anyway, Mom wanted me to mention it to you, in case it's the same thing."

"That sounds really serious." Jacob looked at Hanna, worried. "Maybe you—"

"It's not that serious—I'm not Ashley."

"Well Ashley didn't think it was that serious either," said Joelle.

"I appreciate your concern—all of you," Hanna said, trying to shut down the conversation. "If I have any weird pee episodes, I'll . . ." She shrugged, really not knowing what she would do. It wasn't that she wanted permanent kidney damage, but she didn't want anyone else prying into her life.

"See a doctor?" Jacob prompted, finishing her sentence. He turned to Boyd. "Thank you, for telling us about that. And thank your mom. Is she okay now?"

Boyd nodded. "Yeah, she seems okay. She's back to work."

See? Hanna just had to wait it out; she could endure a few unexpected symptoms.

As the movie started she tried to remember *exactly* how much antifreeze she'd put in Ashley's glass versus what she'd put in her own over the course of two days. She also tried to remember exactly how much she'd been peeing. She had the impression over the last couple of days that she'd been drinking a lot of water. But maybe, due to her altered state, it hadn't really been that much? It must not have been, because otherwise she would've been going to the bathroom more often, and she was pretty sure she'd been going less. A lot less.

As the salty broth slid down her throat, she felt a prickle of fear at the thought that she'd seriously damaged herself. Thanks to her mother's Crohn's disease, Hanna had always been afraid of having a chronic illness. *Mommy was weak and pathetic.* To Hanna, being chronically ill sounded like a fate worse than death; she didn't want either, but was afraid she may have courted both.

64

Dear Goose,

Don't get mad . . . I'll wait while you throw some stuff around the room to get any pent-up anger out of your system.

Ready now? Nice and calm? I really have mostly good news to share with you, but the good news comes via a slightly . . . how to describe it . . . a slightly masochistic path? Shall I share the end results first?

Jacob has been wonderfully solicitous. I finally feel like the queen of my home. He waits on me and dotes on me. He orders and serves whatever I'm hungry for. The other night he gave me a full body massage—without expecting a blow job as payment. For the first time since I've been married, I feel like his Number One Priority. For nearly a week now, it's been all about me, me, me—not Jo, or her homework / dance classes / field trips / school clothes / cool clothes / pimples / periods / appointments / parties / dietary demands, not Jo and her boyfriend, or Jo and the growing fetus. Not Jacob and his work time, or Jacob and his play-time, or Jacob and his sex time. Me, me, me.

"Hanna, how are you feeling?"

"Hanna, what do you need?"

"Hanna, can I get you something?"

And all I had to do to get everyone's attention? Get a little sick.

Don't worry—I'm fine. But I did take a little sip of antifreeze to produce these sympathetic results. I'd totally recovered after a few days, so then I had to walk a delicate line of being "sick" enough to deserve everyone's help while not being so ill that they pestered me about going to a doctor. Even people from work called to check on me—and my boss was fine about my needing "another week or two to recuperate."

Really, I just need another week or two of pampering. Then I'll be ready to deal with my real life again . . . though I haven't yet come up with a workable plan for avoiding my duties as a *grandma*—the word alone makes me want to jump out a window. I'm also still at a loss for conquering Ashley. I guess, aside from these days of being queen of the house, I'm still at a loss in general. But let's not think about that right now!

It probably should've occurred to me a long time ago to do something like this. If I had, maybe Jacob and Joelle wouldn't have gotten so lazy—I made it easy for them to take advantage of me. Perhaps I'll now have to get "sick" on regular occasions, every few months or so. And earn myself a few days off from work, and a few days in the family spotlight.

And there's been another positive development. I've had a lot of time during the day when everyone's out and about, and sometimes I've been a little bored. (I have to make myself *not* clean, and remind myself not to record new TikTok posts.) So one day when I needed something unproductive to do, I went up to the attic, ostensibly for the purpose of snooping around Jacob's studio. And you know what I found? *Beautiful* pictures—of *me*! (Yes, the theme of this letter is *ME*.) :-)

Maybe you're wondering why that was such a surprise—Jacob's a good photographer, right? (And I'm not exactly an eyesore.) But in the last photo I saw of his, I looked a little scary—like, a creature from a horror film—and it worried me that he saw me as uglier than I am. But he processed new prints from that last time I posed for him—and I looked absolutely dreamy. Exotic and otherworldly. There was something of a ghostly quality to my image, but it was alluring and mysterious (not grotesque like his previous effort). I have to say, Jacob is getting really creative with his technique, moving even further away from realism.

Oh, and guess who I ran into? (Like literally, I was out running.) Dr. Yamamoto!

Okay, so maybe I was stalking her a little, but I wanted to see if she was still on Wightman Street and still in business. She caught me skulking around her yard and invited me in. We spoke for a few minutes and she hasn't changed at all. I know I sound all chipper as I write this, but the truth is I was debating whether I should start seeing her again. I feel half out of my mind most of the time . . . Joelle's growing baby bump is like an inflating bomb. Picture someone blowing up a balloon. Bigger (exhale), bigger. And when it pops the world explodes.

Goose, I can't stop this baby from coming. You know I wanted to. You know I tried.

I have to accept reality, but no one understands—except you and Dr. Yamamoto—why this is freaking me out so much. And I can't let everyone see how much it's freaking me out because WHO LOSES THEIR SHIT JUST BECAUSE A MEMBER OF THE HOUSEHOLD IS HAVING A BABY?!

It scares me. That's the truth. But I don't want Jacob or Jo to know just how terrified I am of living with a baby. Little babies are hard enough. So fragile, with their undeveloped skulls and inability to articulate their needs. But then they grow into little children (who, if they're anything like I was, still might be incapable of articulating their needs), and are still fragile, although in different ways.

I CANNOT BE TRUSTED WITH FRAGILE THINGS.

What am I going to do? I can't kill everyone. I can't explain myself. But I don't know how to cope. I'd love to play sick forever and just shut out the world, but I'm pretty sure that's not an option.

I'm sorry. I feel like this letter started so well, and now it's sliding down the chute toward the vat of vipers. (Remember when we used to play Chutes and Ladders? Sorry—a few years too late—if the stories I made up about what was waiting at the bottom of those chutes was a little too scary.)

Well, I hope you can see that I'm doing okay, working things out in my own way, one slightly unconventional step at a time. I haven't been drawing much lately, but I'll try to include a scribble of some kind in my next letter. And since this was all about me, me, me, please tell me all about you, you, you.

Yours,

Hanna

65

Dear Hanna,

Well, you are nothing if not creative. I'm torn between wanting to applaud you and wanting to chastise you—but I don't want to pile on when you're already feeling overwhelmed. Maybe seeing Dr. Yamamoto isn't such a bad idea? I only remember being at a few family sessions, but she was fair, wouldn't you say? And I'm sure it helps that she already knows so much of your history. As much as I wanted to be the person to help you in your time of need, I have to admit that she may be better suited to the task. (At least you aren't still looking to Skog for guidance! That *has* to mean you're not a lost cause, right?)

Not that I want to plant the seed in your head and drive you back into the flimsy arms of your beanbag friend, but . . . the UnderSlumberBumbleBeasts have been on my mind a lot recently. I loved working on crafty projects with you—if you didn't know, I *idolized* you. Maybe I didn't express it enough, but I enjoyed *My UnderSlumberBumbleBeast* almost as much as you did, with its endearing cast of garbage-made misfits, and the clever little human who adored them as treasures. (Don't take this the wrong way, but I've never quite been able to decide if you were more like the girl, Pru, or her collection of under-the-bed friends.) I loved that you wanted to share the book with me—as Dad had with you—and help me make a BumbleBeast of my own.

I didn't have the chance to become so attached to my own beanbag friend, due to his untimely destruction. But if I'd had him as long as you've had Skog, I'm sure I wouldn't be so quick to poke fun at your little beastly pal. ;-) I don't think I ever even told you what I named mine? (I was a little embarrassed by my poor naming skills, even then.)

Butty.

What can I say, I was six and liked the word butt, lol. And he was meant to be my buddy. But the real inspiration came from that one eye, that looked like a piece of butterscotch candy. That eye was my favorite part. You know how sometimes you come across an object, and staring at it makes you dream of other things? I know you never meant for Butty to become such a sore spot with Mom and Dad. They just never appreciated your intentions the way I did. Even though I do sometimes think that you're too attached to Skog, I wish they would've given Butty to you for safekeeping instead of throwing him away. (Maybe if Skog had had a friend of his own, you would've sought other companionship, ha ha.)

Sometimes I really wish we'd been closer in age, so I could've been there for you when you were young—a proper playmate.

Anyway, so that's what's been on my mind.

And now for one very serious thing: Hanna, please don't leave me. Please don't do anything in your desperation that would leave me drifting alone through the dark, cold void of space. You know I don't have a lot of friends either. Promise me? Cross your heart and hope to die? Stick a needle in your eye?

I love you more than anyone in the universe.

Yours,

Goose

66

Hanna's letter to Goose had been an exercise in optimism: it was true, but not the entire truth. Once it became obvious that she was recovering, Jacob was all too eager to return to the way things had always been. He conceded that she wasn't well enough to run around doing errands, but he wanted her to place the online orders for their groceries and necessities.

"You can handle that, it doesn't take too much energy."

He conceded that she wasn't well enough to cook elaborate dinners, but he didn't want to keep ordering in. He suggested she make one-pot meals, like chili or lasagna. (As if the fact that it would all cook in one container minimized how much preparation was involved.) Joelle wasn't much better. She considered it reasonable that Hanna could sit in the passenger seat, cuddling a blankie if need be, whenever Jo wanted to practice driving.

"All you'll have to do is sit!"

There was something unconvincing about the efforts Hanna was making to act as if she was unwell. As much as she summoned the memories of the pain and dizziness she'd felt during her sickest hours, even to her own eyes and ears, it seemed like she was faking it. But she wasn't ready to return to work; her day-to-day life sounded like drudgery. She told herself she just needed a few more days of downtime and being indulged—but she wasn't going to get that if it seemed like she was just being lazy.

Barefoot, she milled around her studio, randomly touching things. She kind of wanted to sit at her table and draw, but in the spirit of being too unwell for her normal activities, she resisted. Now that she'd given up on the idea of a warm shower as a transformative portal, she was intentionally avoiding it. She liked how her unwashed hair hung in her face. And she didn't mind if Jacob thought her too unclean for marital relations.

She crouched down and lifted the top off the box where she kept all of Goose's letters, neatly arranged in their envelopes. It was safer to keep it out of sight, in the closet, but she'd been coming in and rereading everything during her convalescence. But, increasingly paranoid, she needed to put it away. She replaced the lid and slid the box, heavy with letters and drawings, along the floor. The closet was dark and mostly empty. *Like a tomb.* But now if Jacob wandered in, nosy about what she was doing, he'd have less to gawk at.

She hadn't looked in on Skog in a while, so she went to his shelf and gently raised the lid of his velvet-lined bed. Goose wasn't wrong; it was sort of like a coffin. His revelations about Butty had really touched her. Her mother had always wanted Hanna to believe that she was a shitty big sister—the worst ever—because Mommy couldn't handle the truth that Goose liked Hanna better. Everything was a competition for Mommy, who always resented how easy it was for Hanna to steal little pieces of Goose's heart—much as Mommy resented how Hanna had once stolen Daddy's heart.

Skog was sound asleep and she didn't want to wake him. She lowered the lid, and ran her finger across the stuff on the shelf below. A few art books, knickknacks. And there in the middle of the shelf, the set of oil pastels that Jacob had given her for their first Hanukkah together. She opened the beautiful wood box and peered inside at the eighty-four pristine colors. They looked perfect in their little rows, every color in the spectrum. Sometimes she thought it bothered Jacob that she never used the pastels; he couldn't fully grasp that she loved them just as they were, as a collection, as an object to look at.

She'd been the same way as a child, unwilling to damage her favorite art supplies. Mommy, also, felt a rebuke that her gifts went unused, and Hanna couldn't explain to her how it felt to simply touch the flawless little pools of paint. It was like touching rainbows, and dreams, and miniature whirlpools of infinity. Her reasons for not using the oil pastels were somewhat different (as much as she enjoyed visiting them in their immaculate form): as an adult, she was more at home submerged in shades of gray. Working in color was like creating a fantasy, a bright phantasmagoria that gave her a pain between her eyes. In contrast, working in grays felt real and grounded; she could stare at gray forever without getting a headache. Jacob, with his black-and-white photography, understood this on some level. But she knew he still wondered why she never even experimented with the gift he'd given her.

Though her studio didn't leave her much room to pace and roam, it had provided her enough thinking space to reach a decision. Goose's words echoed in her head as she plopped into her chair. "Please don't leave me." She planned to be extra, extra careful this time, but even the thought of disappointing her brother bothered her.

This time she would properly measure the antifreeze, and maybe take as little as a quarter teaspoon. Just enough to produce a sensation that would bring a better performance out of her. Just enough to return her to the heart of her family's attention.

—

First things first, she made sure no one was home. Jacob was at work, but she went through the upstairs rooms, and then the downstairs rooms, just to make sure. She called out for Joelle as she headed into the basement, ready with the lie that she was collecting bedsheets for a load of laundry. The main room was empty, so Hanna knocked on the closed bedroom door. She half expected to open it and find Boyd blubbery and naked on the bed, midnap, but no one was there.

This time she wouldn't hurriedly splash the pink poison into the glass; she would be precise and do it right. First she dropped in a couple of ice cubes. Then she got a bottle of Diet Pepsi out of the refrigerator and opened it. She nearly filled the glass, leaving only half an inch of space at the top. *So I can't overdo it.*

The jug of antifreeze was still quite heavy, having been so sparingly used. She held it over the sink, in case she spilled any, and carefully poured out a quarter teaspoon of the liquid. Sure enough the tiny spoon overflowed, but she left the droplets in the sink for the moment and added the antifreeze to her glass. She stirred it with a chopstick, and the pink poison disappeared into the soda.

Hanna eyed her concoction, displeased. That couldn't possibly be enough, could it? For a moment she debated—and then returned to the sink to pour another quarter teaspoon.

"Hanna?"

Startled, she spun around. The antifreeze in her little spoon splashed onto the counter. Jacob stood there in the entryway. Hanna knew the look on her face was a cartoon mask of guilt-ridden fear. He was dressed for work, but he was here—had he come in the front door without her hearing?

"Did you just get home?" She had to know, because she'd checked the house and had been sure she was alone.

He shook his head, baffled. "I'm leaving now."

"Where were you?"

"In my darkroom. What are you doing?"

Fuck. She hadn't thought to knock on the closed door of his darkroom.

The moment was dragging on, and she felt frozen in place. Jacob sounded more confused than angry, but she didn't think that would last. He looked like a stone statue, intense and unforgiving. Hanna saw the tableau through his eyes.

Her grungy house clothes and greasy hair.

The measuring spoon in her hand.

The jug of antifreeze, now on the counter beside her.

The glass of refreshing, bubbling soda.

Pink splatter.

The chopstick stirrer.

No excuses came to her. No lies that would pass muster. She saw her husband scrutinizing her, fitting puzzle pieces together. The conclusion he would draw was inevitable. Now that the shock of his presence had passed, she felt numb.

Her eyes fell on the knife block. But a spontaneous murder, especially one as messy as a stabbing, would only create more questions that she wouldn't be able to lie her way through. With a sigh, she turned to the sink, turned on the water. Washed away the poison that had spilled in the basin. Saturated the sponge and started wiping off the counter.

Jacob sprang into action. "What are you doing!"

He lunged toward her. Gawked at the jug. The glass. Her.

Hanna calmly twisted the cap back onto the jug of antifreeze. She faced him, leaning against the lower cabinet, and picked up the glass. Before she could decide if she would drink it or not, he snatched it from her hand and threw it in the sink. The violent jangle of shattering glass made her wince. But she crossed her arms and met his stare, refusing to make it easy for him by uttering some sort of overwrought explanation or apology.

"You . . ." Apparently he couldn't decide what to accuse her of. "What's wrong with you?"

She gave a one-shoulder shrug.

"Seriously, what the fuck is wrong with you? Is this why you've been sick?" Things shifted into place, and his eyes widened as an image in his mind came into focus. "Did you—are you the reason Ashley got . . . Did you poison her?"

"A little."

"A little?" The words were like serpents in his mouth, venomous and writhing.

"She's going to take over Joelle's life, the baby's life. I wanted . . . I wanted to keep our family intact."

"Our family intact . . . ?" he murmured. "By . . . ? Oh my God." He stumbled to the island and dropped onto his stool. "Oh my God."

Hanna followed him, and rested her elbows on the island. "I was trying to help."

"Oh my God." He rubbed his face—wiping a vision out of his eyes, smearing impossible words from his lips. The look he gave her was part beseeching, part insanity. "Should I call the police? Take you to a hospital?"

"Why would you call the police?"

"You tried to kill Boyd's mother!" he screamed.

"No! I . . ." She had to switch tactics, fast. "You know how overwhelmed I was, by Jo's pregnancy. But I went to see my therapist last week."

"Your therapist?" Question marks hopped above his head. The way he cocked it made him seem like a robot, unable to compute.

"Dr. Yamamoto. I used to see her, before I met you." An understatement regarding the chronology of events, but true nonetheless. "I'm in over my head, I know that. But I'm getting better now."

"Better? How? You were about to drink . . ." One floppy, addled hand gestured toward the sink.

"I'm getting help. That's the important thing." *That's enough, right?*

"I don't understand what's happening." His complexion had taken on a sickly tinge. He looked too weak to stand up, much less go to work. For a second Hanna feared she'd slipped up and had accidentally poisoned *him*. But no, she'd remember that (wouldn't she?).

A long needle of terror pierced her gut: she was starting to grasp the implications—the magnitude—of Jacob knowing what she'd done. She'd never really thought about what he might do if he found out about her schemes; she'd believed she could keep everything hidden from him—just as she'd hidden everything else she didn't want him to know about. When she and Goose had debated ways of killing Ashley, Hanna had very much been afraid of getting caught—by someone *else*. If Jacob turned her in, where would she end up? Somewhere that wouldn't have the restricted but hopeful grounds of a facility like Marshes. No, adults were sent to places with razor wire and a fortress of locks.

Hanna had to turn this around and exploit his moment of weakness. With Joelle, he could be a doormat, but Hanna was afraid he wouldn't be so pliable with her. A moment ago she'd hoped to avoid explanations and apologies, but now she needed to appeal to his tender side, and seem more pathetic than dangerous.

"I know it's hard—even for me—to understand," she said, her throat clogged with pretend tears. "It's all tied in with stuff that happened when I was a kid. And I've been handling everything badly—thinking about everything made me panic. I've been afraid, that's the truth. I've been really afraid of what might happen if there's a baby in the house, and if I have to take care of it—"

"Didn't we talk about that?"

"Not everything. I didn't know how to tell you . . . It's been really hard for me, and then everything got out of control, in my head. But now I have Dr. Yamamoto again, so . . . Maybe we could see her together, work things out."

"Work what out?" He got to his feet, in spite of being unsteady. "This isn't a problem with *us*—this is a problem with *you*." His expression curdled with disgust, as if he'd tasted something rancid. "I don't know what the fuck I'm supposed to do with you."

He stumbled to the doorway, escaping the noxious fumes of Hanna's presence.

"Jacob, I'm getting better."

"What does that even mean?" He lurched away. "I'm going to work."

This time, the emptiness in the house was palpable, a cold void. Goose's words came back to her, begging her not to leave him drifting alone. Now *she* was the untethered one. The air conditioner was set too low, but the chill enhanced the mood as Hanna imagined herself an astronaut, flailing in her suit, trailing the umbilical cord that had once attached her to a ship. She got smaller and smaller, floating away into the darkness.

67

Already Hanna felt the sting of being ostracized. Joelle wasn't avoiding her because of any knowledge of what Hanna had done; her stepdaughter was behaving in her normal, self-consumed way. But Hanna felt left out as she heard Boyd and Jo in the basement, laughing as they watched something on their little TV. Jacob hadn't come home for supper. Hanna ate alone in the living room.

The instant Jacob stormed out that afternoon, Hanna had been cast to the fringes, far away from the epicenter of the family. She felt herself bobbing there, wondering if she'd be tossed a lifeline, or if he'd leave her there to drown. She cleaned up the kitchen. Did the laundry. She felt sick—in head and body—but now didn't want it to show.

When Jacob finally returned home, she was already in bed. She'd left his bedside lamp on, and sat up when he came in. Without looking at her he headed for the bathroom.

"I'm just getting some stuff. I'll sleep in my studio."

They hadn't talked or communicated since the blowup in the kitchen, and Hanna had no idea what he was thinking—or what he was thinking of doing. She had sixty seconds before he left the room and went upstairs.

"Can we talk?" She quickly added: "I can make an emergency appointment with Dr. Yamamoto and she can help me—us, both of us—make sense of everything."

Ready to walk out on her again, he stopped with his hand on the doorknob and stared at her. She couldn't read him. He'd returned to being a stone statue; his intensity gave away nothing.

"We'll talk tomorrow," he said, crumbling a little with exhaustion. "Noon. Will you be here?"

"Of course." She thought it odd that he was scheduling a time to speak with her, but it was better than silence or avoidance.

He nodded. "I have an appointment in the morning, then I'll be back."

"Okay. Thank you." She hadn't meant to thank him, but it slipped out. In all likelihood she owed him more than a thank-you for agreeing to sit down and talk. She was reminded, again, of how well she'd chosen: Jacob was a good husband and a fair man. He wouldn't just throw away the life they'd enjoyed together.

He pulled the door shut behind him as he left, but Hanna felt the tentacles of worry untangling from her body.

She shimmied across the bed and turned off Jacob's lamp. They'd talk tomorrow. She had time to prepare what to say, reassured that he was willing to listen. She wasn't sure if she could make him understand *everything*, but as a good and fair person, he would want the opportunity to demonstrate his own goodness. Would he, like the superheroes he'd become fond of, want to believe he could save her? Or at least save her from the worst consequences of her own actions?

It's going to be okay. She curled onto her side and shut her eyes, imagining the things she might say to her husband. Tomorrow, at noon.

———

Since waking up, Hanna had found herself in a state of odd nervousness. She was careful with each aspect of her morning routine: shower, hair, clothes, coffee, breakfast. She even wore a bit of mascara, and put in the gold earrings Jacob had given her for their third wedding anniversary. Every action felt ritualistic and important, even as it seemed strange to prepare so methodically for a rendezvous in her own house. What to wear had been a concern: an outfit too fancy would make her look desperate (or out of touch), but something too casual might convey indifference—and she definitely wasn't indifferent. She settled on dark leggings and a loose top that had been deceptively expensive.

What about shoes?

Did she need shoes to attend a meeting in her living room? Or was Jacob thinking of going out onto the deck? She was starting to fear beautiful days, as ugly things always seemed to happen. As noon approached she heard Jacob returning from wherever he'd been. She slipped on a pair of ballet flats, and went downstairs to make sure both the living room and the deck looked appropriately tidy and inviting. She opened the two patio umbrellas, so they'd have the option of sitting in the shade. While she was out there, Jacob poked his head around the sliding door.

"Did you want to talk out here?" he asked.

"Is that okay? Do you have a preference?"

"No, that's fine." He seemed as nervous as she was. He glanced at his watch. "It'll be a few more minutes."

"Okay." She couldn't hide her confusion. Jacob had always been reliably punctual, but not obsessively so—and they were both there, ready. "Do you want something to drink?"

He gave her a glower. "I'll fix it myself."

Hanna followed him inside, but stayed in the living room as he headed for the kitchen. She heard him getting glasses out of the cupboard. She understood why he was being distant, cautious, but appreciated his ability to remain considerate. Ice cubes tumbled into glasses—what was he preparing for them? Iced tea? Something stronger? She stood anxiously by the sliding door, unnerved by the chittering beetles crawling through her gut.

She jumped when the doorbell rang.

The bell's resonant notes thrummed inside her, chiming an alarm. Was it a coincidence that someone was here? Right at noon, when she and Jacob had arranged to talk? Or had Jacob made some sort of plan, involving someone else. Who?

A divorce attorney? Or someone with the power to lock her up.

Shit, what if it's Ashley! What if Jacob was expecting Hanna to confess her sins? She was certain Ashley would *not* be understanding or let it go—she'd charge Hanna with assault and have her arrested.

Jacob sped for the front door. "I'll get it."

With panic setting in, Hanna chased after him. She reached the foyer as Jacob swung the door open. Her jaw dropped in shock, and the beetles quick-froze and shattered inside her. There on the doorstep were her parents.

"Alex. Suzette." Jacob reached out and shook their hands. "Thank you for coming."

68

Hanna and her mother couldn't stop staring at each other. And it was a little unnerving that they were wearing almost the same outfit. The patio umbrella only half shaded Suzette, and the sunlight revealed the small circular scar on her cheek. *I did that.*

She hadn't noticed Mommy's scar in a long time, a reminder of the day when she'd chanted her spell and believed she could set Mommy ablaze with the ease of putting a torch to straw. If Hanna had been smarter, she would've tried setting Mommy's *hair* alight instead of pressing the burning stick into her cheek. Daddy had meant for it to be a spring celebration, singing songs around the little backyard firepit and eating traditional Swedish food. He'd wanted Hanna to ceremoniously cast away her Other self, the one she'd named Marie-Anne Dufosset, but Hanna had been more ambitious: she wanted to get rid of someone *real.* Mommy.

That day changed the trajectory of Hanna's life; soon after they sent her away to Marshes. *No wonder I hate cookouts.*

Across from her now, Daddy smiled at her in his sad way. Most of his hair was gray, and he no longer had a beard. Mommy's hair was dyed a shade too dark, and the skin on her forehead and around her eyes was crisscrossed with worry lines. They'd both gained a few pounds. *Too many cinnamon buns, ha ha.* It suddenly dawned on Hanna that she could barely remember any Swedish—it had been so long since she'd spoken or heard it. *Kanelbullar.* It came to her now, the word she'd once used for cinnamon buns. In a way, Daddy had culturally disowned her after she ruined their Walpurgis celebration.

Alex and Suzette thanked Jacob as he brought out the tray of iced tea and passed the glasses around.

"How are you, *lilla gumman?*"

Hanna gaped at him, shocked to hear her father use her old nickname. Was he feeling sentimental? Surely, if her parents were here, it meant they knew something—that Jacob had told them something awful about her. What was Jacob expecting from them now? That they would reveal her life story, all the missing pieces that explained why she was the way she was? Or did he expect them to step in and parent her—to reprimand her and send her into a time-out for twenty-four minutes (or would that be hours, or years)? *Naughty Hanna, you know it's not nice to poison people.*

Without responding to her father, she looked out across the yard. She almost grinned when she saw Molly, the orphaned three-legged groundhog. *See,* she wanted to tell her mother—*that's what a devoted mother would do, sacrifice her life for her child.* Hanna could've had a happy childhood if Mommy had been out of the picture; with just her Daddy's love, she might have even turned out *normal.* Mommy was the true poison.

Hanna felt her parents watching her and wanted to slither away. Molly limped off into the underbrush. When finally Jacob sat down and the quartet was gathered, Hanna glared at him. Yes, she had made mistakes, but *this* was his fault.

"Thank you again for coming," he said to Alex and Suzette. They sat like dolls, stiff and dazed.

"We were surprised to hear from you," Mommy said, her glass eyes locked on Hanna.

She wondered if her mother thought she looked different, older. Did it pain her more than ever to see herself in her daughter?

At last Suzette blinked and turned to Jacob. Hanna willed her husband not to tell them the worst parts: her parents would make sure she was locked up again. Then again, if Jacob understood what a lifelong fuckup she was, how even as an adult, she couldn't competently kill anyone, maybe he'd see that she really wasn't a threat.

Jacob glanced away from Suzette, almost as if ashamed. "I know, I'm sorry. I've always respected Hanna's wishes, even when I didn't fully understand why she didn't want . . . I'm sorry, I feel like I should've made more of an effort to connect with you."

"Why?" Hanna scornfully demanded.

"I would hate for my daughter to shut me out."

Hanna cringed at how sincere Jacob sounded—how his words begged for everyone's sympathy.

"We tried too, to respect Hanna's wishes," her dad said. "We were proud of her for building her own life." Suzette gave a tiny nod in agreement. "Sometimes, when she was young . . . we didn't always do the right things, or know what she needed. If she was happy here in the life she made, with her career and family, we didn't want to interfere."

"I figured it was something like that." Jacob sighed. The nervousness he'd exposed with their arrival had been replaced by doubt. "Maybe I shouldn't have involved you now, in our problems."

It was Hanna's turn to nod in agreement.

"You must have had your reasons," said Suzette.

"We were worried it was something serious," Alex added.

"It is."

Hanna felt them all looking at her again and tried not to petulantly roll her eyes. Her best way through this was to stay calm and let her husband get whatever was on his mind out of his system. If she fought or complained, she would come off as either childish or crazy. She wanted to remain silent until Jacob was finished throwing her under the bus—then she'd try to impress her parents with a response that was self-reflective and mature. They might not *like* what Jacob had to say, but Hanna hoped to keep her parents from joining sides with him.

"Hanna . . . She talks about how everything ties back to when she was a kid—how all the stuff we're dealing with now, as a family, reminds her of . . . I don't know, she won't tell me. I was running out of ways of trying to make sense of her behavior, and I can't just overlook . . . I don't want to just give up." Jacob looked at her as if she would divulge everything now. She stared at him, let him stew in his own turmoil. "Your parents know you. Maybe they can help me make sense of this?"

"I'm almost afraid to ask," her mother mumbled.

"I thought when you first met . . ." Alex hesitated. "Well, I thought Hanna must have told you—something at least—about her early life? Her . . . difficulties?" His questions were for Jacob, but he directed his confusion at Hanna.

"Not really," Jacob replied. "She's never been interested in talking about her past. I'm not unaware that at her age, in your twenties, you process all your family drama. I thought it was . . . mature, that she didn't want to dwell on rehashing her childhood. But I think I'm missing something. I know about her post–high school studies and work, but prior to that . . ." He shrugged. "She went away to school when she was young. Dysfunctional family issues. That's about all I know."

"*School?*" Alex's chuckle was part amusement, part derision.

"You're just going to let us talk about you?" her mother asked her. "Like you're not here? You aren't going to participate?"

"My husband was the one who called you. I'm just trying to respect whatever it is he wanted to do here."

"You obviously felt you needed our help," Alex said to Jacob. "Is Hanna okay? She looks okay."

"Well, she's not sick anymore—not physically."

She gave him a sneer. *Go ahead, imply I'm mentally ill. They already know that.*

"Hanna had behavioral issues," said Suzette, all too ready to scissor apart the seams of Hanna's adult life. "I guess she didn't tell you that. It wasn't a school but a residential treatment facility. For severely disturbed children."

69

Hanna watched as Jacob absorbed the truth bomb—a small one to start with, really. *School, treatment facility. Po-tay-toh, pu-*tah-*toh.* He bobbed his head as he processed, maybe trying to imagine little Hanna as a hellion. Or maybe the father in him pictured little Joelle instead, crying and hurt. Whatever it was he saw, it wounded him. *Or disappointed him?* Hanna considered getting up and leaving; she didn't need to witness her parents pulling on the threads, unraveling her carefully constructed world.

"I *told* you," she insisted to her husband, "I had problems as a child."

Her mother shook her head, smiled like a knife had parted her lips. "Problems?"

Daddy frowned, perhaps guessing now the magnitude of the half truths Hanna had shared with her husband.

"We've had a good marriage. We were happy," Hanna said to Jacob, to her parents. That was true too.

To her relief, Jacob nodded.

"Things were fine," he said, for Alex and Suzette's benefit, "for a long time. That's part of why this has been so difficult, so unexpected. Maybe it makes a little more sense now, how her experiences as a child . . . It's just—ever since we found out my daughter is pregnant, Hanna's been struggling. Like *really* struggling. I didn't realize at first how bad it was, how she couldn't cope."

Mommy and Daddy mouthed now-we-get-it *Ohs*, then looked at each other with weary eyes, envisioning the past—all the things they hadn't been able to fix. All the specialists and schools. All of Hanna's creative attempts to manage her unmanageable world.

Jacob watched how her parents reacted. "What? What does that mean—you understand why she's . . . ?"

Hanna had appreciated her husband's initial tactfulness; he could've led the conversation with "You'll never guess what she did," or "Your daughter tried to kill someone," but he'd taken a more empathetic route. Unfortunately, that route now risked veering into territory that Hanna sought to avoid at all costs—certain truths really *shouldn't* come out. It almost would've been better if Jacob had simply said, "I need to know if your daughter has a history of poisoning people." Then her parents could've commiserated and explained how Hanna's love could be too obsessive, her attempts to protect people too misguided. But instead he'd wanted to know why she couldn't *cope*, why she was losing her shit because Joelle was pregnant.

"Your daughter was . . . fourteen? When you met Hanna?" Suzette asked.

"She'd just turned twelve. She's sixteen now. We really weren't expecting—"

"You already know I'm uncomfortable around babies," Hanna snapped. "I *told* you that." She looked at her parents, hoping to shut down whatever explanation they were readying. *See, he knows—I do tell him things!* The situation was rolling downhill, and Hanna needed to recalibrate her strategy. Hell, she might have to blurt out her confessions after all—a little bait and switch to change the subject. She glared at Jacob. "You and I *talked* about this." *So shut up.*

"But it still doesn't make sense," he insisted. "The things you're doing are so over the top—so destructive! To us, to you, to other people. And *why*? If this is all a reaction—you're *good* with kids, that's what I don't understand." He spoke faster as he got more exasperated. "You've always been great with Joelle—you know I wouldn't have married you otherwise. And you're great with Goose. I just don't understand, *at all*, why the news of a baby—"

"Wait," Daddy interjected, as if awakened by a tornado warning.

Shit. Fuck. The unraveling was about to accelerate. Hanna had missed her chance to lead the conversation in a different direction.

"Did you say *Goose?*" Mommy asked. The color drained from her face, leaving her pale and haggard.

In spite of what was about to happen, Hanna felt a flare of anger at her husband: her parents didn't deserve to be reminded of this. They hadn't come here for this. And this, more than all other reasons, was why she'd kept her parents at arm's length. Now her husband's indirectness was about to make all their lives exponentially worse.

———

It was too late to offer up a diversion—even one as good as "Guess you were right, Mommy, I can't be cured. I tried to kill again, to protect someone I loved."

Hanna slumped back in her chair, hopeless to stop what was about to happen. She looked away, pretended she wasn't there. Distracted herself with the squirrels at the bird feeder.

Jacob didn't understand the nature of Mommy's bewilderment. "Her brother, Goose—Gustav? Sorry, Hanna always uses his nickname."

Hanna felt the weight, the condemnation, of her parents' fiery stare. They hadn't been confused by Jacob's use of the nickname. They just couldn't believe he'd mentioned Goose in the present tense.

"What have you been telling him?" her mother demanded.

"I'm sorry," said Jacob. "I didn't mean to open a rift, I didn't—we can change the subject, that's not really the important thing."

"No, I think it might be." Alex looked from Hanna to Jacob. "What has she told you? About her brother?"

"That I love him," Hanna said. *Truth.*

"I know they're really close," Jacob replied. "Since he's been away at school, they share a wonderful correspondence, always writing letters."

Her husband had finally said something supportive about her, but it was the worst thing he could've said, given the audience at hand. Mommy and Daddy just gaped, mouths unworking, ribs collapsing. They looked like abandoned houses, empty holes for eyes, walls caving in, doomed to purgatory. In real time they became ghosts of themselves, too haunted to talk.

"Gustav?" Mommy breathed.

"I'm sorry, I don't . . ." Jacob turned to Hanna. "What's happening?"

Had it been about anything but Goose, Hanna would've laughed. Here her husband had summoned her parents, sought their reassurance, and now they were as lost to reality as she was. *Don't mess with the Jensens, we're not altogether reliable.*

"You told him Gustav is *alive*?" Daddy was incredulous. "At *school*?"

"Would that be the fantasy school *you* went to?" Mommy asked, full of hate.

"Wait . . ." Jacob blinked, alert, an android in the act of computing—an android about to trumpet the answer to a complex problem. "Goose isn't . . . ?"

"Our son—Hanna's brother—died when he was six," said Alex's ghost.

"Hanna was babysitting," Mommy's ghost explained. "It was only the second time I'd let her babysit."

She'd never let Hanna forget that.

"Oh my God." The ground shifted beneath Jacob's feet. His reality tilted, dropped him into a place where shadows were solid life-forms, ready to claw away at his substance. *Ding ding ding.* His fears aligned. "Did she . . . ? Was Hanna responsible?"

"Of course she was," Mommy clacked, her cogs and springs starting to rupture.

"No," Hanna countered. "No," she told them all. "It was an accident. I would never hurt Goose!"

"You left him alone," Mommy bleated.

"I went to my *room*—for a few minutes! It was no different than when you turned your back, or stepped into the bathroom!"

"It was longer than a few minutes!" Mommy shrieked.

"No it wasn't!"

Alex held up his hands, silently pleading for them to stop.

"What happened?" Jacob asked, visibly anguished by the nightmare of losing a child.

Hanna read the sorrow he felt for her parents, and wasn't sure if he would believe her. She hugged herself and spoke to the ground. She'd told this story a hundred times—to her parents, therapist, even the police.

"I helped him make a toy, from the book we loved—his own UnderSlumberBumbleBeast. He was really excited, but he could get overexcited sometimes. When it was finished he kept bouncing it around, like it was jumping. He kept bouncing it on me, on my arms, my head. I asked him to please stop but he wouldn't."

The memory pained her. She'd been irritated with him. She'd just done something very nice for Goose, but instead of thanking her or settling down to play, he'd gotten hyper. And then she'd remembered those times when Mommy had screamed in her face, begging Hanna to leave her alone for *just a few minutes*. Hanna had never meant for anything bad to happen. Her father had been more open to her interpretation of events, but her mother always—and still—blamed her. Unlike Mommy, Hanna hadn't screamed at Goose before she marched away.

"I just went to my room for a few minutes, to listen to some music. I hoped he'd calm down on his own, but I expected him to come knocking at my door, trying to bug me. When he didn't, I took out my earbuds and went to see what he was doing. I thought he'd be in front of the TV, or playing in his room with his new toy. But I found him on the floor in the hallway." She hitched back a sob. "Unconscious. I didn't know what happened. His lips were blue. He wasn't breathing.

I called nine one one and they told me how to do chest compressions and mouth to mouth. But it didn't help."

For a moment they were a quartet of muffled sobs. Out of the corner of her eye, she saw Daddy grip Mommy's hand.

"It was an accident," he said gently. He clarified for Jacob: "He'd swallowed a button."

"One I'd sewn onto his toy," said Hanna. "Maybe I didn't sew it well enough. It was the worst day of my life. I love Goose more than anything."

Suzette jumped to her feet. "That's why Hanna doesn't want to be around young children—she's afraid she'll kill them."

"It was an *accident*." But it was true. She was still fearful of her ability to be patient enough, attentive enough. Babies and little kids could be annoying, and what if she needed a break? She looked to her husband. "It was an accident, but maybe I don't have what it takes. To be present all the time. What am I supposed to do if I need a minute to myself?"

"Let's go," Suzette said to Alex. She turned to Jacob. "That's what you needed to know?" Dazed, he nodded as he stood. "That's the tip of the iceberg. Proceed at your own risk, that's all I can say."

"Suzette, that isn't fair," said Alex.

"Isn't it? She's been lying to him about everything." She hurried away, taking the side yard to circumvent going through the house.

Daddy lingered for a moment. "I'm sorry, Hanna. I know you loved him."

He reached for her. She got to her feet and let her father embrace her. He was enough taller that her ear met his upper chest and she heard his heart beating. It brought back memories of how safe she'd once felt in the certainty of her daddy's love.

Before Alex left, he held his hand out to Jacob. Much to Hanna's dismay, Jacob only shook it reluctantly. She knew what that meant: he was readying to turn his back on the Jensens once and for all. Her husband's face was a blank screen, but he wasn't going to forgive her—her mother had prevailed, severed the final stitch that kept Hanna's life together.

"Sometimes she loves too much," Daddy explained to Jacob, even sadder now than when he'd arrived. "I'm sorry. You've been really good for her. I hope you can work things out."

Her father left, following Suzette's trail of crushed grass. Hanna stood there watching in disbelief, a cowering mess, while Jacob, with his hands at his waist, ticked off seconds like a grenade. Frozen in place, they listened as a car started on the other side of the house. The engine revved and drove away.

Boom . . . !

Jacob ignited. He shoved the sliding door open and stormed into the house.

70

The air contracted, like a nuclear bomb gathering in its power before sending out a shock wave. Hanna jogged after her husband as he bolted for the kitchen. He opened the freezer, and her first thought was he intended to grab some ice, or a bag of peas, to put on a black eye. But no one had been punched, not physically. He rummaged around the frozen vegetables and forgotten leftovers until he found what he was looking for. With the vodka bottle's neck in his fist, he slammed the door shut.

Hanna stood at a safe distance, watchful as he glared at her. (He probably didn't intend to throw the bottle at her, but she was ready to duck or flee, just in case.) His eyes were already glassy and bloodshot as he unscrewed the cap and started gulping. He winced from the sting, the flavor, the cold shock.

"What else? What else don't I know?"

She wasn't sure how to answer that.

"Your standing instructions to not bring up Gustav if we ran into your parents? Had nothing to do with their *embarrassment*—they never banished their young children to boarding school."

Hanna meekly shrugged. *I was banished.*

"And your special correspondence—all lies? If Goose has been dead all this time, who have you been writing to?"

"I think of it as therapy. It helps me process my grief. It was something Dr. Yamamoto started with me, a long time ago."

"So plausible. So perfectly plausible—minus the part where you never mentioned he was *dead*. Guess that's why I never saw any of the letters arrive—why you always liked to 'get' the mail."

His words were bullets. Hanna wanted to scream at him, tell him he had no right to call her brother *dead*. Goose wasn't here, not in body, but in her mind he was less dead than most of the people she met. *More alive than Mommy, for sure.*

"Jacob, I'm sorry . . . I know it seems . . ."

"Insane? What did you do when you were a kid? That got you locked up?"

"I'm different now."

"Are you?" His laughter bordered on deranged.

Am I? Maybe not as different as she needed to be.

"I still think it's a good idea," she said, "if we saw Dr. Yamamoto together. She could help—"

"Does she know you've been writing to your dead brother for . . . how many years has it been?"

"Nine. No."

Jacob scoffed. Hanna knew she was grasping at straws. Everything was coming undone, but all she could focus on was how cold Jacob's hand must be, gripping the icy glass bottle. Imagining it made her own hand feel frostbitten. She wasn't sure if she was experiencing a state of surreal disconnection—or if this moment, on the brink of an abyss, was the most real thing she'd felt since getting married. Perhaps the last four years of her life with Jacob had been a dream. A little too good to be true.

"Here's what we're going to do," he slurred, flushed with alcohol. "You're going to leave. Pack up. Get out. Get help. Maybe move out of the city—or at least out of the neighborhood so we won't run into you. You do that, and I won't turn you in. 'Cause you know what? Prison might stop you, but it won't help you. You need to tell that doctor of yours the truth. Maybe someday I'll feel sorry for you. Maybe not."

He turned his back to her.

She knew she had been dismissed. He wasn't turning her in to the authorities—all she had to do was go away. But one matter wasn't finished, at least not for her.

"Can I say goodbye to Joelle?"

He pivoted, lancing her with frigid eyes.

"Please? At least a letter?"

At the word *letter* he barked, "You have a lot of nerve."

"When I was seven my parents left me at the school . . ." She plowed on, even as he rolled his eyes. "I *did* go to school there. They hadn't explained everything to me. I didn't understand what was happening, just that Daddy—who I loved more than anything in the world—got in his car and drove away. And I sat there in the dirt, crying. It ripped a hole in me. And I know this is all my fault, even more so than when I was a kid, but I don't want to leave Joelle with a hole. I love her." *More than I ever loved you.*

She waited while he determined her fate, fairly confident of where he would land. She'd chosen well—he was a good person, with a tender heart. He melted just enough to look wistful, and bereaved. This was how she left the people in her wake.

EPILOGUE

Dear Goose,

Sorry it took me so long to get my paper and pencils unpacked. I've been working at my new job for a few weeks now. It was easy enough to get transferred to a different lab, and I kind of let them decide where I should go, based on their staffing needs. Andrea put in a good word for me, so now I have a full-time position at the lab in Brookline. (Don't tell anyone, but I even got a small raise!) I wanted to live close to work—and Jacob wanted me out of Squirrel Hill—so I'm writing to you from the other side of the Monongahela River. There is a small sense of living in exile (not that Brookline is *that* far away), but . . . it's also been kind of fun?

Can you believe this is my first apartment?? I didn't want to live in a giant rectangle of Lego blocks, with people caged in all around me. So I found an old house that was recently renovated into two apartments, one upstairs and one down. The owner lives on the first floor because he didn't want to go up and down stairs anymore. I have a living room, a tiny kitchen, a bathroom, and a bedroom. Of course it's smaller than anywhere I've ever lived, and it's weird not having my own yard. But there are lots of squirrels in the trees, and one of these days maybe I'll get a bird feeder that can sit on a window ledge.

You know I never wanted to live alone, but it isn't as bad as I thought it would be. I can do what I want when I want to, without answering to anyone—and I don't have to clean up other people's messes or do their laundry or cooking. It's very easy to keep everything tidy here, and I don't have to worry about anyone eating the chocolate chips before I've had a chance to make the cookies (a classic Jo move—though now I kind of miss it a little).

I stayed in a hotel for a while, until I had my job and living situation worked out. Daddy actually invited me to come home for a bit, and I considered it, but I knew it wasn't what Mommy wanted. It felt good that Daddy offered, but I really didn't want to live with them again. He's been making a real effort to connect with me—he took me to IKEA to buy furniture, and then helped me put everything together. We ate meatballs at the cafeteria, and Daddy spoke Swedish that whole day, even when I couldn't understand him.

I think my decor looks very Scandi. Clean lines, nothing fancy. A few potted plants. The only stuff I moved from the house was the contents of my closet and my studio—my drawing table takes up about a quarter of the living room. I have to manage all my own expenses now, so I have to be careful about what I buy. But when I look around, I think, *This is all MINE.* Not Jacob's (or Rachel's), not Mommy's or Daddy's. Mine, mine, mine.

I'm trying to take this new chapter in my life as a time to really appreciate what I have: it isn't lost on me that I got the better end of the deal. Jacob feels betrayed (and I think he hates managing the house by himself). I miss Joelle sometimes. We got to say goodbye, but it was awkward for me and confusing for her. I know my leaving was hardest on her. She sent me an invitation to the baby shower, but Jacob and I agree that's a bad idea. He doesn't want me to see her; he wants a clean end. Our divorce is in the works.

So, little brother, I am a free woman! Truly free for the first time in my life.

As always, thank you for being here for me. I am nothing without you.

Yours,

Hanna

PS Now that I'm unpacked, I've had a chance to do a sketch of the view from my living room. (I may have actually seen a hawk, not a pterodactyl, but I thought the street looks more interesting this way.)

———

Dear Hanna,

I knew you'd land on your feet. I'm really excited for you—for you to finally see what you can do on your own, and discover new things about yourself. I know it was a tumultuous journey to get where you are now, but you learned a lot along the way, right?

And speaking of learning . . .

I want to put this out there now, as a preemptive measure: next time, find yourself a man without kids.

Seriously not joking! No kids = no future grandkids. (And none of the responsibilities that come with having to be maternal.) I know Joelle was part of why and how you worked yourself into Jacob's life. But you've done the Big Sister thing now. Next time maybe look for someone a bit older than Jacob. Or someone who thinks he's a little out of your league. It scares me a little to think just how hot and sophisticated you're going to be at thirty! (Or even twenty-eight, ha ha!) You could bag a billionaire if you tried hard enough.

I know you won't make the same mistakes again, that's the important thing. Take all of this—all the experience you've gained—and devise an even better life for yourself. You can do it—I have faith in you. Grrrl, you're just getting started.

I love you, you crazy little teapot. Don't forget that.

Yours,
Goose

Acknowledgments

Shortly after *Baby Teeth* was published and I started getting my first requests for a sequel, I thought, *Isn't that sweet—people want to spend more time with Hanna!* Back then, I was quick to answer no to the question of whether I planned to write a follow-up novel. For one thing, I considered *Baby Teeth*'s essential story to be complete, and for another, I understood from my filmmaking knowledge that sequels were problematic. A successful sequel has to have enough of the "feel" and elements of the first story to seem familiar and satisfying, while also having enough that's new and original that it isn't boring or derivative. For quite a while I was convinced that was a needle I didn't need to thread.

And then the pandemic happened.

Like many people, I spent the early months of the pandemic as a blob on my couch, watching true-crime shows (any- and everything about psychology and human behavior is fascinating to me). At one point I began toying with the idea of plugging an adult version of Hanna into a fictionalized tale of one of the episodes that especially intrigued me. But I soon realized that while I could write an interesting psychological take on this particular wife/seductress/murderer, the character wasn't *Hanna*. Having determined who Hanna *wasn't*, I then decided to devote real effort to exploring who she might be as a young adult. And from there, I got excited about developing *Dear Hanna*.

True to my understanding of the requirements of a sequel, I wanted to include some familiar things—references to the original story and brief visits from known characters. And I also wanted the book to function on its own as a standalone novel: in my mind, *Dear Hanna* and *Baby Teeth* can be read in either order, each presenting complete moments in their own universes. But most importantly, I wanted to create a portrait of Hanna in adulthood that spoke logically to who she'd been as a child, not unlike Aristotle's famous quote, "Give me a child until he is seven and I will show you the man."

I was influenced and informed by the book *The Sociopath Next Door* by Dr. Martha Stout. She believes that one in twenty-five people is a sociopath—which does not define a person as a serial killer or a criminal, but someone without empathy or remorse. While the rest of us live to *feel* good, people without a conscience live by different rules, often ones they make up themselves. And so, my dear Hanna constructs a life for herself according to the logic of her misaligned moral compass.

I dedicated this book to my readers because, truly, *Baby Teeth* changed my life—and that wouldn't have transpired without the collaborative magic that happened between the book and everyone who embraced it. And it's also my readers to whom I owe the biggest thanks, because without the constant requests to know more about Hanna's life after *Baby Teeth*, I probably wouldn't have ever seriously pondered her future. Naturally I have had my concerns that what some readers really wanted in a sequel was more "bad seed" antics, but in *Dear Hanna* I was passionate about delving into her psyche, her obsessive ideas about what it means to love—and I hope it will satisfy many of you too.

As always, thank you to my agent, Stephen Barbara—I always appreciate your wisdom and honesty, and I could not navigate this business without your reliable counsel. Huge thank-you to Liz Pearsons for giving *Dear Hanna* a welcoming home. I'm grateful to everyone at Thomas & Mercer, especially Gracie Doyle, Jarrod Taylor, and Miranda Gardner. Olga Grlic does the best covers ever, IMHO (see *Baby Teeth* and *Mothered* for more evidence). And let's not forget copyeditor Alicia Lea, who fixes all my commas and blunders (except where I stubbornly stet for idiosyncratic reasons).

Thank you to my friends—you know who you are. Thank you to the authors, past and present, who have blurbed my books (the acknowledgments page is often written rather early in the process). To all you booklovers, BookTokers, BookTubers, booksellers, and book champions of every variety: I am nothing without you.

About the Author

Photo © 2017 Gabrianna Dacko

Zoje Stage's debut novel, *Baby Teeth*, was a *USA Today* and international bestseller and was nominated for a Bram Stoker Award. Her second "mind-bending" (*New York Times*) novel, *Wonderland*, was one of Book Riot's Best Horror Books of 2020. *Getaway*, a "stunning . . . third triumph" (*Booklist*, starred review), was named by LitReactor as one of the Best Books of 2021. Her most recent novel, "utterly harrowing . . . masterful" (Criminal Element), is *Mothered*. She lives in Pittsburgh with her cats.